LOOSE ENDS

NINETTE HARTLEY

———— ♕ ————
HORSTEAD BOOKS

This book is dedicated to my mother
Eileen Hatch 1913-2005

Acknowledgements

First, I would like to thank my husband Geoff Bates, without whose continued support – both financial and emotional – of my writing journey, I could not have completed this novel.

Also my editor, Caroline Petherick , whose patience and understanding over the last few months have been beyond the call of duty (she would delete that cliché for sure).

And my writing friends including The Novelistas (you know who you are) who have stood by me through the rough times of self-doubt and despair, giving me unfailing encouragement to continue. In particular Paula Harmon who, for the few weeks before publication, steered me through the maze of self-publishing.

I must also mention my late husband, Gerald Hartley, whose notes about his life as a private investigator, particularly with regard to blackmail, were invaluable in Part 2 of the book.

PART I

1941

One

Saturday 15th March 1941

In the small industrial town of Ridley, West Yorkshire, two young women walked out of the shirt factory gates together. It was one o'clock in the afternoon. Ness had finished work for the day in the offices, and Eileen had clocked out as a buttonhole and side-seamer on the shop floor. They were looking forward to the weekend.

'I was given a whole *load* of typing today. My fingers are killing me,' said Ness, pulling her gloves on.

'I had to go to the packing department today. They were short – some of the warehouse lads've been called up,' said Eileen.

Then she beamed, fumbled in her handbag and pulled out a packet of cigarettes. She lit one, sucked in the first drag and puffed out the smoke like her life depended on it.

Ness watched her. 'Why have you got that stupid grin on your face? I wish you wouldn't smoke in the street,' said Ness running the two sentences together, then under her breath, just loud enough for Eileen to hear, 'I wish you wouldn't smoke at *all*.'

'I don't care what you think about me smoking. As for the grin on my face, look over *there*.'

Ness looked to where Eileen was pointing with the lighter. A delivery van, with 'Brodericks' emblazoned on the side, was driving out of the factory gates.

'So?'

'There's two shirts in there, with your name and address in the pockets. I wonder where they'll end up?' Eileen threw back her head and laughed like a lid rattling on a pot of boiling water.

'What the ...?'

'I thought it'd be fun to write your name and address on a couple of little labels and put them in the pockets of the shirts I was packing today. You never know what might happen.'

'How could you do that? What on earth ... ? I'm seething, Eileen, bloomin' *seething*!' Ness made to swipe Eileen, and Eileen, ducking out of the way, retorted, 'Come on, Ness. It's just a bit of a laugh. I bet you nothing happens. Nothing at all.'

'You'd better bloody *hope* not.' Ness was furious. She was fed up with Eileen trying to matchmake. It didn't matter how often she told her she wasn't interested – Eileen kept on trying.

'Let me explain,' Eileen said.

'I don't want to know. So you can shut up right *now*.'

The crowds leaving the factory gates dispersed, and the chatter was left behind as the two of them walked on. Ness, burning inside, hurried on ahead of Eileen, who carried on just behind, drawing on her cigarette every few steps.

Some kids were playing football in the street and calling to each other, and some were sitting on doorsteps playing with stones. Ness remembered when she and Eileen had done that. Eileen always won – she was good at those sorts of games – but Ness won the board games. She was better at strategy.

But this little trick of Eileen's really took the biscuit. The fact that work had finished for the week had lost its excitement. The early spring sunshine was warm enough to dry off the showers from that morning, and until the moment Eileen had revealed her surprise Ness had felt relaxed and happy. The war seemed a long way from Ridley.

They walked past their old school, where Ness had so often been told, 'Doodling those dresses will get you nowhere,' followed by a rap on the knuckles. They turned left, then went up over the railway bridge. The Masons Arms was on the next corner, where they sometimes went for a drink on a Friday or Saturday night. On the corner of North Street, where they usually parted company, Eileen asked, 'Can I come back to yours for a while?'

Ness shrugged. She was angry. She'd known Eileen all her life – since they'd been at infant school together, anyway. Then at fifteen they'd both gone to work at Broderick's shirt factory, Eileen sewing, and Ness as a junior in the office; she'd thought there'd be more chance of getting somewhere as a typist. That had been five years ago.

Bickering was normal for them. 'I just wish you'd stop trying to find me a bloke. I can get one of my own if I want one, but right now it's not particularly important to me.'

'It's just ... I wish you had someone so's me and Sid could go out with you as a foursome.'

Ness thought Sid a bit of a wide boy – he could always manage to get the odd extra bit of bacon, make-up, fuel, that sort of stuff. He was full of banter and she didn't trust him. His thin moustache and piggy eyes gave him a shifty air. She didn't know what Eileen saw in him. He was definitely involved in something – but Eileen liked getting her beauty stuff and other goodies, and where they'd come from didn't seem to bother her.

Eileen threw her cigarette stub onto the pavement and ground it with the ball of her foot. She pulled a sorry sort of face.

Ness relented. 'Come on, then. Come back for a quick cuppa and tell me what you've done. Mum and Dad'll be in the shop till five.'

Eileen took Ness's arm to continue their walk. 'By the way, did you hear the bombing over at Leeds last night? Everyone was talking about it on the floor. I was with Sid, and we saw the bombers flying over and heard the incendiaries going off. It was awful. You could see this sort of orange glow on the horizon.' Eileen waved her arm in a dramatic arc. 'Thank God they missed Ridley.'

'Yes, we heard them, and you could still smell the smoke this morning. It made our Tommy even keener to sign up. Now don't try to change the subject – I'm nowhere near forgiving you yet.'

When they went into Ness's parents' corner shop the little bell on the door rang; the sound had been part of Ness's life for ever. When she was tiny she'd played on the floor of the shop with empty cardboard boxes, bashing them with wooden spoons. Later, her younger brother Tommy joined her. He'd used the spoons to hit her, though, instead of the cardboard.

Ness wanted more than this small town where everyone knew the colour of your underwear and your life was pretty much mapped out for you. She might have grown up in the corner shop but she wasn't going to stay there.

Eileen was different. She was content to work on the factory floor until she got married. She was a good looker, a brunette who liked to flirt with the men but was loyal to her Sid. She and Ness were opposites in many ways: Ness read books but Eileen read nothing much at all; Ness was prepared to work for what she wanted but Eileen was content with her lot.

Ness's parents were behind the counter. The shop sold almost everything you could think of, and it smelt of cleaning fluids, soap and newspapers, mingled with vegetables. The shelves held tins of food and jars of preserves, and there was a small glass-fronted cabinet where cheese, ham and other perishable goods were displayed – although these days there was little to show in it.

'Eileen and I are going to have a cup of tea. Got any broken biscuits you want to get rid of?' said Ness.

'No – me and your mum have eaten them,' her dad smiled.

'Give over, Jack, we've done nothing of the sort,' said Ness's mum, Mary, and she came around to the front of the counter with a tin of them, scooped out a couple of small ladlefuls and put them into a brown paper bag. 'There you go, girls. Enjoy your tea.'

It was hard work running the shop, especially with rationing. It made all the transactions more complicated. Ness knew how much her parents wanted to help out the young mums whose husbands had gone off to fight, but everything that passed through the shop had to be accounted for. She was sure they often added a bit of extra to certain shopping baskets when they could. The hours were long, too. They had to get up at six-thirty to open at eight. Jack wouldn't finish until after six in the evening, making sure he'd cashed up and left everything ready for the morning.

Once in the house, Ness and Eileen hung up their coats on the pegs in the hall, and Ness put her hat on the shelf above. Eileen was wearing a headscarf over the pincurls she put into her hair every morning, and she wouldn't take them out until she was home. They went through to the back room. It was the room that was in constant use – a kitchen-cum-dining-cum-sitting room. They were lucky, as there was a fair bit of space in the house They had a front room, back room/kitchen, a scullery and a bathroom downstairs, and three bedrooms upstairs. They had a yard and a storage room at the back of the shop.

Ness made a pot of tea. They drank gallons of the stuff. Tea was the answer to everything. At every opportunity the kettle went on and a pot was brewed. She poured out two cupfuls and plonked them down on the table along with the biscuits. She sat back in her chair and let down her hair, rubbing her scalp as the dark blonde rolls came loose. Shaking her head, she pulled the hair from beside her face and tucked it behind her ears. She was home and relaxed, and she could fix it again later if they went out. She picked up her cup and waited for an explanation, 'Come on, then, spill the beans.'

Eileen sat down opposite her: 'Well, when I got to work this morning I was told I had to go to the packing room – *me* in the packing room! Well, honestly I was – *not* – happy. But the foreman said, "I don't *make* the orders, I just give 'em out." So I had no choice. I guess the warehouse lads've all been called up. Anyway, it was boring – really, really *boring*. Packing up hot weather gear for the Navy. There were four other women in the room, but they were much older than me – I knew them, but not really, if you know what I mean – anyway I worked down one end of the big table on my own. Folding, packing, folding, packing ... you have no *idea* how tedious it was. I could have fallen asleep standing up, it were that dreary ...'

'Get on with it, Eileen.'

'Okay, okay. So, I had this idea, while I was staring at the millionth shirt I was folding – and I thought to myself *Why don't I put Ness's name and address in one of these pockets*? So I got a pencil and a label, and wrote your name and address on it. Then I cut the label a bit smaller, about the size of an Elkes biscuit, and it fitted neatly in the breast pocket of the shirt. Bingo!'

'But I thought you said there were *two* labels?'

'Oh yes, well, after the first one I thought *Why not stick another one in, just to be on the safe side*? So I carried on for a bit, then after I'd filled and closed a few more boxes I put the second one in. I wanted to hedge my bets, keeping them separate, so that maybe they'd go to different places. If you know what I mean.'

'No, I don't.'

'Come *on*, Ness, don't sulk. Nothing might come of it, but on the other hand this could be your chance of a lifetime. A wonderful officer from the Navy with a good job in civvy street!'

'Knowing my luck, if anything happens at all it'll be a snotty-nosed youth from Ridley who finds it.'

Two

Saturday 13th September 1941

All through the summer the war had dragged on. While in the south-east the Battle of Britain had raged and there had been fears of invasion, life in Ridley had been pretty boring. Back in 1939 the government had published leaflets about what to do if the Germans came, so 'Keep calm and carry on' had been displayed on posters everywhere. The residents of Ridley had taken the motto to heart then, and were still living by it in 1941.

And to Ness's relief, nothing had come of Eileen's harebrained idea.

Eileen and Sid were going to the cinema in Leeds, and they'd asked Ness and Tommy to join them. There was a cinema and a theatre in Ridley, but Leeds made it much more of an outing, though Ness was wondering how Sid would have got enough petrol for the trip. Tommy was hoping there wouldn't be any bombing while they were there. Leeds was more of a target than Ridley.

Ness went to Eileen's house to get ready. In Eileen's bedroom she slumped down onto the bed. It was a proper girl's room, with a dressing table, a wardrobe and a small bedside cabinet. Ness thought Eileen should update it a bit, though. She wasn't a kid any more.

'What are you wearing this evening, then?' asked Eileen.

Ness pulled a dress out of the brown paper bag and shook it out. 'I hope it hasn't creased too much. I ironed it just before I left home.'

She took off her skirt and blouse, pulled the dress on over her head and fastened it at the seam on the side.

'That's gorgeous! Is it new? Where'd you get it from?'

'I made it in the evenings last week. I used some old curtain material. It doesn't look bad, does it?' Ness twirled on the spot and the circular skirt spun out from her waist. 'I'm really pleased with it.'

'It's gorgeous – I'd never have thought it was curtain stuff even though it's flowers; they're so tiny and I love the purple and white. It's pretty stylish too, with the white collar. You're wasted in the office. I wish I was as clever as you. Anyway, I can't stand doing sewing when I'm away from the factory.' Eileen started putting the finishing touches to her hair and make-up. 'That's better, bit of rouge and I'll be finished. You ought to wear a bit more make-up, you know. Sid can get you some more powder if you like. I think his friend's got some coming in next week. I can ask what else there is around, maybe a bit of eyeshadow?'

'Thanks, but I'm okay. I like Katherine Hepburn better than Hedy Lamarr.'

'You're kidding yourself if you think either of them don't wear a ton of make-up.'

A car hooted outside.

'Blimey, that's Sid now. Where's your Tommy if he's coming?'

'He'll be here any minute. I told him six-thirty, but if he's late we'll go without him.'

When they got down to the car Tommy was there. He was a handsome lad with a healthy aura about him. Clean-shaven and brown wavy hair, a little on the long side.

'Blimey, Tommy, you brush up well,' said Eileen. 'Pity you're only seventeen.'

Tommy grinned at her.

'Oi,' said Sid. 'Leave it out.'

'Not long now, Eileen – I'll be eighteen next month, ready to join up as soon as—'

'Not *that* again. When're you going to get sensible?' said Ness.

'Even when you're eighteen you'll be too young for me,' said Eileen. 'Sid, talk him out of joining up, can't you? He's working in the steel mill, so he doesn't *have* to go, does he? He's an essential worker.'

'Come on,' said Sid, 'let's go to Leeds and stop all this talk. We can have a good time tonight, at least.'

The trip took about forty-five minutes. The road wasn't busy, and when they left the house it was still light. By the time they drove home, though, it'd be dark, and the drive would be a lot slower with masked headlights.

Leeds was buzzing with people going to each other's houses, to dances, to dinner and to the cinema. As in Ridley, they carried on as if there wasn't a war or any threat of invasion. When Sid had parked the car, they made their way to The Junction, an old Victorian pub close to the Odeon in Briggate. The film was an American one, *Dive Bomber*, with Errol Flynn and Fred MacMurray.

The pub was heaving, too, but they found a table in a corner. The atmosphere was smoky, and Ness thought that the decor was a bit faded, and the place could do with a facelift. It was great to be out of Ridley, though. Ness pushed her way into the corner bench with Eileen, and they left the chairs for Sid and Tommy, who went for drinks; Ness asked for a port and lemon, and Eileen followed suit.

'Oh, and our Tommy's only allowed beer,' said Ness. 'Don't get him on the whisky or anything. He's not even legally allowed to drink *beer* until next month.' She sounded like their mum, but she couldn't help herself.

She took off her coat and settled into the seat. 'It's hard to believe there's a war on, isn't it? Everyone seems so normal. There's not been much bombing in Leeds since the big one last March, has there?'

'Could be because Fritz can't see where they're going because of all the bloody smog pouring out the factories,' said Eileen.

The lads arrived back with the drinks, and the talk turned to Christmas and what they'd be doing this year. Tommy, of course, had to say he'd be fighting somewhere, probably in North Africa. Sid said he'd be steering clear of all that action.

'Don't you *want* to fight for your country?' asked Tommy.

'Course I do, but I'm in a reserved occupation. The country can't manage without railway lines, and I'm one of the chaps who keeps 'em running.'

'Well, they could turn your job over to the women at any time,' said Ness. 'D'you think the Americans'll join us soon?'

'I heard they're helping the Russians – sending money and ammunitions, that is. Must be bloody awful fighting in Russia,' said Eileen.

'And awful on the convoys, said Sid, standing up. 'Now then, how about another drink before the cinema?'

'We're still okay,' said Ness, speaking for Eileen, who scowled at her. 'You're not my mum,' she said.

''Ere, Sid,' said Tommy, 'fancy a quick game of darts?'

'Yeah, all right. You don't mind, do you girls? We'll be just a few minutes. It's not like anyone'll think you're on your own – they all saw you come in with us.' Sid and Tommy walked off.

Eileen and Ness sat in silence for quite a while, watching the people at the bar. Then,

'How's the book-keeping class going?' asked Eileen.

'I quite like it, actually. I have to think hard, and it's very different from sketching.'

'You should be careful – you're going to turn into a boring swot who does nothing but all work and no play. Honestly, I can't *believe* you haven't found a fellow yet.'

'I won't be a boring swot. I'll just know a lot – and for the umpteenth time I've told you I'm not looking for a fellow in any shape or form.'

'Not heard anything from any Navy personnel, then?'

'Be quiet. You're lucky I decided to carry on speaking to you after that farce.'

Eileen downed the rest of her drink. Ness hadn't enjoyed hers much. It was time she turned to something more sophisticated. In Ridley it was just old women who drank port and lemon.

Their men were walking back to the table and they'd been joined by another man. He looked in his mid-twenties and was quite attractive. He wasn't in uniform but he was wearing a stylish brown suit with waistcoat, a white shirt and a multi-striped tie. His shoes were highly polished.

'All right, ladies?' asked Sid. 'This is George, he's a mate of mine from Ridley ... You know Eileen, don't you? And this is Tommy's sister, Ness.'

George smiled. 'Evening, ladies. Pleasure to see you again, Eileen, and delighted to meet you, Ness.' He put out his hand to shake hers. Ness felt his warm dry hand and strong shake. He seemed nice enough.

'It's getting pretty stuffy in here don't you think? I understand you're going to the cinema. Mind if I join you?'

His question was directed at Ness, but Sid answered. 'Course not, mate. Come on, then, let's get going before Tommy wants to try another game. I'm not up for losing a second time – the way he hits the double top makes me think he'll be a crack shot in the army.' He laughed.

It wasn't far to the Odeon. Sid and Eileen linked arms, and Ness took Tommy's arm as he moved up beside them on the pavement.

'Got room for another on the other side?' George asked her.

'I suppose so,' said Ness, 'but don't get any ideas.'

'As if I would.'

In the cinema Ness tried to avoid it, but she ended up sitting next to George, with Eileen on her other side. Then the Pathé News came on. It focused on the Battle of Britain, and they all found it rather depressing.

Dive Bomber was definitely one for the lads, Ness thought it was good but wished they'd been able to see a musical, or something more uplifting. During the interval George asked Ness if he could buy her an ice cream. She was tempted, but she didn't want to give him any encouragement. There was nothing wrong with him – she just wasn't interested. During the second half of the film he tried to hold her hand, but she pulled it away and crossed her arms. She thought he was bloody cheeky and was determined to have a word with Eileen afterwards. It had to be her doing.

After the national anthem they piled out of the cinema with the rest of the audience spilling onto the pavement in a bubbling throng. It was only ten-thirty, but Sid was keen to get back to Ridley before midnight.

'I'd like to offer you a lift, mate, but it'd be too much of a squash in the back of the car with Eileen and Ness.'

'I wouldn't mind at all, I could sit in the middle of these two beautiful ladies – but sadly for me, I'm staying in Leeds for a few days.' He turned to Ness. 'I'll be back home in Ridley at the end of the week. Do you think I could call on you?'

Ness shrugged, relieved she wouldn't have to sit in the car with him. She stammered, 'I'm ... well ... I don't—'

'We're going to the pub in Ridley next Saturday if you want to join us,' said Eileen.

'Great. See you on Saturday, then,' said George, and he lifted his hat and walked off down the street.

The other four got into the car and Ness glowered at Eileen.

'Look,' said Eileen, 'it won't do any harm. He's a nice enough chap, and you'll be with us anyway.'

'I'm just not sure I want to be with *anyone* right now,' said Ness.

'Don't be daft, there's a war on. It'll be a bit of light relief. You don't have to marry him or do anything with him if you don't want,' said Eileen.

'This *was* your doing, wasn't it? I wish you'd stop it. I'm quite capable of doing it for myself.'

'What? You think you might meet someone at your book-keeping classes? Then you can talk numbers, subtraction and addition all night, or maybe even single entry or double entry?' Eileen winked.

'Don't be rude,' said Ness, but she had to stop herself smiling.

They stopped talking, but the men carried on discussing the film. 'Those aeroplanes were fantastic, all flying in formation. Perhaps I'll try for the Air Force rather than the Army,' said Tommy.

'The aircraft carrier was massive,' said Sid. 'Bet it's good to be on one of them. Why don't you try for the Navy? What do you think, girls?'

'I think Errol Flynn's just *gorgeous*, and the American accent's divine,' said Eileen.

'That wasn't the question,' said Sid. 'Which service do you think's the best?'

'Ness,' said Tommy, 'what do you think? Should I join the Air Force?'

'I don't think you should join anything,'

'Well, I've always thought I'd go for the Army. I think you have to be a bit clever to join the Air Force anyway ... and I definitely don't fancy the Navy,'

Sid dropped Ness and Tommy outside their house. When Eileen got into the front of the car, Ness asked if she'd come round to give a hand in the shop tomorrow, to move some of the stock around.

'Yeah, all right, don't mind if I do. We can have a good old chinwag when it's done.

Ness opened their front door – it wasn't locked – but once she and Tommy were inside she bolted it.

'Fancy a cup of tea before we go up?' she asked Tommy as they walked along to the back room.

'Yeah, if you like. Thank God it's Sunday tomorrow. Got any plans?'

The tea had gone over, stewed on the top of the stove for the best part of the day. Ness thought it had been used enough. She emptied the leaves into the slop bucket – it'd go to the pig up the road tomorrow. Everyone in the neighbourhood saved their leftovers for pigs or chickens in the hope of a bit of bacon or an egg flying their way when the time came. Then she made a fresh pot, with enough water for her and Tommy to have a decent cup. The tea leaves could be used again in the morning.

One advantage of the shop was that although they still had to keep to their rations they got first pick of produce. While the tea brewed she went through to the scullery to get some milk from the larder, where it was on a slate shelf. Ness looked at the rest of the shelving in there. It wasn't as stacked as it usually was at this time of year. Not as many preserves or pickles as usual. The war was taking its toll on everyone.

Ness and Tommy sat with their tea and talked over the evening.

'What do you honestly think of Sid?' Ness asked.

Tommy was surprised at the question, 'Why are you asking? Have you heard something?'

'No, I just worry about Eileen, really. I think Sid dabbles in the black market and there'll be trouble. I think she sees through it, though.'

Tommy laughed. 'Everyone dabbles a bit, Ness. I mean, it's going on all over the place. He'll be all right.'

'I never accept anything Eileen says she can get for me. Have you ever taken anything from Sid?'

'Nah, not really.'

'What kind of an answer's that? Do you want a biscuit?'

'Why are you being so nice to me? It's not my birthday till next month.'

'I know. Are you still going to sign up? Because I've been thinking about it this evening, after the film and everything. You were really keen, and I was thinking maybe you should volunteer for the Home Guard. I mean it'd keep you happy, wouldn't it? We need to have some younger men at home looking after us all, in case the Germans invade. Eileen says they do proper training and everything – bit of first aid, PE and boxing – you'd be good at that, you're quick on your feet.'

'I'm a step ahead of you. Hadn't told you before, because I wanted to tell all the family together, but you've brought it up now. I put my name down for them this morning before I went to work.'

'But in the car tonight you were going on about joining up again!'

'I know, but I'd already told Sid and George about the Home Guard when we were playing darts. I just thought I'd get you going a bit.' He laughed. 'I'll be collecting my uniform when I go to my first session on Thursday at St Andrew's church hall. Once I'm trained, I'll get paid for any duties I do. Good, eh?'

'That's great, Tommy. Mum'll be really pleased. And you'll be able to stay home and wait until you're nineteen or twenty. It might be all over by then.'

'I'll tell the folks in the morning.'

It was the first time Ness had felt Tommy was growing up a bit. It was a relief to know he'd made the decision to stay at home.

'I'm going up now, Sis,' said Tommy. 'It were good fun tonight.'

Three

Petty Officer Robert Granger took a swig of tea to wash down the sticky bun. He only had a half-hour break before he had to be back in the communications room, and although the mess deck was still a lower deck, it was preferable to being down in the bowels of the ship. He tried to take as long over the tea as possible.

Earlier in the day he'd seen enemy aircraft circling above, but this was normal. He knew they were always scouting the Med to see where the fleet was heading. He was used to it, and like the rest of the crew he could see that they probably were reconnaissance aircraft, so hopefully no chance of them taking a pop at the ships.

'Just time for another cup I reckon,' he said to a fellow officer as he stood to refill his tin mug. As he began to pour, there was a thunderous roar and the ship made an almighty lurch, Robert's mug went flying and as he grabbed the table his teapot crashed onto the deck.

'What the hell was that?' he said.

'Christ knows, a bomb or torpedo I guess … whatever it was, I'm not hanging round here. C'mon, let's get topside!'

Robert grabbed a lifejacket from beneath the table and ran for the companionways to the upper deck. His shoulders bumped the walls of the passageway as he lurched along with other sailors racing to escape. His heart thudded as fast as his feet were moving, as if the rhythm of the one dictated the speed of the other. Once out in the open he struggled to keep his balance on the sloping deck. It was hard to see anything, thick smoke everywhere. Seamen were scrabbling around and falling over each other. Robert tried to find his way and get his bearings, but there were too many other men all looking out for themselves.

He fought without success to make his way to the bridge, knowing that's where he should be, but his legs floundered. Standing upright was almost impossible. Then he was hit in the back, knocking the wind from him – a large sailor had elbowed him. He recovered and glanced around, looking for other officers or somebody taking charge, but nobody was around. His eye was caught by a young lad in overalls, his face pale and strained, mumbling to himself as if praying. He looked at Robert and then up towards the bridge, presumably waiting for the signal to abandon ship, but it didn't come.

'Save yourself, lad,' Robert shouted. 'The order'll come soon enough.'

'Yes ... sir!' the boy shouted, and attempted a salute.

Robert watched him sit down and take off his shoes, then slide down the deck, to jump over the side.

After a few minutes a bell rang and the captain ordered all hands to abandon ship. Robert knew there was nothing for it but to follow in the footsteps of the rating. He looked around for a few moments. The ship was broken and listing. The deck was sloping at forty-five degrees and he'd have to make a jump for it before it was too late. He checked his lifejacket, removed his shoes and slid to the railing, then hoisted himself up and launched himself out, as far from the sinking ship as he could. He bobbed around for a while, swimming away as fast as he could, but as the ship went under he was sucked down; so far down, he thought his lungs would burst. He didn't expect to come up again. His chest burned – he was going to die, he was sure of it. But suddenly his head was above the surface. Spitting out seawater mixed with oil, he gasped for breath while trying to assess his position. The ship was gone and he was surrounded by floating debris, screaming men, dead bodies and the stench of burning cordite.

He saw men grab for the larger pieces of wreckage as they floated past. Some pieces had many as six sailors holding onto them. It was impossible to recognise anyone, as their faces were black, covered in oil, leaving only a couple of blank, staring eyes. Robert presumed he must look the same. He managed to hold onto what appeared to be a door; it wasn't very big, but it was buoyant enough to support him. He dragged the top half of his body over it and let his legs dangle in the sea. The energy had drained from him. He lay there, listening to the carnage going on around him, unable to make sense of it all. He felt a tug on his right foot and immediately thought he was in danger of being dragged back into the water. So he strengthened his hold on the door, then pulled himself up until he was sitting on it.

But whatever was hanging onto him was still there.

He heard a desperate voice: 'Help me!'

Robert rolled onto his side and put his hand down to find the body belonging to the voice. 'Here, grab my hand – but don't pull too hard, leave that to me.'

He got hold of the sailor's lifejacket and yanked on it with as much strength as he could find.

'Now, kick with your legs, man, and try and help yourself up.' Robert pulled him onto the door with him and the sailor lay there on his stomach beside Robert, then began to cough, and vomited violently.

'Sorry, sorry, can't help it.'

Robert patted the man on his back. He didn't imagine it'd help him, but it was the only gesture he could think of. 'Don't worry, get it all out.' He gave him a minute and helped him to turn over and sit up, then the two men were side by side.

'It's a good job the sea's calm. This door'd be no good in heavy weather.' The man laughed. 'Sorry, it's not funny at all, can't think why I did that.'

'Don't worry, old chap. It's a bit of an unusual situation. Nervous reaction probably. What's your name and rank?'

'Brown, sir. I saw you up on deck, before the ship went down. You're Petty Officer Granger, aren't you?'

'Yes. I think we may be stuck here for a while. With a bit of luck, one of the other escort ships will turn back for us as soon as they think it's safe enough.'

'Before dark, I hope, otherwise we're going to have to keep each other going until the morning, and we might not make it.'

The two fell silent for a while, watching what was going on around them and searching the horizon for signs of a rescue ship. The initial panic and confusion had eased off and everyone around them were survivors who were clinging, like them, to bits of wreckage. There were only two inflatables, and they were some distance from Robert and Brown. Robert tried to make out how many men were on each craft; they were meant for only ten but were obviously carrying more. He watched a body being pushed over the side of one of the boats. Presumably the man had just died. People were praying.

'Do you think we should pray too, sir?'

'I'm afraid I'm not really a believer, but right now I'd be prepared to send up a prayer or two just in case.' He paused, 'I think it might be better if we sit back to back; we can take support by leaning on each other. I'll turn around first.'

Robert didn't find it easy to change position; the door rocked alarmingly as he swivelled around. Once settled he told Brown to turn, and eventually their shoulders and backs were touching and their heads resting together.

Several minutes passed in silence.

'Feels a bit odd, this,' said Brown.

'It's more comfortable, though. We ought to keep talking, you know, otherwise there's a danger that one of us might fall into unconsciousness.' Robert thought he sounded a bit overdramatic. 'What's going through your mind, Brown?'

'I've been thinking about my people back in Blighty, actually. What about you? Anyone there for you, sir?'

'Yes, my parents and my sister. She's twenty-three, two years younger than me. They're all in Devon, in the countryside, thank goodness. Don't think they've seen much action. Although Plymouth's taken quite a hammering.'

'I've only got my mum. My dad died in the last lot, when I was just a baby. She never married again.' Brown rubbed his head. 'I did have a girl – but I've had the letter, the one that says she's found someone else.'

'Another one'll come along I expect,' said Robert. But then, thinking he sounded a bit insensitive, he added 'I mean, you'll find another girl soon enough.'

'I hope so. You not got a special girl, then?'

'No, not really, I've never had a serious girlfriend.'

'When did you join up, sir?'

'As soon as war was declared. I did my training, and then some more, so I could be a petty officer. What about you?'

'I waited until I got called up. Didn't want to leave my mother alone in London ... sir.'

'Oh, I can understand that.'

'What do you do in civvy street, sir?'

'I'm a journalist.'

'That sounds interesting, sir. More interesting than my job as a salesman, anyway. Still, it's got prospects ...' He paused as the whimpers of the injured rose above the lapping of the waves. 'I can't stand the way some of these men are calling out for their mothers. It's awful.' Brown shifted his position and the door rocked violently.

'Woah – careful!' said Robert, anxiety in his voice.

'Sorry, sir. Finding it hard. Can't bear to think of all these men injured and dying.'

'Try to concentrate on saving yourself,' said Robert. Talk about when you were a boy or something. Tell me more about yourself.'

'I don't know what to say, sir.'

'No need to keep calling me sir all the time ... a sinking ship's a great leveller. Save it for later. Where did you go to school?'

'I went to the local primary school. The head teacher of the infants was a bit of a witch. We all hated her. She was tiny and wrinkled and shouted in a high-pitched voice. We reckoned she put spells on the kids.' Brown laughed. 'Ridiculous when you look back. She seemed about ninety years old but that wasn't possible. When I moved into the main school that was better, but I used to get into trouble for talking too much. Plenty of knuckle raps with a ruler for me.'

'What about the next school?'

'I didn't get to the grammar school, if that's what you're wondering, but I did all right. I liked a bit of football – still do as a matter of fact. But I probably spent too much time and energy on the field instead of at my schoolwork.'

'What about you?'

'Boarding school for me. Makes you pretty self-sufficient and I made a few friends – but, well, I missed out on home life, I think. I wasn't that keen on sport, I'm afraid. I might have had a better time if I'd enjoyed rugby or hockey but it just wasn't for me. More the academic type, English and history in particular. It all seems a very long time ago ... and a long way from here.'

The men fell silent again. Too silent. The long swells made the door move rhythmically in a gentle rocking motion. Mesmerising. Men were still calling out, but the sea was still fairly calm. Robert could feel himself drifting. He knew it was important to keep talking, but it was so hard to keep it up. He could feel Brown's body getting heavy on him, and realised he too was fading. With enormous effort, he forced himself to dig Brown in the ribs with his elbow.

'Brown, come on, keep yourself awake and talk to me.'

Brown moaned, 'I just want to sleep for a bit ...' His voice had a drunken drawl to it.

'I'm the same, but we've got to stay focused. Think of that witch of a head teacher. What was her name?'

'Can't ... remember.'

'Yes, you can! Think, man, think!'

Robert thought he was doing a good job of keeping himself alert by going on at Brown. The dreadful thought of losing him was a scenario he didn't want to take place.

'Was she Miss or Mrs? Smith? Jones? Come on, man, what was it?'

'Something ... short ... to do with a kitchen ...'

'Hey! Look – over there! It's a ship, it's a ship!'

One of the men in an inflatable shouted, 'Anyone got a flare?'

'I think there's one on here,' returned the first voice.

'Send the bloody thing up, then.'

'Here, here, over here ...'

Everyone shouted at once, the panic and noise rising as it had earlier in the day, but this time there was more enthusiasm than despair. Robert and Brown leapt into action, the adrenaline rush taking Brown from near-unconsciousness to alertness in a matter of moments.

'Here! We're over here!' Robert waved his arms. The door rocked violently.

'Careful – you'll tip us over and then no chance of rescue.' Brown grabbed at him.

Others were crying and calling out until the ship, a destroyer, came close enough to help the survivors aboard. Seeing the scramble nets being thrown over the side, the men didn't hang around. They paddled to get as close as they could to the ship, then took the plunge into the water for the second time that day. This time they swam to the nets and hauled themselves up.

A seaman called over the side, 'Come on! Fast as you can. Help those who need it. We don't want to hang around here any longer than necessary. We don't know where that bloody U-boat might be now!'

Robert and Brown joined the other survivors on the upper deck. They were glad to be out of the water, but some of the others seemed close to dying. As he looked around, Robert thought that on the whole they were a motley-looking bunch, dirty and oily. And there weren't many of them. He was glad to take a swig of rum when some jugs were handed out. He and Brown sat down together.

'Where do you think they'll take us?' asked Brown.

'Alex, probably, or Port Said – but I'm sure they'll tell us soon. As long as it's somewhere warm and dry I don't care.' Robert laughed, but his eyes suddenly filled with tears.

'I know how you feel. It's a bloody miracle we're here. There don't seem to be that many of us saved after all. We're the lucky ones.'

The men drifted in and out of sleep. At one point they were woken and given some soup, bread and tea. The night passed quickly and without incident except for sailors crying out in their sleep. They were told they'd be landing in Alexandria in a couple of days and that under no circumstances were they to write home and tell any of their families or friends what had happened. The incident would be reported officially when the time came.

When they docked they were sent to a submarine depot ship and as they walked down the gangway they were each given a packet of five Woodbines and a bar of soap, then sent to wash up.

'This'll be the best shower I've ever had,' said Brown.

'Not before time,' said Robert. 'I was beginning to think we'd never get rid of the stink.'

They were handed a basic kit with hot weather rig – pants, shirt, shorts, socks, canvas shoes – plus some toiletries and a little spending money.

After they had washed the information came through to say they'd be going back to England via Gibraltar, sailing within forty-eight hours. They were to be billeted in Alexandria for two nights and were given shore leave until embarkation. Robert and Brown decided to find a bar and enjoy a couple of bevvies before turning in for the night.

'Here's to a quiet trip back to England,' said Robert.

'Cheers, mate! Here's to us,' said Brown.

Robert reached into the breast pocket of his new shirt and pulled out the packet of Woodbines. As he did this, a small card fell out onto the table. He picked it up and looked at it. His eyebrows rose.

'What's that?' asked Brown.

'Nothing, just a size ticket.' He had no idea why he hadn't revealed what he'd read on it. 'Here, I wanted to give these to you. I don't smoke cigarettes, only a pipe, and I don't do that very often. You might as well have them.'

'Thanks. That's very kind of you.'

To Robert, Brown seemed much younger than himself, although there were only a few years between them. Despite both of them saying they'd write, Robert didn't think they would keep in touch. Although they'd kept each other going for what seemed a long time in the water, what Robert wanted now was to forget the experience. He hoped he'd never see Brown again. There wasn't any point in pretending. War was like that. You could never be sure which ship you'd be assigned to or where you'd end up.

Four

Saturday 27th September 1941

On Wednesday 24th it was Eileen's twenty-first birthday. She'd wanted a party that day, but as there was a dance on at the local Empire Theatre on the Saturday, it was decided they'd go there to celebrate instead. They all met up at the Masons Arms for a drink before walking over to the dance hall.

Ness wore a sleeveless dress she'd made over the summer from an old evening dress she'd bought at a Red Cross sale. It had a pale pink silk lining with a soft net covering. The bodice was fitted and the skirt swung away from the waist. She had sewn several thin strips of darker pink velvet running down from the scooped neckline to the hem, and finished them off with occasional tiny embroidered flowers.

'Blimey, Ness, you should be making clothes for a living. You're a brilliant advert for 'Make do and Mend' said Eileen.

'I've always done that. I don't need a government pamphlet to encourage me.'

The weather during the day was still warm enough but the evenings cold, so they both took a covering with them to wrap around their shoulders. Eileen's was a fur stole – Sid had bought it for her, of course. Ness chose a knitted shawl her mother had made ages ago. Ness wasn't keen on fur, although she had to admit she loved the feeling of her mum's beaver lamb coat, and had snuggled up into it when she was a child, finding comfort in stroking the soft pelt.

They left the pub after a couple of drinks and headed over to the Empire. Sid had the tickets for everyone. The proceeds of the dance were going to the war effort, so nobody minded paying. George had joined them again, and Ness felt his eyes on her as soon as she walked into the pub. Tommy had brought a girl with him, Emma. She was sixteen, and worked at Brodericks as a side-seamer. Ness didn't know her – she thought Eileen might – but anyway she appeared to be a nice girl. It'd be good for Tommy to have someone. Ness wondered if they'd been together long but he hadn't let on – perhaps Emma was the reason why he'd decided to stay home and join the Home Guard. Perhaps Eileen knew more. She'd have to quiz her about it later.

It was dark as they walked along, and George came up beside Ness.

'Take my arm, why don't you? Can't have you tripping over in your dance shoes.'

'These aren't my dancing shoes – I've got those in my bag. These are my day shoes. A girl can never have too many pairs of shoes, you know. Although at the moment the choice is a bit limited.' Ness smiled at George and, deciding not to be belligerent, accepted his offer. She couldn't be bothered to waste the energy on being mean. She put her arm through the crook of his. 'Don't get any ideas, though,' she said.

'Just a friendly night out. I get the picture,' said George, and he patted her hand.

***

The queue for the Empire was long but it moved quickly. Everyone loved to go dancing – it took you right away from the war and the news. Ness and Eileen went to the ladies cloakroom and Emma tagged along.

'Isn't this nice? Tommy with Emma here' – Eileen smiled at Emma – 'me with Sid and you with George.'

'I've already told him not to get any ideas,' said Ness. 'So bear that in mind, please.'

They changed their shoes and checked their make-up. Eileen's of course needed a touch-up but Ness couldn't be bothered.

When Eileen had finished, 'Come on, let's get dancing,' she said.

All three marched into the dance hall, which was packed. People milling everywhere. There were a number of small tables and chairs around the edge and Ness heard Sid shout to them. Waving his arm, he called to them to come over to where the men had saved some places.

There were already drinks on the table; beer for the men and port and lemon for the women. The band were playing a foxtrot to get the evening going.

'Come on, Sid, I can't *wait*!' Eileen dragged him off.

Tommy and Emma followed, and Ness sat still.

'Do you want to dance, then?' asked George.

'Shouldn't we stay here to watch the drinks and bags?'

'They'll be fine. Look around, everyone's leaving their table. And your things are over the backs of the chairs. Nobody will touch anything. Anyway, I can watch them as we dance if you're worried.'

Reluctantly – she couldn't think of another excuse – Ness stood up and went onto the dance floor. The band were good – a big local dance band with older men who had not been called away – so it wasn't long before she was enjoying herself. George was a good dancer, too, so good that she stayed on the floor with him for three more dances before insisting they go back to the table for a drink and a rest.

At the table, George told Ness that he'd asked the band to play Happy Birthday immediately after they'd taken a break, so that people would be seated.

'That's a lovely thing to do,' said Ness, and she meant it. He was a thoughtful bloke.

The band stopped playing and announced a half-hour interval with an opportunity to buy tea and sandwiches, Ness was tempted, but nobody else in their party fancied any, so she just shut up. She didn't want to be a spoilsport. They stuck to the alcohol.

After the break the bandleader called Eileen's name out through the microphone. She feigned being embarrassed as the whole audience sang Happy Birthday to her. Sid began singing, 'For she's a jolly good fellow,' and the others joined in. When they'd finished everyone hugged and kissed. George took the opportunity to give Ness a gentle, caring kiss on the lips.

She drew back immediately. 'Please don't, George. You're a lovely chap, but I'm not really wanting any of that right now.'

He smiled kindly and said he was sorry.

***

In bed that night, Ness was more determined than ever to get herself out of Ridley. She didn't know how she was going to do it. She wasn't religious, so she didn't think praying would help her. As she turned over to go to sleep she made a promise to herself, and said the words aloud: 'I'll get my book-keeping exams, then maybe I'll learn short-hand, and then I'll get a job with a big firm in London.'

Five

Saturday 27th September 1941

Whilst waiting for his train Robert found a telephone box and called his parents' house.

'Hello, Rose. Did you get my letter? About my ship going down?'

'Robert!' It was wonderful to hear his sister, but she sounded surprised. 'No, we didn't – are you all right? Are you injured? Where are you?'

'I'm absolutely fine. Honestly. It was pretty awful but I'm not injured. I'm at Paddington, catching the next train to Totnes; it should arrive at six this evening but it'll probably be late. Can you come to meet me?'

'Of course I will. Mother and Father will be so pleased to see you.'

I doubt that, thought Robert. 'Well, I'll certainly be pleased to see *you*. I'll tell you everything when I get there. I won't chat now, save it for later. You'd better call the station to see what time the train is due in. As I said, there's no guarantee it'll be on time.'

***

Rose was at Totnes to meet him. The train was only forty-five minutes late. He jumped into the car and kissed her on the cheek before they drove off towards Dittisham.

'So, how are the parents, then?' asked Robert, once they were under way.

'Father's very busy – he's had to take on extra patients from Donald, because he's left the practice and joined up as an army doctor.'

'What about Mother?'

'She's helping Father, making appointments and keeping records. His secretary left to join the land army. Honestly, everyone's leaving and going off to war except me. I wanted to go into the QA's but father was adamant I'd be useless – 'Much better to use your brain, girl'. I registered to work for the war effort ages ago – we all had to – but I'm still waiting to hear back. In the meantime I've been knitting socks and sewing blankets. But I want to go to London and I don't care what I do, though I'd like to use my shorthand and typing.

'Well, it's good that Mother's got something to do other than coffee mornings and the church roster.'

'I think she enjoys going into Dartmouth every day – I wouldn't be surprised if she carried on after the war.'

'How are Jim and Mrs Leach?'

'Same as ever. Jim wanted to come and fetch you – he thought it was his duty – but I stopped him.'

'Well, I'll see him later. Has he been growing stuff?'

'Yes, of course – and Mrs Leach is making the most of things, cooking up a storm in the kitchen with his veg and fruit,' Rose laughed.

'Do you think the war'll end soon?'

'No idea.'

They fell silent.

It was after 7 by the time they arrived back at the house on the outskirts of the village, Robert got out of the car to open the heavy wooden gate for Rose to drive through.

'I'll walk up to the house,' he said. 'Nice to get a bit of fresh air.'

He lingered, then followed the car up the driveway, his feet crunching on the gravel. It was the only sound that could be heard; there was no breeze, so no clinking from the boats moored in the Dart, nor any owls out yet, and the daytime sounds of cows, sheep and country life had stilled. Robert took a deep breath; he could smell the river, a mixture of diesel, tar from the ropes, and water. A wave of tranquillity passed over him. He always missed Devon while he was in London, and right now he was far away from sinking ships, the smell of death, screaming men, blood, pain and the absolute shambles that was the war. His ship going down and the subsequent saving of selected crew members was hard to live with. Who makes the selection? he wondered. He didn't believe in God.

A light came on in the porch, and he could see his mother coming out to the car and helping Rose with his kitbag. He wished he could run to her arms and feel a motherly affection, but he knew he'd get a better welcome from the dog, Paddy, a golden retriever who ran to his side whining and wagging his tail.

'Hello, boy,' said Robert and bent down to stroke the dog's ears. 'Come on, let's make the best of this, shall we?'

He stood upright, forced a smile on his face and walked with determination to the front door. 'Hello, Mother.'

'Hello, Robert. Good to have you home, even if it is only for a short visit.' She hesitated for a moment, then stepped forward and pecked him on the cheek. 'Come on in.'

Once inside the house Robert took off his coat and shoes replacing them with the slippers that had been left for him in the hallway. His father, he knew, would be sitting in his study and Robert would be expected to go to him, which of course he did. Ever the dutiful son. Except he had joined the Navy instead of his father's regiment – he had served in it as a doctor during World War I. Robert could have had a commission, begun as a second lieutenant and worked his way up to captain within a short time. But he had the sea in his blood. His family had moved to Devon in 1919 when he was just a boy of three. His father had been invalided out of the war in 1917 and had spent two years recuperating, and then, when the opportunity had come up for the practice in Dartmouth the family had moved there from London. For a while they'd lived at the surgery but then, when Donald joined the partnership, he lived in Dartmouth with his family while the Grangers had moved to the house in the countryside.

Robert knocked on the door and waited.

'Come in, come in. What *are* you waiting for?' The familiar boom of a voice.

'Evening, Father. How are you?' Robert shook his father's out-stretched hand; the other was on his stick. The doctor stood up from his seat behind the desk and walked round it towards Robert.

'Not too bad. Leg's playing up a bit, but then it always has and always will. Can't expect to have all that shrapnel in your flesh without a few problems. How about you? Got torpedoed, I hear. Are you allowed to talk about it?'

'Well, not the details – but it wasn't too bad.' *Why do I find it so difficult to be honest?* 'I was lucky and managed to grab onto something and someone after I ended up in the water, then we kept each other going until we were rescued.'

'Nothing like a bit of action to keep you on your toes. Good for the soul. A bit of a scare, humph?'

Robert looked down at his slippered feet. Incongruous. His head swam with the memory of the sinking ship, the fear of the men and the panic and chaos.

'Yes, Father. It was a bit of a scare,' he replied. He just couldn't tell him the truth; his father wouldn't want to hear it, anyhow.

'Well, I know all about that. It's probably not as bad at sea as fighting on the land, man to man and all that. I saw plenty of sights in my time. Makes a man of you.'

Why did his father have to pretend all the time? He must have had a rough time during the First World War but he would never talk about it. Now he was pretending it was all jolly hockey sticks. Stiff upper lip and all that, and behaving as though the Army was so much tougher than the other forces. Robert wondered if his father treated his patients in the same off-hand way: *What, Mrs Baker? You've got stomach ache and you're vomiting blood? Pull yourself together! Take this pill and you'll be right as rain.*

They heard the dinner bell ring and Robert's father stood up immediately and began to walk towards the door. He indicated for Robert to do likewise.

'Come on, better not be late to the table Robert.

They sat in the dining room, which was spacious and beautifully furnished. Both this room and the drawing room next door had French windows leading out onto the terrace and garden.

'I hear you're growing plenty of vegetables in the garden, Mother,' asked Robert.

'Well, not personally – I'm a bit too busy working with your father in his practice – but Jim's doing his best.'

'How are the Leaches? They must be getting on a bit now.'

'Yes, they're both in their sixties, but quite fit. We couldn't manage without them. Do you realise, it's over twenty years they've been with us?'

Robert's father waved his hand over the table, 'Pass the wine, would you, Robert?'

'Yesterday I spent a bit of time with the sailor who I'd floated about in the Med with after the ship'd gone down.'

'Will you be seeing him again?'

'I don't think so. There's was a sort of bond, I suppose – but really, you can't get sentimental in these times. Anything can happen. In fact, I'll probably never see him again.'

'Yes, mm, that is the trouble with times like these. So many of my close friends lost in the first lot. It's best not to dwell on it, lad. People come and go during the war, that's how it is.' That was the closest Robert's father got to talking about it.

The dinner seemed to go on for ever, but eventually the evening came to an end.

Robert slept well for the first time in ages. It was good to be back in Devon. He was up by eight o'clock and ready to go out in the autumn air.

'I'll take the dog down to The Ham for a run, shall I? I'm not in any rush. I might get the ferry to Dartmouth. Would that be all right?'

'Fine by me,' said his mother. 'I don't have time to run him today, I'm due in the surgery at nine with your father, so I've got to go now. If you're still hanging about in Dartmouth by noon we can give you a lift back, probably. Just come and find us.'

'Thanks, Mother, I'll do that. Come on, Paddy, let's go.'

Their house was on high ground above the village, and the views down to the Dart were stunning. The river was wide and deep, and several small boats were moored there. On the opposite side from Dittisham was Greenway. Robert had heard that the authoress Agatha Christie had bought the big house there, although he'd never seen her.

He wound his way down the track and past the backs of some houses, then crossed a stream and eventually arrived at the large grassed area they called The Ham, beside the river. He threw a stick for the dog several times, the last one landing in the river. Paddy didn't hesitate to retrieve it and rushed back, dropping it at his feet. He shook himself violently and Robert was soaked.

'Bloody hell! Oh well, I'm wet now, might as well take a walk along the river bank, see what we can find, eh?' he said.

His step was light as he walked as far as he could, picking up shells and stones and putting them in his pockets, just as he'd done as a boy. They'd always had a dog and he'd whiled away many hours and days by the river. He caught sight of his dinghy, turned upside down and wintered, the way he'd left it so many years ago. He was amazed that some youngster hadn't taken it by now. He pulled back the tarpaulin and looked at the state of it.

'It's in a pretty bad way, Paddy, not sure it's even riverworthy. Perhaps I should spend this week fixing it up. What d'you think?'

The dog lifted his leg and peed on the bow.

'You think it'd be a waste of time, eh? But I've got to find *something* to do down here for the next few days.'

He sat on one of the benches that looked out onto the river. Most of them had plaques on them dedicating them to lost loved ones who'd spent time there and loved the place.

He put his hand in his pocket and pulled out the label he'd found back in Alex. He read it again for probably the hundredth time; this time aloud.

'Eunice Proctor, 44 North Street, Ridley, Yorkshire.'

Six

Saturday 11th October 1941

'I'll see you at my house at eight, then,' Ness said to Eileen when they parted company on the corner of North Street after work. 'I hope this damn wind has dropped by then, or I might stay home in the warm with a good book.'

'Don't you dare! It'll be a good night, I'm sure of it. I'll be dragging you out to the Masons Arms. Make sure you're ready in time.'

'Is George definitely coming?'

'Sid said he was, so yes. Why? Have you decided you're interested now? I saw you enjoyed dancing with him last time.'

'No, not a bit of it. I just wondered who you'd got lined up for me this week if it wasn't George.'

'I've given up, honestly I have. I promise not to interfere again.'

'I'll believe *that* when I see it.'

Ness hurried off along the last bit of the road, her head bowed against the wind, thinking she was mad agreeing to go out. Still, Tommy could come along, and everyone had been so pleased at home about him joining the Home Guard that it'd be something to celebrate this week.

Inside the front door she noticed a duffel coat hanging on one of the pegs and a kitbag on the floor. Her stomach dropped. A lump of panic zipped from her head and dropped like a stone to her feet. Her brain flashed back to that day in March. *Damn* Eileen! Ness had put that business behind her, but this could only mean one thing ...

'Ness, is that you?' her mother shouted.

'Yes. I'm just hanging my coat up.' Her voice was squeaky. She made her way past the stairs and stood by the door to the back room.

'Ness, this is Robert. He just got here, about half an hour ago. What have you been up to, my girl?'

There was an attractive man sitting at the table with a large cup of tea in front of him. Mary had a big grin on her face – he'd obviously charmed her already. Ness connected the note in the pocket with this man and cursed Eileen again.

'Hello Eunice, I'm Robert.' He shook her hand. It was a warm affectionate shake.

Ness was motionless for a moment, wondering what to say, and then came out with, 'Nobody calls me Eunice. I'm Ness.' She was furious. Eileen must have written her full name on the label.

'Sit down, Ness, and have a cup of tea,' said Mary, ever practical.

Ness pulled out the chair opposite Robert, 'How is it you're here, then?' she asked.

'I thought ...' said Robert, 'well, I wasn't going to do anything, but I had to go to Liverpool to pick up my ship and I thought, well, why not?'

'Why not *what*?' Ness asked rather stupidly. She couldn't get her head around it. 'Why didn't you write to me first?'

'Well, I thought, why not go and knock on the door and say hello to the woman who sent the address. So here I am.'

'Yes, here you are,' she said. Her tongue stuck to the roof of her mouth. She took a gulp of tea. 'Sorry, I'm a bit shocked. I'd completely forgotten about the note. It was ages ago. My friend Eileen did it. We never expected anything to happen. Well, at least *I* didn't.'

'What note?' asked Mary.

'It was a silly prank Eileen played, way back in March. *Stupid* girl!'

There was a bit of a pause in the conversation and they both looked at Ness, waiting for an explanation, but she couldn't give it, not now.

'Oh, what about tea?' said Mary. 'I've not got enough in the house to feed an extra one.'

'Don't worry about me – I'm used to meagre rations,' said Robert.

Tommy appeared in the doorway, 'What's going on here, then?'

Ness introduced Robert and there was a buzz around the table, everyone talking at once.

At that moment their father came into the room. 'What's all this chatter about, then?'

'I don't think I've got enough to feed everyone, and there isn't time to get any more in.'

'Why don't we have fish and chips?'

'Great idea, and I can pay!'

'Aye, that'll be grand. Come with me to fetch them.'

Robert and Tommy left, leaving Ness with her parents.

'You kept that quiet, didn't you?' said Mary. 'The note.'

'It was just a joke. I didn't really think anything would come of it. I was cross at the time but you know Eileen – she meant well. She's always trying to palm me off with some bloke.'

'He seems right enough,' said her father, 'but you never know. Take care, Ness.'

'Look, I'm not about to run off with him, so you can relax, Dad. Don't get overexcited or you'll have a turn.'

'There's no need to be rude, Ness. No need at all.'

'Leave your father alone – he doesn't need any of your teasing this evening. We had a busy morning in the shop, and now this chap turns up and ... well ... I think we're a bit shocked by it all, to be honest,' said Mary.

'Well, you didn't look shocked when I came in! You looked thoroughly happy with Robert'– she accentuated his name – 'sitting with you, having a cup of tea and chatting.'

'Well, there were a brew on and we didn't want him to feel awkward. I mean he had your name and address clear as anything.'

Ness could barely grasp what had happened. A complete stranger turning up on the doorstep, just like that. Eileen had a lot to answer for.

Tommy and Robert came back with the fish and chips, and some beer and pop. All five squashed around the table. They didn't bother with plates, just ate straight from the paper. Everyone put a liberal amount of salt on their chips. At least that wasn't rationed yet. The conversation was lively. Robert talked a little about being in the Navy but he didn't want to elaborate too much.

'What made you choose the Navy?' Ness asked him.

'I figured it if I were going to die, then at least at sea it might be a clean death. No wallowing in all that mud like they did on the Western Front in the last lot. You know what I mean? But now ... having been on a ship that sank ... I'm not sure I was right ... about the sea being clean, I mean.'

No one reacted. There was an embarrassed silence.

Ness wanted to know more, so she asked him. 'Was it bad?'

'Stop it, Ness,' said her father. 'The man doesn't want to talk about it. He's only got twenty-four hours' leave left. He wants to forget about it all. Where are you from, Robert?'

'I'm from Devon, actually. A little place upriver from Dartmouth, where my father's a doctor.'

'That's nice. Any other family?' said Mary.

'I have a sister, Rose. She wanted to go into the QAs, but my father was adamant that she shouldn't. She wants to work for the war effort but hasn't heard anything. I saw her just last week and she said she was fed up with making socks and blankets.' He laughed. 'She wants to go to London, and she's good at shorthand and typing.'

'I'm a typist, too,' Ness said, and it sounded rather weak. 'I work in the office at the shirt factory. I ought to do shorthand too, but I'm learning book-keeping instead. Thought it'd be handier.'

'What do you do when there isn't a war on?' Tommy asked, turning to Robert.

'I'm a journalist, actually. 'I used to work for a local rag but now I work for the *Daily Herald* in London.

'That sounds right good. You should've been a war correspondent or something.'

'Belt up, Tommy.' Ness frowned at him.

'It's all right. I could have done that, but I had my heart set on joining the Navy as soon as war was declared. I don't know why, but there you are. The paper'll still be there when the war's over.'

'Let's hope you are too.'

'*Really*, Tommy.' Ness scowled again. 'What a thing to say. Why don't you take Robert into the front room while I go and get changed to go out? Try and stop asking him too many questions, though. Why don't you talk about the film we went to see last month or tell him about the Home Guard?'

'Righto,' said Tommy. 'This way, mate.'

'I'll come too,' said Jack, who just wanted to get out of the back room.

Ness and Mary began to clear up.

'You go and freshen up and get changed,' said Mary.

Ness went to the bathroom and splashed a bit of water over her face, all the time thinking about Robert and how she was going to handle this. Despite her insistence about not wanting a boyfriend, she was just a little bit fascinated by him. A doctor's son. At least he could hold a decent conversation. And she didn't think he'd be 'after one thing', as her mother would say.

The front door banged and as Ness came out of the bathroom she heard Eileen's voice. 'Hello! Anyone around? You ready, Ness?'

'*You*!' Ness threw her arm out and pointed her finger like a teacher about to give her a good telling-off. 'You have *no idea* what you might have done putting those labels in the shirt pockets. And you wrote *Eunice* on them! I could *kill* you!' Ness spoke in a loud whisper as she didn't want the people in the front room to hear her.

'I'm not exactly sure what you're on about,' said Eileen, 'but don't get yourself all worked up, there's nothing attractive about that.'

'Go into the front room, why don't you? Ness growled. 'You'll soon see what I'm on about.'

***

Half an hour later they were all in the Masons Arms and joined by Sid and George. It was a squash and very smoky.

'Do you smoke?' Ness asked Robert as they stood in the entrance.

'I did, but I just use a pipe now and not that often. I know practically all sailors smoke, but I wanted to try and cut down – well, cut out really – so I got myself this pipe.' He produced it from the pocket of his coat, and stuck it in his mouth then thought better of it, put it back in the pocket and hung the coat up. 'I don't think I'll bother right now. I'll inhale enough smoke just from being in here.'

Tommy, Robert, Sid and George went to buy drinks. Ness and Eileen went to secure a table in the corner of the lounge bar and waited for the men to come back.

'He's okay, Robert, isn't he? Nice-looking, and he seems well educated. Too educated for me, but I bet he's right up your street.' Eileen nudged Ness in the ribs.

'Yes, he's nice. But I'm still not forgiving you.' Ness made no further comment as the men came back with the drinks. They fitted neatly around the table. Sid sat at one end of it with George next to him, then Tommy, and at the other end was Eileen, then Ness and Robert. Sid got into conversation with George, and Tommy with

Eileen. Robert leant in close to Ness. It was quite noisy in the bar, and for that she was grateful.

'I'm so glad I came here before going to Liverpool. You never know … when you go away … when or if you might come back.

'I understand. Yes, it's nice you came. Do you know where you're going when you get to the docks?'

'Off on the Atlantic convoys on an escort ship – not exactly sure where we're heading, but we report tomorrow and then sail on Monday 13th, Liverpool to somewhere – probably Scapa Flow to start with, at least.

'It'll be cold, then.'

'Yes, you're right there. They've given me a heavy coat, but I think we'll be supplied with a lot more.'

'Will you be away for long?'

'I don't know … I think the initial sailing, out and back, will be about three weeks, but then we might get sent out there again, or somewhere else, so proper leave could be a while away. Who knows? Nobody knows anything, it seems.' He cleared his throat. 'Anyone for another drink?'

'I reckon we'll all be up for that, said Sid. 'Why don't we have a kitty to draw on? If we all put two and six in, that should be plenty.'

'Good idea,' said Robert, 'but I think we men should put in for the ladies too. I mean, we shouldn't expect these lovely, attractive girls to pay for anything.'

'Oh, you're such a flatterer,' Eileen puckered her lips. 'You can buy my drink any time, sailor.'

'You're going to have to keep your eye on that one, Sid,' said Robert, and threw an extra shilling with his half-crown into the centre of the table. The other men followed suit.

'C'mon and help me with the drinks, would you?' Robert said to Sid.

George took the opportunity to speak to Ness while the other men were at the bar. He'd been desperate to talk to her since she had come in with Robert and the others. 'Where did you find him?'

It was Eileen who answered him, and she proceeded to tell him the whole story, embellishing it as much as she could.

George laughed, not unkindly. 'I bet you didn't expect anything to come of it, eh? You could've just put Ness's name and address in *my* coat pocket. At least she'd know what she was getting.' He laughed again and, turning his head to Ness, said, 'I know you enjoyed last Saturday. I hope you don't push me aside too quickly.'

'You're right, I did enjoy the dancing. But that's as far as it goes, George. You know that. Anyway, it's nice to meet someone different who's not from round here, that's what I think.' Ness said. She felt she wasn't being very kind.

George didn't answer, but the others were back now, and they chatted together about the Leeds bombings and the London Blitz, which had thankfully ended back in May. They discussed where the war might be going. The evening went on, and Robert and Ness moved on to talking about books and films they liked. She told him her favourite book was Gone with the Wind, and she asked him which was his favourite. He said he liked P. G. Wodehouse, but couldn't pick a favourite. They focused on each other, while the others were discussing rationing– but Ness could see George glancing over at her every so often.

The time went fast; Ness was surprised when the bell went for last orders. They drank up and made their way out of the pub. Ness shivered outside after the stuffiness and smokiness. She pulled her coat more tightly around her and wound her scarf so it covered her ears. She should have worn a hat, she thought.

They all stood around on the pavement looking at each other.

Sid spoke first. 'What time do you have to leave in the morning, Robert?'

'Pretty early I think, around six probably.'

'Where were you thinking of kipping tonight, then? There's no room at Ness's place.'

'I hadn't really thought about it.'

'Well, you'd best get your bags and walk back with me. My house is closer to the station. You'll be able to get a train first thing to Manchester and from there you can get to Liverpool. You'll have to kip on the floor, I'm afraid.'

Ness jumped in quickly, 'You can kip on the floor in the front room at our place. Mum and Dad won't mind, I'm sure. They'll be in bed asleep by now, anyway – but Sid, thanks for the offer.'

'What about me?' said George. 'You've forgotten about me.'

'You can just get on home,' said Ness.

'Not nice,' said George.

He'd had a skinful, and Ness actually felt a bit sorry for him, 'You'll feel better tomorrow, George. Come on, let's get going.' She moved between Tommy and Robert, and linking her arms through theirs she marched them off down the street.

Seven

Ness put the kettle on and made a cup of tea.

'There's only a couple of biscuits I'm afraid. Baking day's tomorrow. Mum does quite well, considering the rations we get.'

'Don't worry – I'm sure I can manage without,' said Robert.

'I'm off to bed, said Tommy. 'Think I've had more than I ought. See you in the morning.'

Ness and Robert sat at the table.

'I'll go and find a couple of spare blankets for you. The bathroom and toilet are out the back. In the morning, if you want a shave you might have to boil a kettle for hot water. It depends on the stove, if it stays in or not. It heats the water, you see.'

She poured the tea, then said, 'I'll just go and get the blankets, then.'

When she came back downstairs she went straight into the front room, where she found Robert waiting. She hesitated when she saw him, and he immediately said, 'I thought it might be a little more comfortable in here so I brought my tea in. I hope that's all right. I've brought my kitbag in, too.'

'Of course. No problem at all.'

'I took the liberty of bringing in your tea.' He gave her a smile.

There were a couple of armchairs and a small sofa, a rather dull brown with equally dull and weird orange swirly blobs all over that looked like snail trails.

'The furniture's a bit old. I think it might have even belonged to my grandmother before us. My mother has tried to liven it up with a few non-matching cushions and some white antimacassars she picked up at the market.' Ness suddenly saw the whole room in a different light. She was embarrassed when she thought about what Robert's house might be like. 'It's not very fancy in here, I'm afraid. We hardly ever use it. Stupid, really, having a front room sitting empty. We sometimes come in here and listen to the radio, but that's usually in the summer. We stay in the back room during the winter. My mother keeps the room clean, though, it's just the furnishings are a bit—'

'Look, it's fine. My parents don't have the same taste in decor as I do. So I know what you mean. Let's sit down, shall we?'

He waited for Ness to go first and she chose to sit in an armchair. He sat on the sofa, which was at a right angle next to the chair.

'At last we're by ourselves,' Robert said. 'I know it must seem very odd for me to come here and just land myself on you and your family. But ... well ... to tell you the truth I was fascinated by the little note. It was such an unusual thing to happen. Personally I'm glad Eileen did it. I guess it lit a small spark of interest in me. I thought the name Eunice rather unusual, too. You must tell me why you were given it. I know you like to be Ness, though. That's a pretty name too ... Am I waffling?'

'A little bit,' said Ness. 'Why don't you tell me more about what happened?'

'Well, after the ship went down and so many of the crew were lost, I suppose it came home to me rather quickly that I could actually die at any time. I don't mean to be morbid but, you know, most of the time you just get on with it and don't think too much about what might happen – but we were under pressure from the U-boats for several days, other ships had gone down and well ... I don't really want to talk about it, but it just makes your own mortality very real.'

Ness looked at him and saw a sensitive man who had faced death and then decided he was going to live his life to the full. 'I think I know what you mean. It must have been an awful experience. I can't imagine how it'd feel.'

'Yes – and it's not just facing death. It's accepting that I was one of those saved. It makes one feel a terrible guilt, and then a sense that you have to live for those who died. You know, take chances and don't think about the consequences.'

'You're making it all sound very dramatic.'

'Am I? I suppose it was, in a way. All those who went down, sucked under, and the rest of us left floundering in the sea. It wasn't a pleasant experience. We were the last to be sunk at that time. After that the U-boats disappeared ... but you can never be sure they'll not turn up again.'

'It must be really frightening. How were you rescued? If you're allowed to tell me.'

He shifted in his seat. 'We were picked up by one of the other escort ships. In quite a short time, actually. They came close and then dropped nets down. Those who could, clambered up, helping those less able. The sailors on the rescue ship hauled us all over the rail and onto the deck. Never been so glad to see a rating. I even hugged the chap. He must have thought I was bloody mad! Anyway, we were taken to Alex, where we were given some clean kit and a shower. It was the best shower I've ever had.'

'When did you find the note?'

'It was a while later. I was sitting at a bar having a drink with another chap, and when I pulled out a packet of cigarettes I'd been given earlier and put in my pocket, the note came out with it. I was going to swap the cigarettes, you see, because I don't smoke now – well, just the pipe, and I only do that for show, as you know.' He laughed. 'The note dropped onto the table. I picked it up and glimpsed what was on it, and shoved it back into my pocket, keeping quiet about it.'

'Did you show it to anyone?' She asked, hoping he hadn't. She could feel herself getting hot and bothered about the whole incident.

'No. Oddly, I didn't. I rather thought I'd ignore it, so I just held onto it. Then we were sent back to England on the first available ship and given a week's leave. When I changed into my other kit for landing in Portsmouth, I took out the note and put it in a wallet in my kitbag.'

He stopped for a while.

'What happened next?'

He smiled, and paused again. Ness felt it was a bit annoying. She just wanted him to finish the story.

'I spent some time at home and it was while I was there that I looked at the note again. Then I got my orders to go to Liverpool, and I realised the address was up here in the north somewhere, so I thought *Why not go and visit the lady, hoping she isn't as old as my mother?* He smiled, 'I'd got nothing to lose. So here I am.'

'Yes, here you are.' It was the second time she'd said it, and it sounded as feeble as the first time.

'I'm really glad about the whole thing. I mean ... look, if the ship hadn't gone down and I hadn't needed a new kit then, well, we'd never have met, and that'd be a shame.' He put his hand out and covered hers.

It was all a bit fast for Ness, so she gently removed it, 'I'd better be getting to bed,' she said.

'I'm sorry, I shouldn't have done that. But it's so lovely to touch a soft hand.' He smiled. 'But I do understand. We've only just met, so maybe I should hold fire.' He laughed, not at her but more at himself.

'Well, like I said, I should be getting to bed.' Ness stood up and made to leave the front room.

'Would you write to me while I'm at sea? It takes an age for letters to get through and I don't know what it'll be like on the convoys, wherever we go, but I can't tell you how wonderful it is to receive a letter or two. My sister writes to me, but it'd be lovely to get a letter from you.'

Ness smiled and agreed without hesitation.

***

In the morning Ness heard him moving around downstairs. She couldn't make up her mind whether to leave him to it or go and help. It was really early. Still dark, around five-thirty. She heard the kettle, a chair being scraped back, and a clattering of crockery. About fifteen minutes went by, and she couldn't resist the temptation to go down any longer. She threw on some clothes and shoved her feet into her slippers. She tried to walk down the stairs in a nonchalant sort of way but couldn't pull it off. As she reached the hallway, there was Robert standing by the door. He smiled at her when he saw her.

'Morning,' she said. 'You're off, then?'

'Yes, just collecting my things. I'm glad you came down.'

He went towards her. 'Thanks for putting me up. I've left everything tidy in the front room and managed to wash and shave.'

'Did you find anything to eat?'

'A cup of tea was all I needed. I'll get something at the station, if there's anywhere open.'

'Let me make you a sandwich or something. It'll only take a second.' She pushed past him and began to head for the kitchen.

'No, honestly, it's fine. You keep your food. There'll be something for me somewhere.'

He took her hand and squeezed it tight, 'I'll write just as soon as I get a chance. It'll give me something to think about and look forward to. I'll tell you more about Devon. I've not had nearly enough time to find out about you, so you can keep me up to date with what's happing here in Ridley.'

She really laughed then. 'That won't take much time or paper. The most exciting thing that's happened in the last five years is you turning up.'

'I've got to go, or I'm going to miss the train. Not that they stick to the timetable these days.'

She let go of his hand and stood by the door as he left. It was a cold morning, but she watched him walk off up the road and waited to see if he'd look back before he turned the corner. He did, and he gave a little wave. She waved back, and he was gone.

She went back inside. Excitement over for the day. The clock in the back room read five-fifty. Ness decided to make a cup of tea and take it up to her bedroom. Nothing for her to get up for this Sunday morning.

Eight

Saturday 18th October 1941

A whole week had gone by since Robert's visit. Ness hadn't written to him in that time, and she wasn't sure why. She walked round to the library with the express intention of sitting at one of the desks and composing a really good letter. It would be easier away from the prying eyes and questions at home. Her mother had not stopped going on about it all week. Quite annoying.

The first thing she did was to change her library books. She thought she'd find a book by P. G. Wodehouse. She chose *The Inimitable Jeeves* because it had been the first one published, according to the imprint page.

She sat at one of the tables. It was quiet. Ness could hear herself breathing, and the occasional turn of a page and cough from behind the shelves. There was a smell of wood polish, paper, books and leather. The air was serious. The librarian behind the counter was stamping books and sticking labels onto the flyleaves of new ones. A woman came in, shushing a couple of children she had with her. They reached up to hand in the books they were returning, and then she took them over to the children's section to choose some more. Yet again, it was hard to believe there was a war going on outside. Here in Ridley library, it felt no different from any other Saturday afternoon in peacetime.

Ness took out her pad and pen and stared at the blank page. She began by writing her address, which made her smile because she thought of the little note. After five minutes she wrote, *Dear Robert* and after another five minutes she wrote, *It was lovely to meet you last Saturday.* She was getting nowhere fast. She looked at the Jeeves book beside her on the table. Picked it up and opened it and began reading. Immediately she could see that although this was a different world from hers, she was going to enjoy the book. She was drawn in, and an hour passed quickly. She had to make a note of a few words she didn't quite understand – what was a whangee, for goodness' sake? She put two and two together, and reckoned it must be some kind of umbrella.

She went back to her letter. At last she had something interesting to write about. She screwed up the first piece of paper and stuffed it in her handbag. Just like a real author, she imagined. She began writing the letter again.

Saturday 18th October 1941

Dear Robert,

I enjoyed meeting you last weekend and I'm sorry it's taken me a whole week to write. It's Saturday afternoon and I have come to the library. I looked for a book by P. G. Woodhouse and chose the first one published. At least I think it is. I began to read it right away and I'm rather enjoying it, and I can see why you would like it. It's not a world I'm familiar with at all, but it is good to read something different.

It's been a pretty quiet week here in Ridley. I thought about you in that awful cold place and I hope that you have been given all the kit you might need to keep you warm. The nights are drawing in here and it will soon be winter. Can't imagine we'll be as cold as you are, though.

It's hard to know what to write so I thought I could 'talk' you through my week.

Monday: Went to work, and my typewriter ribbon broke. It's not usually a problem, but there were no new ones so I had to try and fix the old one and wind it back onto the spool. Thankfully, it worked okay, but my fingers are still stained with red and blue, so add that to my white hands and I am being rather patriotic.

Tuesday: Went to work. Typewriter ribbon held up fine. In the evening I began to make a dress from some remnants I picked up from the shop floor. But I soon realised there wasn't enough material for a dress, so I made a blouse, which I haven't finished yet. I have a rather ancient sewing machine which works by hand. It's okay, but slow. Sometimes I think I'd be quicker just using a needle and thread!

Wednesday: Went to work. It rained all day so I didn't go for a walk at lunchtime, which I often do. We only get half an hour, but it's good to get out of the place. In the evening I went to my book-keeping class.

Thursday: Went to work. Nothing much else to report except that Gladys, who I work with, is expecting a baby, so she will have to leave. At least I think so, but maybe because of the war they won't insist. But I think she wants to give up work anyway.

Friday: Went to work. Nothing else to report at all. Didn't even go to the pub with anyone in the evening.

Saturday: (today) went to work this morning and now I'm in the library writing to you. Might go out tonight. It depends.

So as you can see a week full of so many exciting things. Oh I did manage to read a good book this week and it wasn't Gone with the Wind. It was another old favourite, by one of the Brontë sisters. I'll let you guess which one. No prizes for getting it right, though.

Well, I'd better close now. Hope this letter finds you, and finds you well. Write back if you get time.

From

Ness x

She added the x on second thoughts, because she didn't think 'from' was very friendly but didn't want to put 'love' or anything similar.

She folded up the paper, put it into the envelope and addressed it. She would post it on her way home. She was looking forward to the rest of Saturday at home with a good book and no pub, dance or cinema. She liked to do that sometimes. Just shut herself away. Eileen was disappointed because she'd hoped Ness would come out with her, Sid and George, but Ness knew it wasn't fair to encourage George. He was okay as a friend – in fact, she liked him a great deal. There was nothing wrong with him, but there was no spark. She wasn't sure there had been a spark between her and Robert, either. She knew that meeting with him was a bit of a novelty, but maybe that's as far as it would go. He might never come back. She had sent the letter, but that might be the end of it. Why would a doctor's son from Devon even be interested in her?

Nine

Wednesday 19th November 1941

When Ness got in from work there was a letter for her from Robert. She waited until she'd eaten and then took it up to her room to read.

Dear Ness,

Thank you for your letter. Sorry I didn't write before, but we were busy learning the ropes on this new route. It was so nice to meet you too, and your friends, back in October. I liked all of them, and Tommy and your parents. The fish and chips were good – nice they're not rationed. At least not yet.

I love the idea that you're reading Wodehouse and that you're enjoying it. Let me think, would the Brontë book be Jane Eyre? It's not my favourite, I must admit. I like Wuthering Heights. I'd like to visit Haworth sometime if I ever get the chance. I don't get much chance to read at the moment but I have brought a book of poetry with me. It's a collection, so there are lots of poets featured – easy to dip in and out of.

*It's very cold where we are in the **XXXXXXXXXX** (not sure if they'll leave that in) anyway, it's really freezing. I can't say much*

about what I'm doing, but the bad news is I'm stuck here, in this job,
XXXXXXXX XXXXXXXX

Devon, London, Ridley – they all seem a very long way away at the moment. Hope you can write again soon. Sending it via sea-mail seems to work.

Kind regards

Robert

Ness's instinct was to reply immediately, but then she thought she'd wait until the weekend. She wasn't sure what to make of his mention of a book of poetry – it wasn't something she'd ever been interested in, but perhaps she'd have a look in the library next Saturday. She didn't know anything at all about poetry, and couldn't imagine that Eileen or any of her friends would know anything either. What she did know was that her father had talked about some poets from the last war. Poets who'd written from the front line. She'd ignored him at the time. Funny how things your parents talk about are often not interesting when you're young. She decided to ask him about it this evening before she went to her book-keeping class.

She changed out of her work clothes, put Robert's letter in the top drawer of her dressing table and went downstairs to find her father, who was sitting looking at the rather depleted version of the local paper.

'Dad?'

'Hmm?' He lowered the paper enough to peer over the top. 'That sounds like a cry for help. Hope it's nothing too complicated – I'm not in the mood.' He smiled anyway.

'I just wanted to ask you about poetry.'

'Me? Poetry? What gives you the idea I know anything about *poetry*?'

She explained about her remembering him saying something when she was younger about the war poets, and she was thinking of maybe reading some poetry and didn't know where to begin.

'I don't really think I'm the right person to ask. Your mother used to read a bit of poetry to me when I was in hospital. She didn't read the war poets, though – that would have been a bit too close to home, if you get me. I think she used to read from a mixed book, you know? One with a few different poets in, but I can't remember what it was called. I think your best bet is to ask at the library. Sorry not to be more of a help. Mind, if you do find something, I'd like to have a read myself, or maybe we could all sit round of an evening and read some.'

That wasn't exactly what Ness had in mind but she hadn't the heart to say so. 'Can't you just give me some idea, a name or something?'

'Your mum'd remember better than me.'

Ness felt like the whole conversation was a waste of time. She sometimes thought there was more to her dad than he ever let on. War does terrible things to people. He hardly ever spoke about his experiences, nor did her mother. Ness used to press them sometimes because she thought it was so romantic that Mary had nursed Jack when he was injured. That was how they'd met. She imagined them now with her mother reading poetry to her dad, but somehow she couldn't really bring the picture to mind. They didn't seem the sort of people to do that. It's strange, Ness thought, how little she knew about her parents.

She asked her mother the same questions about the poets. She came up with Kipling and Wordsworth and Byron, and then she said,

'Of course there's always the Poet Laureate, John Masefield. Everyone knows his poem 'Sea Fever' – *I must go down to the sea again ...*'

Ness was surprised, and wished she'd had this conversation before, 'Didn't you ever think of introducing me to some poetry?'

'Not really. I thought you'd do it at school.'

'I don't think I paid attention. I was more interested in reading novels and doing the country dancing. Thanks anyway. I'll go to the library on Saturday.'

'What's brought all this on, anyway?' asked Mary.

'Nothing in particular. I want to broaden my reading, that's all.' Ness wasn't ready to share her reason yet, although they would know she'd received a letter and probably guessed it was from Robert.

Ten

Saturday 21st March 1942

Ness lay on her bed. Her parents were working in the shop and she was staying out of the way. Tommy was out with the Home Guard. She loved Saturday afternoons, especially when nobody was around. She'd not had a letter from Robert for ages and couldn't be bothered to write to him. She wasn't sure why she'd been writing to him anyway. It was over a year since Eileen had put the labels in the pockets, and nearly six months since she'd seen him that one time.

She looked at her room and wondered if she could change things around a bit. She liked to do that every so often. It kept things fresh and made her feel as though she were somewhere different. She was inventive – she could turn an old bedcover into curtains, a dress, a pair of trousers – anything, really. She was always drawing designs in a sketchbook she'd been given for Christmas one year. The bedroom was rectangular, and at the moment the bed was on a long side under the window, which looked out over the back yard and to other houses. Ness thought about moving it to the short wall then putting her dressing table in its place. Then she could perhaps make some long curtains down to the floor, although that might be too much. Anyhow, it was easy enough to move the bed, so she began there.

After shifting everything around Ness sat back on her bed and surveyed the room. She decided she didn't like the mirror on the dressing table; it obscured the view through the window and made closing the curtains difficult. She decided to ask Tommy to take it off when he came home. She didn't really need it anyway. She could hang it on another wall. Otherwise she was satisfied with the changes she'd made.

It was time for a cup of tea, and as she made her way down the stairs she heard a knock on the front door. She hoped it wasn't Eileen, just a hawker she could get rid of. She didn't want her afternoon at home alone to be messed up. It was no good guessing who might be out there, though, so she went ahead and opened the door.

'Hello, stranger.'

Ness couldn't believe her eyes when she saw Robert standing there. 'Are you going to make a habit of turning up uninvited and unexpected?' she asked, in a not particularly friendly way.

'I'm sorry, I know I should have written – but I've got twenty-four hours before the ship leaves again from Liverpool. Not enough time to go home to Devon.'

'That's no excuse. Honestly, I'm a bit shocked.'

'Aren't you going to ask me in? Aren't you pleased to see me?'

'I'll let you in – but I'm not going to answer your second question for a moment,' Ness said. But she couldn't resist a little smile behind his back as he walked into the hall past her. She took his coat and hung it by the door. Now it only seemed a minute ago it had been hanging there in October.

'How have you been?'

'So-so. I was just thinking about you a little while ago. Thinking it had been a while since I'd heard from you. I thought you must have forgotten all about me. Now you're here, it feels like you only left a week ago. Come on, I'll put the kettle on. I was going to have a cup of tea anyway.'

'That'd be lovely. It'd go down very well indeed.' Robert smiled at her: 'You've no idea how much I've looked forward to a decent cup of tea.'

'Come on, then, come and sit down.'

'Thank you for your letters. It was sometimes difficult to write back because we were at sea for long periods of time, backwards and forwards with the convoys. I'm not supposed to say where, but let me just add that it was freezing cold the whole time.' He laughed.

'Well you're here now.' Ness thought it was all a little bit awkward and hoped that by the time they sat down things would be a bit more relaxed. 'Sorry, there's no biscuits again. I could pop into the shop and get a couple if you like. Mum and Dad are in there now. Saturday afternoon's usually quite busy, so they both work in there. Sometimes Eileen and I do a stint.'

'I don't need a biscuit. Just tea'll be fine. Okay if I plonk myself down here?' He didn't wait for an answer.

For a minute they sipped their tea in silence. The realisation that they didn't know each other at all well hung between them. They'd written letters, yes, but that wasn't the same as spending time together. Even so, Ness felt a sort of connection with Robert and wondered if he felt the same. Surely, he wouldn't have written and wouldn't be here unless there was something.

'I've enjoyed reading the P. G. Wodehouse books. They made me laugh out loud sometimes. I'm glad you told me about them. I need a few more recommendations now.'

'I never stopped thinking about you the whole time. Your face in my mind kept me going through some bad times. It's been tough, Ness. Really tough, I've seen a few sights, I can tell you.' He moved his hand towards hers on the table.

Ness swiftly wrapped both her hands around her cup. 'Not much changed around here, as you can see. Tommy's enjoying being a member of the Home Guard, which keeps him out of mischief. He's got pretty good at boxing, of all things.'

'I kept thinking about your name – Eunice – and wondering how you came to be given it. It's quite unusual, isn't it?'

'It means 'good victory', and it's Greek. My parents met during the last war. My dad was injured and Mum nursed him. I'd like to think there was a real story behind them giving me the name but so far they've haven't told me anything. At least anything they want to share. I wondered if it had been the name of a long-lost relative. But actually they said that they just liked the name. Thank goodness they only ever call me Ness, though.'

'How did they decide on Ness?'

'It was because I couldn't say Eunice when I was little and I called myself Ness.'

'Interesting.'

'No, I think you mean boring – which pretty much sums up my life.'

'Come, now. It's not that bad. You're *seriously* down in the dumps today. Perhaps I shouldn't have come after all.'

Ness felt a sudden rush of guilt. She didn't know why she was being so miserable, so she said, 'In answer to your second question at the door, yes, I *am* pleased to see you. Despite the fact I'd been enjoying having the place to myself for a few hours until you came in to spoil my solitude.'

Robert looked taken aback, and Ness laughed and took his hand. 'I'm only joking. Just, next time you come please let me know in advance and then I can prepare myself.'

'What like a meal? I don't need to eat you.' Robert squeezed her hand. 'Talking of food, what'll we do tonight then? Will it be fish and chips again? Old habits die hard.'

'That'd be good. We can go and fetch them together. We'll just pop into the shop, say hello to Mum and Dad and tell them what we're up to.'

***

At the chippie they met Eileen, Sid and George who were all, except for George, delighted to see Robert again and greeted him with enthusiasm.

'Hello, stranger,' said Sid. 'What have you been up to? Sunk any U-boats lately?'

'Not allowed to say, but it's been a successful, if not a freezing, few months, thank you.'

'We must stop meeting like this,' said George with a sour face.

'Well, Ness, you're not keeping him all to yourself this evening,' said Eileen. 'We're going to pop down to the Masons Arms. You must come too – it'll be like old times.'

'Bring Tommy too,' shouted George.

Ness wasn't too keen on the idea and she wondered what Robert thought, then he said, 'I don't mind going to the pub, but I wondered if we could go to the pictures instead? Do we have to go to Leeds for that? Surely there's a cinema in Ridley.'

Ness was relieved. 'There's the Globe, but I don't know what it's showing. We can find out when we get back to the house. It'll be in the paper I expect. We could take the long way home and have a look – but if we do the fish and chips'll get cold.'

'I'll take a chance on the paper.'

Back at the house Robert didn't need to find out from the newspaper which film was showing because Tommy knew. 'It's *Mrs Miniver*, if you can face it. Load of twaddle as far as I'm concerned.'

Robert and Ness went to the cinema and sat side by side. He held her hand at one point and she didn't object. She couldn't concentrate on the film. She didn't want to let go of his hand. It was warm and dry. She didn't want to do more than hold his hand either. She hadn't planned any of this, and she scolded herself for writing to him, which would have only encouraged him. She decided she was just confused.

Walking back to the house they chatted about the *Mrs Miniver* but as Ness hadn't watched it properly she couldn't contribute much.

'I think they portrayed the London Blitz pretty well, don't you?' said Robert.

'It was frightening,' agreed Ness. 'The bombing's been pretty bad in Leeds, but they seem to always bypass Ridley. We've been lucky.'

Before they went in through the front door. Robert pulled Ness towards him and kissed her softly on the lips. Ness enjoyed it, but pushed him gently away from her. 'Don't rush me, please.'

'I'm sorry. I couldn't help it. You're a very beautiful girl. But there's no hurry.' They went into the house, holding hands.

Once again, Ness brought the blankets downstairs to the front room for Robert to make up a bed and stay the night. They sat in the front room and talked about their childhoods. Ness's parents came in and joined in the conversation for a while, as did Tommy, then everyone went off to bed.

Mary was very pointed about Ness coming up with them. 'Come on, lass, you need to get up them stairs. Robert'll be tired after all the travelling he's been doing. You best leave him to get his beauty sleep, too.'

Although Ness was embarrassed by the way her mother spoke, in some ways she felt relieved, as it took the pressure off her having to make any awkward rebuffs. She was sure Robert would want to take things a little further than he had on the doorstep, but she just wasn't quite ready. At least she didn't think she was.

Eleven

Sunday 22nd March 1942

When Robert arrived back at the docks in Liverpool and walked up the gangplank he was met, as usual, by the quartermaster. This time, though, he handed Robert a telegram.

As he read it the colour drained from his face.

'All right, mate?'

'It's my father – he's gravely ill. My sister wants me to go down to Devon. They say he won't last more than a couple of days. How ironic! I was thinking my family would receive this kind of message about me, not the other way around.'

'Not sure the Navy'll let you go. You'll have to speak to the captain.'

'I've no doubt they'll spare me if they can. Thompson had a similar situation last Christmas, and they gave him compassionate leave for a fortnight. I'll need a week at least.'

'Well, good luck, mate.'

Robert was given ten days' leave. He should have felt glad to be going back to Devon to see his family, but he was unsettled. It was a nightmare journey from Liverpool to Totnes, and he only hoped he'd get back in time to see his father before it was too late.

His sister would be there to meet him, just the same as last time. He thought about Ness. It was extraordinary the effect she'd had on him. He'd tried to fight it, but seeing her again had just fired up his feelings. Bloody war, bloody Navy, bloody everything. He stared out of the train window as it neared his station and pulled hard at his pipe. He wouldn't be able to smoke once in the car or back at his parents' house.

By the time Rose and Robert arrived back at the house it was gone 10 pm. The dog was as happy to see him as ever, although Robert thought he detected the old boy was a bit unsettled.

'What's up, boy? You can tell something's up, can't you? Down now, there's a good dog. I'll take you out in the morning.'

He saw his mother approaching down the stairs and moved towards her. 'Hello, Mother. How are you bearing up? It's an awful business. Rose told me Dad's had a stroke and it's pretty bad. Is he conscious?'

'Hello, Robert. So many questions. Yes, it's a bad stroke; they think he must have had more than one. He hasn't come round at all since it happened. It was after work last Monday and I was out that evening, unfortunately, as was Rose, so he lay for some time slumped on his desk. The ambulance came, and Doctor Bligh from Totnes, but they decided we should keep him at home. I think they know nothing can be done. I've tried to look after him as best I can ... with help of a nurse and Rose of course ... but he just doesn't respond ...' Her voice broke into a sob and she moved to sit down on a chair in the hallway.

'Well, I'm here now. I don't have to be back for a few days, so I can help.'

'That's kind of you, Robert. Perhaps you'd like to go up and see him now. The nurse is with him, settling him for the night, but she'll be gone soon.'

Robert went up the stairs with a heavy step. He didn't know what to expect. He'd seen enough men sick or dying, and he'd always assumed his father would die before he did, but now it was actually happening he found a torrent of thoughts and regrets storming his brain.

It was dim in the bedroom, and the nurse was leaving as he opened the door.

'He's quiet now and his breathing's very shallow. I don't think it'll be long. Possibly this evening. It's Robert, isn't it?'

'Yes. It is.'

'I'll be downstairs if you need me. I won't go home tonight.'

Robert closed the door gently behind her as she left, grateful for her presence, yet grateful too that she was gone from the room. He was anxious to spend time with his father and speak to him alone while he had the chance. Even if his father couldn't respond he hoped he would hear him. He wanted to tell him things he hadn't spoken of before, or at least for a while. He sat down beside the bed and tried to take in what he saw. His father's face was pale and like marble, expressionless, as though he'd already gone.

'Dad, it's Robert,' he said, taking his father's limp hand in his. The skin was paper-thin, from dehydration he thought, not just age. How old was he, anyway? Robert wondered how it was he couldn't remember his father's age. *He must be well over sixty,* he thought.

'I hope you can hear me. I wanted to tell you how well I've done in the Navy and to say I'm sorry if I let you down by not joining the

Army. I wish we'd had a bit more time together lately, since I've been a man and not a boy. I think we could share more now we've both seen action in the forces ...' Robert hesitated, 'I do love you, Father. I hope you know that, and I know you love me. We haven't always agreed, but that would have been boring.'

Robert paused again, wishing the words would come more freely. 'I don't know what else to say, even though I've not said nearly enough.'

His eyes tingled with tears, but he held them back – his father would not appreciate emotional weakness in him, a man. Robert sat silently, holding his father's hand and waiting.

Rose and his mother came into the room, and then they were all waiting. There didn't seem anything for any of them to say, so they sat, lost in their own thoughts.

Robert's father died in the early hours of the morning. The doctor came, the vicar came, and the undertaker. The family saw to the formalities without saying too much. Robert was glad he'd managed to get back before his father had passed away, and he thought his mother was pleased he'd been present, although she never said so. He and Rose felt a little closer after the night was over.

The next morning, after a late and rather stilted breakfast around the large kitchen table. Rose and Robert decided to take the dog out for a walk.

'You sure you'll be all right, Mother?' asked Robert.

'Yes, you two go on out. I've got some telephone calls to make, and I think I'd rather be on my own.'

Paddy was obviously glad to be away from the gloom and restrictions of the house, and he ran everywhere sniffing and poking at the side of the path and, when they got to The Ham, rolling over and sliding along, rubbing his back along the wet grass.

'I thought I'd feel much worse than I do now that Father's dead,' said Rose.

'It's the relief, probably. You had to spend a bit more time here before the final hour than I did. You might be in shock, so don't be surprised if you feel dreadful later.'

They walked side by side, Rose kicking the stones on the pathway and Robert breathing in the smell of the estuary – a cross between salt water and fresh, crabs and seaweed, meadow flowers and grass. It seeped into his lungs and he loved it.

At last Rose spoke. 'I've been asked to go to London, to work at the Air Ministry. It's not really come at the right time, but I'm ready to go – have been for ages, really – so I've accepted.'

'What about Mother? Do you think she'll be all right on her own?'

'She's much stronger than you imagine, Robert. You've been away from home too long. She'll be fine. It'll take a little time, and I'm not thinking of bunking off before the week's out. I'll introduce the idea gradually, after the funeral, and see how things play out. What about you? Will you have to go back immediately?'

'I expect so. I'm glad they've arranged it in just two days – amazing. I've got ten days' leave but I might go back a couple of days earlier. There's someone I want to see.'

'Is it someone I should know about?'

Robert didn't want to say too much but he'd spent a great deal of the night thinking about Ness. His father's death had come out of the blue, and probably his father had not managed to achieve many of the things he wanted, because he'd run out of time. Robert wasn't planning on dying any time soon, but you never know – and he wasn't exactly leading a safe life right now. He wanted to go back and see Ness again, and this time make the situation less tenuous. He was sure she felt the same way, even though she'd been a little reluctant when he was there.

'Are you going to tell me or not?' asked Rose.

Robert threw a stick for Paddy and without facing his sister said, 'It's this girl, you see – Ness she's called – I've fallen in love with her.'

Twelve

Saturday 4th April 1942

Ness sat behind the shop counter reading a copy of Vogue magazine. One of the women in the office had passed it on to her, it was a few months out of date but Ness liked to read the ideas about dressmaking and keep up with what the latest styles might be. Her parents had gone to visit relatives, a thing they rarely did, but her mother's sister was ill and as it was the Easter weekend they'd taken advantage of Easter Monday off and left on Friday night. Ness didn't need to go to work on the Saturday morning so had gone straight into to the shop. Tommy was out as usual with the Home Guard, honing his boxing skills. He'd taken to skipping in the back yard as often as he could.

The doorbell rang. Ness put the magazine on the counter and stood up.

'Hello Ness.'

Ness raised her eyebrows quizzically when she saw Robert just inside the door.

'Sorry, I've done it again. But this time I really *am* sorry.'

'How come you're back here so soon?' was all she could think of to say.

'I meant to write to you, but it's all been very difficult. When I got back to the ship last time there was a telegram waiting for me. My father was seriously ill and my sister wanted me back home at once. I didn't think they'd give me leave because I'd only just had twenty-four hours, but I went to the captain anyway. I said I'd need at least a week, but he gave me ten days. It was a nightmare getting home from Liverpool to Totnes, but I did it.

'Did you ... did your father die?'

'Yes, sadly he did, but I got there in time. But I'm not sure he was aware of me sitting by the bed. We didn't get on, you see. He'd never liked the fact I joined the Navy. He was all Army, but I had the sea in my soul. I hated the idea of joining the Army. I don't think he ever forgave me.'

'Did you make your peace, though?'

'Well, I made it with myself, I suppose. I just hope he heard me.'

Ness sensed he was still upset with everything. She waited a second before asking, 'How's your mother coping?'

'All right, I think. She's ten years younger than Dad – not that it makes a difference, but I think she'll be fine. She didn't seem that keen to see me. We're not a close family. At least my sister and I are, but my parents are not that loving. Never have been. I had the feeling my mother thought I was in the way.'

'People react differently to death, though. Perhaps she's just grieving.'

'Yes. That's very true ...

'Look, I can shut up shop here in a minute. Nobody's been in this afternoon except you. I'm wasting my time in here, and if anybody needs anything urgently they'll just come and knock on the door. That's what usually happens.'

Back at the kitchen table, Robert began to laugh. 'Well Ness, here I am again drinking tea in your kitchen. Please don't let's have fish and chips tonight, and don't let's tell anyone I'm here.'

'Why did you decide to come back?'

'I'm here because this is where I want to be ... with you ...'

'But ...'

'I know I shouldn't be. I know it's all too soon for you, but I've thought of little else but you over the last few days. Especially after my father died. I know he wasn't young, but life can be snatched away at any time – and particularly now with the war on. Plus ... I've grown very fond of you very quickly.'

'I like you, too.'

'Do you think you could like me more?'

'I'm not sure.' Ness smiled, put down her cup and took his hand.

Robert cupped her hand in both of his and pulled her up so they were standing beside the table. He stroked her cheek with the back of his hand. He let his finger move across her lips and then took her head in his hands, drew her face towards his and kissed her. Ness enjoyed it. This time there *was* a spark – no mistaking it. She kissed him back. They stood holding each other for a short time. A warm, close embrace.

'Shall we go up to my bedroom?' she said. 'It's more comfortable in there. One thing might lead to another.'

'Are you sure about this, Ness?'

'Well, it's not *proper* – but yes. I'm fine with it.'

'Will anyone come home?'

'Tommy won't be home until much later this evening. My parents won't be back until tomorrow, late.'

'How convenient. It's almost as though it was arranged for us,' said Robert, and then added, 'but what about any shop customers who come knocking?'

'They'll go home empty-handed, won't they?'

***

Tommy arrived home around ten o'clock to find Ness and Robert in deep discussion in the back room. They were sitting each side of the stove in the easy chairs usually occupied by Ness's parents.

'What's on here, then? You can't be on leave again already,' said Tommy.

'No, I'm not really on leave – well, not proper leave.'

'Robert's father died, and they gave him some compassionate. He's off again tomorrow for Liverpool.'

'Sorry to hear that, mate. Really sorry. If I'd known you'd be here I would have skived off tonight.'

'Don't worry. Ness and I are getting along very well. We've had a good time getting to know each other.' Robert looked at Ness directly, and she blushed.

'Well, that's all right, then. I'll be off to bed now. Do you want me to help make the bed up in the front room for you?'

Ness butted straight in. 'No, you get off, I'll do it.' She ran off upstairs to get the bed linen and blankets.

'Righto then. I'll go and use the bathroom and then leave you both to it. Goodnight.'

Robert went into the front room and put the cushions on the floor. He hoped Ness would join him in there, but realised they would have to pretend they slept well apart.

Ness came in through the open door and handed the bedding to Robert. 'I'm going to use the bathroom and then go up to bed.'

Robert looked dismayed. Ness smiled and came up to him and, putting her arms around him, she whispered, 'Want me to come back down again?'

He buried his head in her hair and held her close, breathing in the very Nessness of her. 'You *bet* I do. Don't be long.'

***

Once Ness was sure Tommy was asleep, she crept down the stairs and joined Robert. They made the most of the night. It had all happened rather fast for Ness, but once hooked she was enjoying being caught. Afterwards, they talked in hushed tones well into the night.

'We should probably have talked more before we got up to no good,' said Robert.

'There'll be plenty of time for talk in the future. And more letter-writing. I know it's ridiculous, but I do honestly feel like I've known you for ages.'

'Yes, I know what you mean.'

'Let's get some sleep now, shall we? I'll have to get up early, before Tommy does.'

***

Around seven in the morning, Ness went to the bathroom and then ran up the stairs back to her bedroom. She shouted for Tommy to wake up and come down for his breakfast, knowing he would most likely grab something and run out of the house. It was Sunday, but since he'd joined the Home Guard he never missed a Sunday training session.

'Bye, Sis. Bye, Robert. See you next time. Give my love to the Atlantic, or the Med or wherever you're going now.'

Robert and Ness sat quietly for a while. Ness made some toast and they ate it with a scrape of dripping and some homemade jam.

Both of them knew that the last few hours had been precious and not likely to be repeated for a good few months. What was supposed to be a happy time was turning into a heavy weight of gloom.

Ness held back the tears and tried to sound positive. 'My parents will be sorry to have missed you. We don't get many visitors from away, so I know they'll wish they'd been here. They like you anyway.' She felt she sounded pathetic. She really wanted to shower Robert with talk of undying love and throw herself at his feet. It was so out of character that she was frightening herself, so instead of being romantic she just said, 'It was good yesterday and last night wasn't it?' She'd not done it before so she hadn't got anything to judge it by, but didn't want to say too much. She was sure Robert was experienced, at least it seemed that way.

'It wasn't just good – it was *wonderful*,' he said.

They smiled stupidly at each other.

'I don't like this,' she said. 'I can't stand it. I'd give anything for us to have the pleasure of being together for a bit longer. I'm not asking for months, just a little more time, enough so we can know each other better before you have to leave. I know that it's important for you to go off and fight – but right now I don't care, I don't care about anything, only us.'

'I understand, I really do. But sad as it is, we have met at a difficult time. It's not possible for me to just up and leave the Navy. I have to go on and do what I can to make sure the future for us is what we'd want. I'd happily give it all up for you – but right now I have a duty, to my country and to our families. Sadly, I have no choice but to leave.'

'Don't say any more. I understand,' said Ness.

Robert stood up and walked around to where she was sitting, pulled her to her feet and held her close. He savoured the smell of her hair, the feel of her tiny ears and the look of her eyes. He would take the memories with him, tucked away in a pocket in his heart. He knew he was in love. He thought her wonderful. Right now, she was perfect. He pushed her gently away and held her at arm's length.

'I have to go. I can't stay any longer.' He pulled out a piece of paper from his kitbag. 'Here, my sister Rose knows about you. Please, if you need anything, here's my address and telephone number in Devon. You can call them. I don't believe you'll have any privileged access via the Navy to my whereabouts or my possible fate – we're not connected officially in any way. But really, if you're at all worried then you must contact my family.'

She took the piece of paper and read it quickly before putting it in the pocket of her trousers. 'Another address in a pocket,' she said.

After a pause, Robert said, 'I love you, Ness.'

'I love you too, and I can't *wait* for you to come back. I'll write, I promise.'

'Do you by any chance have a photograph of yourself I could have, please?'

Ness ran upstairs to her bedroom and took out a tin containing a few photos. There was one of her leaning on a wall in Harrogate, taken on a works outing they'd gone on in the summer of '39. She took it down to Robert.

'It's a couple of years old, I'm afraid.'

'It's lovely.'

Robert put the photograph safely into his wallet, then said, 'It's best not to linger too long over goodbyes. Remember, I love you and I *will* be back.'

Just inside the front door they kissed and hugged. Outside they stood for a moment longer.

'Goodbye,' said Ness.

'Goodbye,' Robert said. Then he was off.

Ness watched him as he walked down the road and waited for him to turn and wave again as he got to the corner. Again, she returned the wave. Again, he was gone. She tried not to cry, but she couldn't help herself. She pulled out a hanky from her pocket, and the piece of paper with the Devon address on it fell out. She picked it up and remained standing outside her front door until there was no point in staying there any longer. 'Goodbye,' she said to the empty corner.

Thirteen

Sunday 5th April 1942

Y ou all right, mate?' The man sitting next to Robert on the train nudged him. 'Only you've gone a bit of a funny colour and your hands are shaking.'

'I'll be all right, thank you. I was drifting off ... Sorry to disturb you.'

'That's okay, I know what you fellows have been going through, doesn't matter which service you're in, it can be bloody difficult. I was in the Army in the last lot, you know, but too old this time. I would've gone, though, if they'd let me.'

'Yes,' said Robert, 'I know.'

He shook his hands and rubbed them together. They were clammy and sticky. He leant back onto the headrest of the seat and closed his eyes. He could see Ness's beautiful face, and he knew without a doubt he held her above everything and everyone. What a week it had been. His emotions were all over the place. Bereaved and in love. *Can't get more diverse than that,* he thought. He longed for the bloody war to be over. With his eyes tight shut he let himself daydream and think of life when it was all over. London with Ness. That would be amazing.

Holidays in Devon. Dogs, kids. These thoughts and dreams would get him through the next few months. He was lucky.

'Where are you off to, then, when you get to Liverpool?' asked the man, disturbing Robert's thoughts.

'Joining the convoys. Not sure where we're going – the Med perhaps, Gibraltar, Malta, probably.'

'This war's a bad business, so I hear. I've seen it on the Pathé News at the cinema. North Africa looks bad.'

'Yes,' Robert replied, and hoped the man didn't want to carry on talking about it. He was trying to resist the dark thoughts that crept over him. Nobody really knew how bad it was; they'd read stuff and seen the news bulletins, but Malta seemed to be holding out. The German bombing of supply ships had been heavy, Malta was under siege, and had been since 1940. Robert closed his eyes again and willed the man to take the hint that he really didn't want to talk.

'Got a girl, have you?' The man winked. 'One in every port, I bet.'

'Two in every port, actually.' Robert hoped that would shut him up.

The train began to slow as it entered the outskirts of Liverpool; the devastation from the bombing raids was still evident, with streets destroyed and rubble everywhere. The sight of it silenced the man. He took off his hat and held it in his lap, and Robert followed suit, as they passed a bombed school, one half of it completely obliterated and the other half with blown-out windows.

'Let's hope they weren't at school when it happened. They're probably in another area now. They'll treat it all as a bit of fun perhaps, being somewhere new,' said Robert.

'I've noticed the kids round our way treat the bombsites as playgrounds. What a time to be growing up, though.'

Lime Street station was heaving with soldiers and sailors. It was pouring with rain, April showers at their worst, and the wind whipped around the corners of the buildings. Robert pulled his duffel coat around him, hunched his shoulders and put his head down. He put his pipe in his pocket, adjusted his kitbag on his shoulder, and walked fast. He wanted to lose the man and get to the docks as quickly as possible.

He hurried along from the railway station, pushing his way through the throngs walking in the road as much as on the pavement. He was surprised to see the trams still running, although he imagined there must have been some disruption. He marvelled at the way people carried on as though nothing had happened. 'It's the British fighting spirit,' his father would have said.

Robert didn't have to report to the docks until early Monday morning, so he found a pie shop before going to his digs, a small B&B. He asked the landlady for some paper and envelopes, which she gladly gave him: 'I like to keep a stock here. Most of the fellas who stay here like to write home before they go. They're all off somewhere that could be dangerous, and not sure when or if they'll be back.'

Her words were not exactly cheering, so he took himself off upstairs. There was a small chest of drawers in the room and a chair, which he sat on but at an angle, because there was nowhere for his legs to fit under. It was uncomfortable but bearable. He wrote first to Ness.

My darling Ness,

I'm staying in a Bed & Breakfast not far from the port. Just hope I don't get bombed this evening! The landlady here is plump but perhaps not too jolly. I think she'll serve a good breakfast, though.

I'm missing you so much already, and when I look at the single bed here in my room, I think of how cosy it would be to snuggle up with you. I understand what you meant about knowing each other so well even though we've hardly had any time together. I know you like reading, and I wish so much that I could share my books with you. We have so many of them at Dittisham. Send me a list of everything you have read, and we can compare notes. I love a good murder mystery. I've read most of Agatha Christie's. She lives not far from our house, on the opposite side of the water. One of my favourites is Murder on the Orient Express. I wonder if we'll ever get to travel on that train? Doubt it on a journalist's pay!

What else do I know about you? You're good at sewing and you like going to the pictures – and I think you're a little bit ambitious. It's wonderful you're learning book-keeping. It wouldn't suit me. You're far too interesting to be an accountant, by the way.

When I was at school I had to write home every week and it rather put me off letter-writing. However, writing to you is proving to be a joy.

I can't wait to see you again. I must stop writing now. I'll write again as soon as I can. Take care, my beloved. I'll see you again soon.

With all my love - until we meet again.

Robert xxx

PS don't forget to write to Rose at some point. She may write to you first, I suppose, but I would really like you two to meet up.

He wrote to his mother without mentioning Ness – she wouldn't understand – and then he penned a quick letter to his sister.

Dear Rose,

I hope things are not too bad at home. Mother will be fine, I'm sure; she's got so many friends to support her. Get on with what you want to do as soon as you can. Head to London, and you can stay in the flat.

I wanted to tell you about Ness. I declared my feelings to her and it appeared she felt the same. I won't go into detail, but let's just say we sealed our relationship. It's early days, but I've never felt so sure about anyone before. I've given her our Devon address and telephone number and told her to call if she needs to. Actually, I've told her to write to you anyway. It would be lovely if you two could make contact.

I'm not planning on doing anything stupid, and I'll try not to put myself in danger – but it could be tough out where I'm headed. I've written Ness's address at the end of this letter, and if anything at all should happen to me I want you to get in touch with her straight away, please, especially if you haven't written to each other before. She doesn't have a telephone. You'll like her very much, and I'm sure you'll be good friends when this bloody war is over.

I'll call when I'm next on leave, if I get any, but I may not get back to Devon because any time I do get I'll use to go and see Ness.

Good luck with the new job!

Much love

Robert x

Fourteen

Tuesday 7th April 1942 Southall, Middlesex

Alf looked at the stew on his plate. He didn't have much appetite. He and his mum Gladys lived in an Edwardian semi-detached three-bedroom house, the same as all the others down the road. Alf's dad had died from tuberculosis and left his mum a widow. The house was too big for just the two of them, so she took in lodgers – there was one staying at the moment, but he'd gone off for a few days.

Alf's room, though, was always kept free in case he came home unexpectedly. Which is what had happened today. His ship had gone down in the Med in the middle of March. and after being picked up he had ended up in Alexandria, then, after a week there he was sent home. He'd not liked Alex – he didn't really like the Navy, and he was not happy right now. Tonight he was feeling particularly miserable. The last letter he'd had from his girl, Judith, she'd written and given him the push. Passed him over. She didn't say she had anyone else, but she did say she didn't want to hang around for him. But they'd been together for a while. Local kids together, then as a couple. Alf was angry, and he couldn't keep his feelings hidden.

'Cheer up, Alf. It might never happen. I'm pleased to have you home even if it's only for a short while. Pity you didn't make it for Easter Sunday – we could have gone to church together.'

'Look, Mum, I've just spent the last few weeks being sunk, rescued and sent back here. I wouldn't have gone to church with you anyway, even if I had been here on Sunday. On top of everything else, Judith's not my girl any more – and there's hardly *any* meat in this stew.' He knew he wasn't being very nice to his mum, but he didn't care.

'Well, there's plenty of vegetables in it.'

Gladys loved her garden and even kept a few chickens for fresh eggs, which were hard to come by for most people. Since Alf had last been home an Anderson shelter had been installed – only small, but enough for four people to sleep in. 'It's quite cosy in there if we're all in it. I share it with my neighbours – there's just the two of them at the moment. Bill, the husband, he helped me put the thing up so it's only fair we share it. I'm grateful for the company sometimes. This lodger I've got at the moment is a bit quiet, he keeps himself to himself. He works for the War Office.'

Gladys and Alf were sitting in the front room to eat. It was just about big enough for a dining table by the window, and a sofa with a couple of armchairs around the fire in the back part of the room. On the side was a wireless which Gladys kept on as much as she could, even though the reception was a bit crackly. She mostly listened to the Home Service during the day to keep up with the news about the war, then in the evenings the Light Programme for music and plays.

'Looks like there's been a fair bit of bombing round here. I guess they're aiming for the airfield at Heston,' said Alf, trying to get off the subject of himself.

'It's been pretty bad. I wouldn't be surprised if the sirens didn't go this evening. It's too bad when they go during the day, too – sometimes I start a job in the house in the morning and I never get the chance to finish it. I'm in and out of that shelter like a jack in the box!' Gladys laughed, a hearty loud laugh. She was relaxing for the first time in a long while. It was good to have her son back with her. She carried on: 'You know, right down the street on the other side of the road there was a bomb dropped but it didn't go off. They evacuated everybody from the houses close by, and the poor people had to stay in the church hall for four days and four nights until it was safe for them to go back.'

'What did they do with the bomb?'

'They've left it. Apparently, it wasn't set on a time fuse so it won't go off now. I suppose they'll lift it sometime.'

'Mum, I'm tired. If it's okay with you, I'll pop down to the pub for a drink. I'll not be long.'

As he walked down the road. Alf noticed more devastation. When he got to the corner of the road his face dropped when he saw that the house next to the pub was broken in half. It looked so weird with the wallpaper showing, part of a staircase sticking up in the middle and a mess of rubble and brick with an armchair on the top of it. Alf hurried into the pub and leant on the bar, his face pale. It had been Judith's house.

'Evening, Alf. You all right? What'll you have to drink? The first one's on me, I like to treat all the servicemen who come in here to at least one.'

'What happened next door? Are the family okay?' asked Alf.

'Didn't your mum tell you? They were away when it happened. It was Judith's wedding day – she married a butcher from Brighton, and they all went down there for the wedding.'

'My mum probably didn't want to upset me.' Alf took his beer to a table in the corner of the bar where he sat brooding. He ordered more beer. There was nobody else in the pub that he knew. He let the whole Judith business eat into his head. *Why did she change? We'd made plans. But when I was away fighting she was at home messing about with a bloody butcher of all things. And I didn't have enough meat in my stew. This thought almost made him laugh until he realised how true it was. Well, I'll show her. I won't hang around, I can find someone else, no problem. I'll have one more before I leave.*

He pulled out his wallet for the fifth time that night. When he drew out a pound note he saw the little ticket with the name and address on it. He'd found it in the top pocket of the uniform shirt he'd been given after the sinking of his ship. Now he read the ticket again, and in that moment made the decision to pay this woman in Ridley a visit. He'd go back to Liverpool early and visit her on the way. He was pretty sure it was doable, but he'd check on the road atlas when he got back home, to see which station he'd have to get to.

Fifteen

Wednesday 8th April 1942

'Why do you have to leave so quickly? I thought you said you had a week, and you've only been here a *day*.'

'I'm sorry, Mum, but I got a telegram to say I had to report to Liverpool as soon as I could. I'm fit and well so I can't refuse.' Alf was a bit uneasy about lying to his mum – she could see right through him – but he just couldn't stay here a day longer.

'When did the telegram arrive, then?'

'This morning while you were out doing the veg and the hens.'

He thought she was going to ask more details or ask to see proof, but she let it go: 'Well, let me pack you up some grub for your journey. How will you get there?'

'Bus into central London then train.'

'Better pack you up enough for the day, then.' She went off to the kitchen. Alf went upstairs, rolled up the hot weather gear he'd been given and shoved it into the bottom of his kitbag. He had no idea where he'd be sent when he eventually got to Liverpool. He'd just be turning up a day or two early. He might hit it off with this Eunice woman, but he thought it unlikely with a name like that. And then he could always hang around in Liverpool – it was a great city for women.

***

Alf had to change trains three times to get to Ridley. It was a bloody long day. His body ached and his fists hurt from being clenched for most of the journey.

The trains were crowded with servicemen from all the different branches. Their kitbags, some green and others an indeterminate white, took up a lot of space in the aisles. The men's uniforms all stank of god knew what, and almost all of them smoked, including Alf.

He kept thinking about Judith, and then about this flighty bit who'd put her name and address in the pocket of a sailor's uniform. What kind of a name was Eunice? He decided she was either a swot with short brown hair and glasses or a foreigner, which wouldn't suit him at all.

At last his train pulled into Ridley. He shouldered his kitbag and fought his way through the bodies to get down onto the platform. The weather was overcast, not very inviting. He pulled his duffel coat around him and headed out of the station.

''Scuse me, mate, can you tell me which way to North Street?'

'That'll be about a fifteen-minute walk, I think. Ya go straight down tha'n road o'er there, right at t'corner and keep straight on 'til you coom to Broderick's factory then take a left. North Street's just along there.'

Alf found it difficult to follow his strong accent, but he set off in the direction he thought he should follow. After a short walk he found

North Street. Nothing too exciting to write home about, he thought. He wandered along it until he came to 44. It seemed to be connected to a corner shop, which was closed. He knocked on the house door, and waited.

Sixteen

Wednesday 8th April 1942, Ridley

Ness loved Wednesday evenings ever since she'd signed up for the book-keeping classes. She was hoping they wouldn't stop running, either because the teacher was called up or for any other reason the government decided on. It was the one evening of the week she could go out and forget about things. Robert, of course, had been on her mind, and the fact that things had progressed as far as they had made her more determined to learn more about him.

She took care getting ready to go out, pulling out a nice skirt from her wardrobe and a blouse and cardigan to go with it. She heard the clock downstairs strike six – an hour before the class began. Her parents were eating their tea in the back room, having shut up the shop at five-thirty. Wednesday was sometimes a half-day but as they'd been closed over Easter they'd decided to stay open today and risk the council's disapproval – it wasn't as though they had any employees, after all.

As she was walking down the stairs there was a knock on the front door.

'I'll go,' she shouted to her parents. She put her books on the bottom step then pulled the door open a little, to see a sailor on the doorstep. He removed his hat, revealing a mop of curly fair hair, and gave her a rather bizarre grin, a bit like an orangutan trying to please her. But it didn't work.

'Hello, Miss. My name's Alf Taylor, and I found this label in the pocket of my uniform.'

Ness tried to smile but the muscles in her face wouldn't work properly. She opened her mouth to speak. 'I'm sorry?' was all that came out.

'I found your name and address in the pocket of my new kit. You are Eunice, aren't you? And this is 44 North Street, Ridley, right? I mean, I've come all the way from Southall, near London, so ...?'

She hesitated. His attitude wasn't very pleasant, but she thought that the best thing would be to invite him in. At least her parents would help her out.

'Look, I'm sorry, you may have wasted your time, but do come in, please. Come and have a cup of tea. My parents are in the back room and the pot's full.' She thought she was being ridiculous; whatever did 'the pot's full' sound like?

'Well, I'd appreciate a cuppa, that's for sure.'

He pushed past her and plonked his kitbag on the floor, then took off his coat and hung it on the peg. It looked just like Robert's, but it wasn't, of course.

'Quite warm for this time of year, really,' he said, then walked on through to the back room as though he owned the place. 'Evening, everyone.'

Ness, right behind Alf, said to him, 'This is Mr and Mrs Proctor. Mum, Dad, this is ... Alf, from Southall, near London. You'll never guess what. He found the other one of those labels that Eileen wrote.' She tried to sound light-hearted about it and gave a little laugh.

'Well I never,' said her mum. 'How about that? It was well over a year ago, wasn't it?'

'Would you like a cup of tea?' This was from Ness's dad.'

'Wouldn't say no. Thirsty work, travelling.' Alf pulled out a chair and sat down at the table. Ness couldn't help comparing him with Robert. There was no contest. Alf was rude and slightly obnoxious. God, how was she going to get rid of him?

Ness plonked the tea in front of him.

'Any chance of a biscuit or something a bit more substantial?' he asked.

Ness glanced at her mother and raised her eyebrows, then she frowned at her dad as she could see he was about to offer him something more *substantial.*

'I'm afraid we've just eaten tea, and there's no more tonight,' said her mum.

Ignoring Ness's warning, her dad said, 'You could find a bit of bread and dripping for the bloke, surely?'

'Don't worry, I'll do it,' said Ness, and she went to the larder to get the jar of dripping and a slice of bread. After she'd slapped the dripping onto the bread she brought it to the table. 'Here you go, then.'

It was all very awkward as the three of them sat and watched Alf eat the food and slurp the tea. His manners weren't great, but then Tommy's weren't either, so Ness thought she shouldn't be so judgemental.

'I have to go out soon. I've got an evening class tonight.'

'Really? Doing what?' asked Alf, and smirked as he said it.

She told him book-keeping, and he scoffed at that. She said she had to leave in about fifteen minutes. She also told him about Robert and that he'd found another of the labels Eileen had put in a uniform, and that she and Robert had promised that they would write to each other and they were sort of making plans. It sounded a bit weak, but she didn't want to say 'engaged' as she'd not even told her parents how much things had progressed.

'I'm really sorry, Alf. You've had a wasted journey. And by the way, everyone calls me Ness. I don't like Eunice.'

'Well, I'm glad to hear that. I thought it was an awful name. No offence, Mr and Mrs Proctor.' He gave a rather smarmy smile as he shoved the last piece of the bread and dripping into his mouth. 'Well, sounds like I arrived too late to the show doesn't it? Well, never mind, plenty more fish in the sea. Now then, Eunice, how about I walk you to your class?'

Ness winced at the way he said her name. 'I'm fine, honestly I'll be fine walking on my own.'

'Well, if you've got a toilet, perhaps I could just use it before I go. I suppose I'll have to head back for the station. Bloody waste of time this was.'

'Look, I really am very sorry, but I didn't put those labels in the shirts, my friend Eileen did. Anyway, the bathroom's just through there.' She pointed to the door leading out of the kitchen to the back of the house.

While he was gone Ness and her parents whispered to each other. Her mum suggested she should just let him walk her and if necessary her dad would come too. 'Just don't aggravate him, he's already upset,' Mary said.

'Well, I can't see any harm in him,' said Jack. 'You want me to come?'

But Ness said she'd be all right and as Alf came back into the kitchen she put on a big smile: 'Right, then, we'd better be off. I don't like to be late for the class. It's on the way to the station anyway. It's in the local school. I'll just pick up my bag and books.'

They walked together down North Street, Ness praying they wouldn't meet anyone.

'Nice to have the lighter evenings isn't it?' she said.

'Won't make much difference to me when I'm back on board tomorrow.'

'No, I suppose not.'

'It's a pity you've taken up with this Robert bloke. Hope he's nice to you. I'd have given you a good time, you know. We could've painted the town red together, as they say.'

'Well, I'm not one for too much going out. really.'

'No, I imagine you aren't.'

After a few turnings they came to the school. She shook Alf's hand and pointed out the way back to the station.

'You should be all right. It's not far. Nowhere's very far in Ridley. I hope you don't have to wait too long for your train.'

'Righto. Thanks for nothing. Have a good life.'

With that he walked off up the street and didn't look back.

Seventeen

When Ness came out of her class it was very dark. She and the other students chatted for a while – a few were heading for the pub, but Ness said no – she wanted to get home. It was coming up to nine-thirty. She pulled out her torch so she could see a little more clearly, but the thin thread of light barely helped. It had clearly been raining while she was at her class – she could smell the damp rising from the ground, and there was a fresh earthy scent as she passed the waste ground next to the school. She imagined the weeds would be popping their heads out early the next morning. She thought about the sailor who'd turned up at her door and hoped he'd found the railway station and was well on his way to Liverpool. She'd not liked him much.

'Hello.'

His voice came out of the dark, making her jump.

'It's me, Alf. How did the class go, Eunice?' His voice was low and he was slurring his words a little.

'Hello Alf, I was just thinking about you.' Ness tried to sound friendly, 'It was fine. Very good in fact.'

'You shouldn't be walking home alone at this time of night, I mean I know there's not many around, but those who are might not be the kind you'd want to meet.'

'I'm okay, really I am. I'm used to walking home in the dark.' Ness shone her little torch towards the edge of the pavement. It was pretty useless, but nobody was allowed anything much brighter. 'I'd better get going – my parents'll be wondering where I am.'

Her heart began beating faster and she quickened her pace, trying not to let him notice she was anxious. She could smell the threat of his closeness. They were just passing a ginnel and with a swift step to the side he moved behind her. His arms came around her, his right arm hugging her shoulders and chest, and his left hand over her mouth. Her torch fell to the ground and he kicked it away into the gutter. He pushed her, forcing her towards the dark alley. Once inside, he shoved her against the wall, his full body weight behind her.

'Now then,' he paused, then said in a mocking tone, 'Eunice.' His mouth close to her ear. 'Don't go shouting and don't struggle, we're just going to have a bit of fun. You and me. I didn't come all this way for a cup of tea and a miserable piece of bread and dripping. I've no doubt you've done this sort of thing before so it won't be a problem for you. I reckon you're right up for it. Let's see now.'

His head was on her shoulder and his mouth close to her ear. Ness's face was pushed against the bricks and she could taste them. His breath was foul. She could smell the drink on him – he must have spent the last two hours in the pub. She wanted to scream or run, but she could do neither. She thought if she just closed her eyes and let him get on with it then it'd be over more quickly.

'I'm gonna take my hand off your mouth, but you better not make a sound. It'll just be worse for you if you do. Nod your head if you understand what I'm saying.'

Ness nodded and felt her forehead graze the cold wall. She prayed someone would come down the alleyway. But this path was a short cut from the school to the park and she guessed nobody would be going through to the park at this time of night.

'You're gonna love this as much as me. I can tell you're begging for it.'

With his left hand he fumbled with his own clothing and lifted up her coat and skirt from behind. He ripped her knickers down, tearing them, then with his right foot spread her legs apart. She held her forehead away from the wall but her chest and body were pushed up against it over and over as he shoved at her. She ended up with her head turned to the side and her face squashed. His breath got faster and his spittle sprayed onto her left cheek as his chin dug into her shoulder. She held her eyes tight shut.

It was over pretty quickly.

Alf pulled away from her. He fastened his trousers and tidied his clothes. He ran his fingers through his hair, and smirked. 'That wasn't so bad, was it, sweetheart?' He sniffed, and Ness stood stock still. 'I've left me bag and coat in the pub. I'll be just nipping back to get them before I head for the station.' He turned Ness around to face him and pointed his finger at her an inch from her face. 'Don't you go following me or mention this to anyone, you whore. That'll teach you to go sending out your name and address to the sailors. A bloody big disappointment you are. A bloody big disappointment. Now go home to Mummy and Daddy, and don't say a fucking word. Got it?' He leant towards her and kissed her full on the lips, shoving his tongue into her mouth. 'Bye, darling, take care now.' He staggered off, leaving her alone in the dark and silence.

Ness couldn't move. She stood still, leaning against the wall, and waited for his footsteps to go. Then the tears came. Lots of them. She bent down and picked up her torn knickers, which were grubby from where he'd trodden on them. She stuffed them into her pocket, found her hanky and blew her nose. Picking up her bag, her books and her torch she began to walk slowly out of the alleyway.

Her head became filled with the kindness and the lovemaking she'd experienced with Robert. He'd been so gentle with her for her first time. It had been real lovemaking. She'd wanted him, and he'd recip-rocated. But now, how could something so beautiful be turned into something so sordid? She was afraid she was going to be sick. The thought of that man's hands mauling her where Robert had touched her with such tenderness. What had just happened to her? How could she have let it happen?

Her instinct at that point was to run away, to flee from the scene, find refuge with Eileen or at home. But she knew that this was some-thing she couldn't share with anyone. So instead of running, she walked. Her feet were heavy as she dragged herself along the pavement towards nowhere. She was sore, she was exhausted. She was ashamed. She felt dirty and used. This was the worst possible thing that could have happened, but she knew she could tell no-one. So she was relieved to be alone. Not a soul was out on the streets to see her.

Ness walked around aimlessly in circles for a while, avoiding the pubs and the station and the main roads. She walked until she thought her parents would be in bed. As she sometimes went for a drink with the other students after the class she knew that'd be where her parents would think she'd gone. After what seemed like hours, she guessed it must be about eleven. It should be safe to go home.

She opened her front door. It was quiet inside. She took off her coat and hung it on the peg. It didn't look too dirty. She imagined it covered in brick dust and dirt, but as she'd walked she'd brushed it down as much as she could. Her stockings were torn. She pulled her knickers out from her coat pocket and wondered what on earth she could do with them. She thought of putting them in the stove, if it was still alight. She opened the door and shoved her knickers in, digging at them with the poker until she was sure they were burning. She took off her stockings, too; they burnt more easily than the knickers. She walked out to the bathroom. What she wanted to do was run a bath and sink right down into the water until her whole body, head and all, would be covered. But if she did, it'd mean questions and her parents were very strict about not using the water. *Damn war, damn restrictions.* She got a jug from the larder and brought it back to the bathroom. After she'd stripped down naked, she filled the jug, sat on the toilet and tipped the water between her legs, scrubbing at her skin with a flannel, over and over again until she'd rubbed her skin raw. But she knew no matter how many times she did it she'd not be able to get rid of him.

Eventually she got up, washed her face and cleaned her teeth. She hoped she'd be able to wash her hair and have her weekly bath tomorrow. She felt numb. Completely numb. She'd allowed it to happen, and she wished she'd been brave enough to fight him off. The guilt clung to her like a leaden corset which she couldn't rip off. She went upstairs to her bedroom. Put on her nightdress, which thank God was clean, and a pair of clean knickers. She hoped tomorrow some of the soreness would have eased, otherwise she didn't know how she'd get through the day. She had no more stockings. She would have to go bare-legged to work. She didn't know what she'd say to her parents. She didn't know what she'd say to Eileen. But she knew, with certainty, that she could tell no-one the truth.

Lying in bed, she let the tears come quietly. She spoke softly, 'I'm so sorry, Robert. I've ruined everything. I can't believe it. I should never have let him in. I should've turned him away. I've spoilt it all. I can never tell you, and I'm not sure I can ever see you again. I'm sorry.'

Eighteen

Monday 13th April 1942

Ness didn't know how she got through the days after the awful attack by Alf. She'd stayed off work Thursday and Friday, pretending she was ill, but on Saturday morning she did the usual half-day, and avoided Eileen's questions after work. They parted at the corner of North Street when Ness refused to go out with them all on Saturday night. Eileen was worried and came round with George later in the afternoon to try and persuade her, but she was adamant.

'I'll be fine next week, honestly. I shouldn't have gone back to work this morning. I've had a really nasty bug and need to just get into bed early tonight and rest again tomorrow. I'll be back at work on Monday good as new, I'm sure.' She smiled at them, pushing her true feelings as deep inside her as she could manage. She needed to box them up and shut them away if she was going to be able to carry on with her life as though nothing had happened. If she could get through the weekend, she was sure that by Monday she'd have filed away as much as possible, and eventually – maybe in a week, a month, a few months, a year …

who knew how long it would take ...? She looked at her friends again. She saw real concern on their faces, which only made her feel worse.

On a sudden impulse, she hugged them both. 'Get going to the pub, now, and have a couple for me. I'm going to tuck up in my bed with a cup of tea and a good book.' She put her hand on Eileen's chest and pushed her gently on her way: 'Bye, you two.'

Ness had received Robert's letter on the Friday morning and still couldn't bring herself to even open it. She wasn't sure she could correspond with him until she'd got over what had happened. But then she thought she'd probably never get over it. She thought about going to the police – but thinking about it was as far as she got. She didn't know Alf's address. She remembered his surname – she'd never forget it – and that he was from Southall, near London. But a lot of good that'd do her. She didn't think the police would believe her, anyway. The whole story sounded ridiculous. They'd blame her, anyhow, because her address had been in his pocket.

Ness put Robert's letter under her pillow and did not touch it all weekend. She went back into work on Monday. The physical pain had almost gone away, but she couldn't stop replaying the event over and over in her head. She hoped work would be her saviour. She went into the office determined to put all her effort into it; no loitering in the toilet, no slacking at the desk and not too much chatting. Until then she'd enjoyed the banter between the typists, but now it had lost all interest for her. But she knew she had to put up a good front, otherwise too many questions would be asked.

She got through the day, but only because she made a tremendous effort to forget the whole incident. To block it from her mind. After work, she walked home with Eileen. It was an effort to keep her secret, but she knew it was the only way; to carry on as though nothing had happened. The girls parted company on the corner as usual, with promises to go out the following weekend. Ness told Eileen she wanted to get on with her book-keeping so wouldn't be doing anything during the week. Eileen was satisfied that Ness had just had a 'bug' and now everything was back to normal.

By the time she got home she felt tired, but determined not to let what had happened ruin her life. She went straight up to her room. Kicking off her shoes, she flopped onto the bed. She lay there for a minute and then, feeling stronger, pulled out the letter from Robert.

She read it through twice. She tried hard not to cry, but she was asking too much of herself. Then, after the third read-through, she sat up, shook her head, blew her nose and reaffirmed to herself the decision she'd made earlier. She would not let the incident rule her life. She'd carry on as though it hadn't happened.

She knew she was lucky to have Robert, and he was so obviously in love with her. He need never know what had happened. She heard her parents come in; they would all be eating in a short while. Afterwards, she'd write her reply to Robert. It'd be better if her parents knew she was writing. It'd all be normal.

13th April 1942

Dear Robert,

Thanks for your letter. It's Monday evening here and your letter arrived today. I'm writing straight back. I hope the breakfast that your plump landlady served you was good enough to last you all day!

I'm missing you too, and yes, it would be wonderful to snuggle up with you. I think about you all the time, when I'm at work, or out with Eileen, but especially when I'm on my own, at home and in bed.

I love the idea of travelling on the Orient Express. I've not read the book, but I will now. I think I might like Agatha Christie, I mean, if you do then I surely will.

I love the idea of going to London and to Devon. I've never really been anywhere except Leeds. Although we did all go to Blackpool once for a holiday, but it was a disaster as it poured with rain and was very windy. My umbrella blew inside out!

Write when you can, and I will write back. I understand it will be difficult for you and I know some people around here don't receive a letter from their relatives for ages and then they get three at once!

I will take care and so must you. I will write to Rose soon.

All my love

Ness xxx

She kissed the letter before she put it in the envelope. She thought it a stupid action, but it made her feel better. She decided that writing to Robert was a good thing to do; she'd drawn strength from the action. Her mood lightened. Perhaps she could get through this after all. What happened would be her secret, and providing Alf kept away then everything'd be okay. She couldn't imagine he'd ever dare to show his face here again. She hoped not, anyway.

Nineteen

Friday 26th June 1942

Ness tried to deny the signs and pretend it wasn't happening. She looked at the calendar, the one she'd got last Christmas. It was a homemade thing she'd bought at a Red Cross fair. A picture of the Tower of London stuck on a piece of card. A piece of red string stuck onto the back made a loop to hang it up by. On the front at the bottom there was a paper calendar attached and you could pull off the months as they went by, but Ness hadn't bothered. Now she tore off January and February. Studying March, she tried to remember when her last monthly had been, and then she knew it was the weekend of the 21st March. She remembered because that Saturday they'd all gone to the cinema in Ridley to see *Ghost Train* and she'd had to go to the ladies in the middle and sort herself out. She hadn't got a pad, so she'd used a handkerchief until she got home.

When she first noticed her monthly didn't come, she thought maybe her body had gone into shock because of what happened, a sort of reaction against the assault. Then she just ignored the next two months. If she didn't think about it then it couldn't be true. How *could* she have been so bloody stupid? She'd banished it in the same way as she'd tried to put out of her mind the horrendous experience she had with Alf. It really was the worst of situations; pregnant and no idea who the father might be. One man she loved, the other she despised. It *had* to be Robert's. She would believe it was Robert's. She convinced herself that that was the way forward. She would only ever think of it as Robert's, otherwise she couldn't contemplate her life having any meaning at all.

She didn't know how she'd get through the next few days, never mind a lifetime. For now, she had to carry on as though nothing was wrong. She headed into work as though life was a breeze

***

After work on the Friday, Ness and Eileen went back to Ness's house to talk about a dress Ness was going to make for Eileen. They were sitting in the kitchen having a cup of tea looking at the pattern, when Ness felt nauseous.

'You all right, Ness? You look as though you're going to be sick,' said Eileen.

'It's the heat, I think. Never known June so warm. I'll just pop to the toilet for a minute.'

Ness was sweating – but it wasn't the heat, it was the nausea. Her stomach churned and she felt it surge. She held her hand over her mouth as she rushed to the toilet. Her stomach emptied itself of the tea she'd drunk. Then she washed her face and rinsed her mouth. Pulling herself together, she went back to face Eileen.

'Are you going to tell me what's wrong?'

'I've just got a bug or something. There's a lot about.'

'Not *your* kind of bug, there isn't. I've been watching you over the last week or so and I think I know your symptoms. Not that I've experienced them myself, but ... let's get out of here and go for a drink, shall we? Then we can talk about it.'

Ness knew she was going to have to tell Eileen about the pregnancy. She was going to have to tell somebody, anyhow, and Eileen was the best person. She'd only tell her what was necessary, though. It'd be a relief to share at least one secret.

***

'Right, then,' said Eileen as she plonked the glass in front of Ness. 'Lemonade for you – that should sort your stomach out – and a port for me. Come on then, spill the beans.' She lit a cigarette, tilted her head back and blew the smoke up and backwards. 'I'm guessing you won't be too keen on breathing that in,' she said.

'You're right there. It turns my stomach.'

Eileen stubbed out the cigarette.

Ness told Eileen that she suspected the worst. She hadn't been to see the doctor, but all the signs pointed to the fact she was expecting a baby. She didn't cry, she didn't laugh, she just gave the facts. As though she were talking about somebody else and not herself.

'Have you told anyone?'

'No, of course not. I don't know who to tell. My parents'll be disappointed, to say the least. And there'd be no point telling Tommy.'

Eileen pulled her chair closer to her friend and put her arm around her, which made Ness swallow hard to stop the tears.

'Look, it might not be as bad as you think. I mean, how do you actually *feel* about having a baby? Are you a little bit excited or just completely devastated?'

'I'm scared. It's all so complicated. More complicated than you know.'

'Robert'll stand by you, I'm sure. He's not the kind of bloke who'd leave you high and dry. Not that I know that much about him but from what you've told me.'

'It's not going to be easy. It's the last thing I need. If only it hadn't happened ... any of it.'

'Well, the government'll be pleased – they're encouraging all us women to have more babies for the war effort.' Eileen roared with laughter until she saw the look of despair on Ness's face. 'I'm sorry, it's not at all funny. I probably know of someone who can help, if you're not too far gone, if you think you want to, you know ...'

'I'm way too far gone. I worked it out this morning. I'm over thirteen weeks. It's surprising it doesn't show. I can't feel anything' – she put her hands to her stomach – 'except a bit queasy some of the time. I suspected for ages but just kept pretending it wasn't happening. Not very bright, really.'

'Well, it's the first one, and often it doesn't even begin to show until four months, and you're a slim fit person. I expect you'll carry it well.'

'I just wish I wasn't carrying it at *all* – and I don't like the way you say, "first one" as though there might be more.' Ness managed a weak smile.

'I think you should tell your mum. She might not be as shocked as you think.'

'Tell her mum what?' It was George. He'd come into the bar without either of them noticing.

'Nothing you need to know about,' said Eileen.

'Sorry, none of my business what young ladies talk about. Now then, can I get you something to drink?'

'We're fine, thanks, just leaving in fact,' said Eileen.

'Blimey, I'm not *that* bad, am I? I was on my way round to see Tommy and thought I'd pop in here first to see if he was in already. I can walk you home if you like, Ness. You look a bit pale, like you could do with a helping hand.'

'Thanks, George.' Ness stood up.

George smiled.

'You look pleased with yourself,' said Eileen.

'Not every day a bloke gets to walk his favourite girl home.'

'Come on, then, George, let's not hang about,' said Ness.

'Remember,' said Eileen. 'Let me know how it goes. Maybe we can chat again at lunch break tomorrow?'

Ness took George's arm. She felt a complete fraud. She thought, maybe if the opportunity had come up she would've told Eileen the whole story, but they'd not had the chance. She tried to keep up a front of cheerfulness even though her insides felt like the jelly on dripping ... and the thought of dripping or jelly was not at all pleasant.

Ness and George walked out of the pub and into the warm evening air. It was still light, and for once it was quiet, apart from a few children playing in the streets. Ness looked at the boys kicking an empty tin can along the street, some of them barely out of nappies. She placed her hand on her stomach and wondered what was inside her. Girl or boy?

What – or more importantly who – would it look like? What did the future hold for her and her baby?

'Are you listening to me?' George asked.

'Sorry, I'm a bit preoccupied. It's been a hard week at work.

He put his arm casually around her shoulder. 'You know, if you were my girl you could give up work and I'd look after you.'

Ness pulled away gently, although it flashed through her mind that if she acted quickly all her problems would be solved. It would have to be an extremely premature baby, though.

'That's kind of you, George, but you know Robert's my man.'

'I suppose a local lad isn't good enough for you?'

'It's not that.'

'That's part of it, though. I know you don't want to stay here. I'm not saying you've got ideas above your station, just that you think the world's a bigger place than Ridley. Maybe it is – perhaps I should think about moving on, too, but it's difficult at the moment. What with the war and everything.'

They had reached Ness's door and George pulled her back for a moment, stopping her from going in.

'Think about it, will you? I'm fond of you and your family. I'm not in the war. Perhaps you think I'm a coward, but I tried to sign up, but I've got flat feet. Seems the Home Guard don't mind, though.'

Ness smiled at him and gently removed her arm from his. She told him it'd be unlikely they would ever be a couple but she'd certainly look upon him as a good friend. If George felt rebuffed, he didn't show it. He opened the door for her, grinned and allowed her to walk into the house ahead of him.

Ness's mum smiled at them both as they came into the back room.

'Looks like we've got one more for tea this evening, then. Move up, Tommy, you've nearly finished anyway.'

'Don't worry, Mrs Proctor, I'm fine. I came to get my friend and take him to the pub.'

'Young men today, spending all their hard-earned on drink. Wait till you've got a wife waiting for you – she'll soon tie a bit o'string around your wage packet.'

'Don't look at *me*, Mum,' said Ness. 'I'll not be marrying any time soon, and certainly not George.'

'Well, that's nice, isn't it? You bring a girl home and she just makes fun of you.'

'You could do a lot worse than George.'

'That's a bit steep, Mrs Proctor. I'd like to think she couldn't do any *better* than me!'

'I didn't mean it like that,' said Ness. 'Look, are you blokes going out or not? Because I'd like to tidy myself up, then sit down and eat my tea in peace, so get going.'

'All right, we've got the message. C'mon, George, let's go.' Tommy and George got out of the house like they'd been given the all clear.

Ness sat in the chair by the range. 'What's for tea?'

'It's not much, I'm afraid. I've made some vegetable pie, the pastry's got mashed potato and flour in it. It's not bad. Tommy had some soon as he came in and he didn't complain for once.'

'What's in it?'

'Carrots and leeks. Couldn't get much else at the market today. Tomatoes were all gone when I got there.'

'I think I'll give it a miss, Mum, thanks.'

'Not like you to turn your nose up. Aren't you feeling well? Look, go and wash your face and I'll make you a bit of toast and a cuppa. Would that suit?'

'No, I don't want anything, thanks. Sorry.'

Ness went up to her room and lay down on the bed. It was cool compared to outside, and although it was a summer's evening, and light, there weren't any kids playing out the back, so it was quiet.

Ness's eyes closed and she felt herself drifting into sleep. The next thing she heard was her mother's voice,

'Ness, love, I've brought up some tea and a bit of toast. You look awful peaky.'

'What time is it? I must have fallen asleep.'

'Aye, it's gone eight-thirty. I've woken you because you won't sleep tonight if you sleep now. Do you feel like coming downstairs after? Your dad's gone to the club. Maybe we could listen to the radio – there'll be some music on at nine and then the news.'

She helped Ness sit up and gave her the tea.

'I'll leave you for now, then, see you in a minute.' Mary went back downstairs.

Ness wondered when the baby would be born. She thought about the girl down the road who'd got in the family way at the end of '40, but at least she'd been going steady with a fella. Even so, the neighbourhood wasn't kind. Lots of talking behind hands at the wedding, because she'd had to wait for him to come home on leave and it was obvious to everyone.

Ness thought again about who the father might be. The only thing she could do was to blank out the Alf experience. It couldn't be his.

123

The baby had to be Robert's. She couldn't cope with the idea that the baby could have been conceived in any other way except love.

She wanted desperately to tell Eileen what had happened with Alf. She'd kept it to herself for so long, and now she needed to share it more than ever. A problem shared and all that ... but she had the feeling that sharing this particular incident might not solve anything. Just make it worse. The situation was horrible.

Ness thought that if she wrote to Robert he'd want to come home immediately, but he wouldn't be allowed to. It was a miracle he'd had compassionate leave after his dad had died, and this situation certainly wouldn't get him any time off. In any case, she didn't know how she'd cope with seeing him. This was the biggest mess. It had all begun because of the bloody labels in the pocket. Perhaps Eileen would feel really bad about it now, if and when Ness told her what had happened – she'd blame herself for the whole sorry story.

The toast was welcome, but she couldn't face the tea. She'd gone right off it. She put on a summer dress and some old shoes, and thought about what Eileen had said about telling her mum. There was no time like the present. She went downstairs to have the chat she didn't want to have.

Twenty

After Ness had blurted everything out, between bouts of crying, the two women sat in silence in the kitchen. Ness's mother didn't take the news well. She drank her tea slowly; it was as though she was sorting out everything she'd been told, before weighing it all up and giving her verdict.

It was gone ten when Tommy came in. He was worse for wear, banging the front door then tiptoeing as he came into the living room, making more noise than if he'd walked in as normal. He could tell straight away things weren't right. His mother's eyes were red from crying and Ness was curled up in an easy chair.

'What's up with you two? Looks like someone's told you the weekend's been cancelled.'

'This is between me and your sister. You'd best go straight upstairs, Tommy.' Mary glared at him.

'But I need to use the privy first.'

'Get on, then, and be quick about it.'

He went out to the bathroom.

'You're *not* to tell him,' said Mary. 'We need a bit of time to think things through. This has come as a terrible shock. If only it had been George's. He'd have married you in a trice and been happy to do it.

That's what you should do. You could do a lot worse. I mean, Robert's a nice bloke, but I don't think his family would approve, do you?' She didn't want an answer – she was set to go on all night. 'I'm not telling your dad, neither. What were you *thinking* of, girl?

'There's a war on, Mum.'

'Well, there was a war on when I was your age too, but we didn't go gallivanting about with any man who came our way.'

'It wasn't just any man, Mum. It was Robert and I know it was all quick, but I love him and he loves me.'

Tommy came back into the room, looked around and opened his mouth but thought better of it and went upstairs.

'I'd hoped that by telling you about it you might want to help me out, but I can see I was wrong. It was Eileen who thought you'd be understanding.'

'Well, she got that wrong, didn't she? All very well for her – she's got a steady bloke in Sid. If it happened to her she could wed quick and there'd be no tongues wagging.'

'I'm going up, Mum. I'm exhausted. I won't tell Dad, and I won't tell Tommy, but they'll have to know at some point and probably soon. The first thing I'm going to do is write to Robert.'

Mary stayed quiet for a moment. She blew out her breath between her pursed lips and her cheeks puffed out. Shaking her head, she said, 'It's a shock, you see, a shock. I thought you were a good girl, never expected this from you. Let me sleep on it, and we'll talk again in the morning.'

'Come on, then, let's go up before Dad gets home.' Ness pulled her mother up from the chair and guided her towards the stairs. The two women leant on each other, neither of them understanding their own emotions, both wishing they weren't in this situation.

Twenty-one

Saturday Afternoon 27th June 1942

Ness hadn't thought that writing to Robert would be easy but she'd never imagined it'd be this hard. She'd been sitting at the kitchen table for over an hour.

At breakfast her mum had been very quiet. The night before hadn't been mentioned, but when Ness went off to work Mary handed her a few broken biscuits in a brown paper bag.

'Here, take these with you. You might find a little snack now and then will keep the sickness at bay. Also, while you're feeling a bit off colour, you want to stick to some bland food for a while.'

'I don't feel too good either, Mum. Can I have a couple of biscuits too?' Rubbing his stomach, Tommy pulled a sad face.

'Give over, Tommy. There's nought wrong with you.'

'Oh, it's just women's business, is it?'

Ness was pretty sure he hadn't got a clue, but she was glad he didn't push it any further.

Her mother was upset, she could understand that, but she was relieved that her mum had at least spoken to her. Maybe in a few days things would improve.

She pushed the thoughts away and got back to writing. If she could get the words right, she knew Robert would stick by her. He was that sort of man. She rubbed out everything she'd written and remembering that Robert's birthday had been on the 20th June she began again:

27th June 1942

Dear Robert,

I hope you are well and that you managed to celebrate your birthday last week. Maybe next year we can have a celebration together.

Well now, I have some important news but before I tell you, I want you to know that you don't HAVE to do the right thing, even though that would obviously be the best course of action for me.

She put down the pencil down for a moment and chewed the end of it. She was going to change her letter until she was happy with it, then she'd copy it out in pen. Now, she crossed out the last few words she'd written and put a full stop after *'thing'*.

We have been a little unlucky. I'm afraid we got a bit carried away in April, not imagining what the consequences might be, and the result of that, is that I'm going to have your baby. Maybe not good timing and we wouldn't have chosen for it to happen, but it has and we can't change that.

Please write to me and tell me what to do. You asked me to marry you after the war was over, so would it be okay to bring that forward a bit? Is there any chance you will get some leave to come back to England any time soon? You said you might be home in August. Perhaps we could do it then?

She thought a bit, then added *If you want to, of course.*

I love you very much. I am so sorry that this has happened. It must be hard for you away at sea. and this news won't be easy for you. Please take care of yourself.

I'll wait to hear from you.

All my love

Ness x

It wasn't a very long letter but, satisfied she'd done her best, she copied it into the form, folded and stuck it, and addressed it. It was so frustrating not to be able to telephone Robert or to know exactly where he was.

There was a knock at the front door, then Ness heard it open and George walked into the kitchen. He really knew the wrong time to appear.

Ness swiftly hid the letter in her pocket: 'What are you doing here? Tommy's out and Mum's at the market.'

'It's a beautiful day, Ness, I've borrowed a car and I want to drive you down to the river. I've got a picnic and we can sit on the bank and enjoy the sun.'

'You don't give up, do you?'

'Not easily. But, honest, I'm just being a friend. I think you need one right now. I've got a feeling, can't put my finger on it, but I don't think things are going as well as you'd like. Perhaps you might want to talk about it?'

George was turning out to be too good to be true. She could really do with someone to lean on right now. 'No strings attached? Really? Just a friendly picnic?'

'Agreed. We can post that letter on the way.' He smiled and Ness blushed.

'It's to Robert. Wanted to keep him up to date with all the Ridley news.'

'That'll be a short note, then. Come on, let's go.'

'How did you manage to get petrol?' asked Ness as she got into the car.

'You've got to know people in this war, Ness. It's the only way to get through it. I don't like taking advantage, but there are times when you just have to pull a few strings.'

Ness looked straight ahead but had half an eye on George. She thought he was unlikely to be up to anything, but from the day she'd met him, she'd thought he'd be easily persuaded to turn a blind eye to some things. There was something endearing about him – he was a good looker and considerate, and her parents were very fond of him – and he made no secret of how he felt about her. But she just couldn't think of him in any way except as a friend. Especially since he'd teamed up with Tommy. She wondered if it'd be possible to confide in him, but decided it would be too unfair, given his feelings towards her. What a pity that mixed friendships were frowned on. What could be wrong with having a bloke as a best friend as well as, or instead of, a girl?

'Will here be all right?' he asked her.

She looked up to find they'd left the town behind and were well into the countryside. George had pulled up the car onto a verge, and she could see the River Gryme only a few yards below them. George told her that the people of Ridley thought the river was named after their ancestors, a filthy lot. Ness laughed, not believing a word he said. When they got out of the car George collected the picnic while Ness carried the blanket. The bank was steep but the grass was long and the wildflowers high, so they made their way down, walking sideways, to where the ground levelled out. There was a flat area, perfect for sitting.

'It looks as though we're not the only ones to picnic here,' said George picking up an empty glass bottle. 'I don't like litter. We'll take it home.

This was the side of George that Ness really liked – he was caring and had a good sense of humour. But he was lacking in any kind of ambition or drive.

'We've got some spam and lettuce sandwiches. My mum grew the lettuce – she's getting to be a dab hand at vegetable gardening, like a lot of people. We've got a small allotment, but we have to share the produce around a bit – family and friends and that.'

'Do you like reading?' asked Ness.

'Not much. I look at the papers sometimes and a comic or two. I was never one for book reading though.'

The food was plain but good. Ness couldn't summon up the energy to make more conversation, and all George talked about was football, the pub, work and the war.

She was about to suggest they made a move when she heard a distant rumble. 'Was that thunder?' she asked.

'I hope so – it's not the right time of the day for bombing, although I wouldn't put it past them.

The sky darkened; there was a storm on the way. 'We'd better get out of here before it gets any closer,' said George.

'Too late.' Ness felt the massive drops of rain, slow at first and then heavier and faster. They bit into her back as she struggled to climb up the now slippery bank.

'Hang on, Ness, let me get this stuff to the car then I'll come back and help you.'

'Help me first, won't you?' Ness shouted, and put out her hand as her feet failed to grip the surface. Her hair become soaked and stuck to her face. She couldn't believe how fast it was all happening. George got himself up beside her, but their wet hands felt oily and didn't grip securely. Ness grabbed the grass, found her feet gaining some leverage and managed to gain some ground. She was almost at the top when lightning struck a tree some ten yards away. The shock of it threw both of them back and Ness plummeted down the bank, rolling over and over.

At the bottom she lay motionless. A second later George lurched down after her, concerned she might have broken something. 'Ness, are you okay? Can you hear me?'

She opened her eyes and saw a man looking at her and cradling her in his arms. In her confused state she spoke with an urgency: 'I'm sorry, Robert – I'm sorry about everything. I just fell. I might have lost the baby.'

George remained calm. 'It's fine, Ness, it's all fine.'

By this time the wind was fierce and the rain had saturated them both. George looked around for some shelter but there was nothing. It wasn't 'fine' at all. He reached for the rug they'd been sitting on earlier

– he'd thrown it down when he was trying to help Ness up the bank. It was sodden.

'It's a summer storm, Ness, it'll be over in a minute. They go as fast as they come.'

Ness's eyes were closed. George lay her down on her back and got himself onto all fours, his knees on one side of her head and his hands on the other side, shielding as much of her as he could, and waited for the downpour to ease.

***

Two hours later they were back at the house. Ness had changed her clothes and been put to bed by her mum. George had borrowed a pair of trousers and shirt from Tommy, then sat down, tucked into a biscuit and a cup of tea and told the story.

'... so poor old Ness was out for the count. But I kept the worst of the rain off her, and after about ten minutes would you believe it the sun came out! The warmth must have made her come to. She was a bit drowsy, but we waited until she felt a bit better and then we had to work out how to get up the bank, because even though everything was drying out pretty fast, it was still slippery. Guess what I did?'

'I can't imagine,' said Mary.

'You gave her a fireman's lift and ran up the bank like Jessie Owens!' suggested Tommy.

'Not quite. But I remembered there was a tow rope in the car, a long one. My mate had left it in there after being towed by a tractor a few weeks ago.'

'Reliable car was it, then?' said Tommy.

'Be quiet and let him finish,' said Mary.

'I got the rope out and tied it round a tree. Not the one that had been hit by lightning of course, but another one. Then I let the rope down the hill. '

'Hill? I thought you said it was just a bank,' said Tommy.

'Will you please stop interrupting him?'

'I let the rope down the bank, and then Ness was able to hold on to it and walk slowly up, with me behind her, giving a helping hand, like.'

'I'm not sure that sounds quite proper,' said Tommy.

'Don't be daft. I had my right hand on the rope just behind hers, and the other hand on the loose end, which I'd put around her waist, pulling it shorter as we made progress. It was a bit slow, it took us about twenty minutes to get up, whereas Ness had gone down in about thirty seconds.'

'Well, I'm glad it all ended safely and nobody worse for wear, except the clothing – but that'll dry out,' said Mary, and laughed aloud. This started them all off – by the end of it Tommy was crying and rolling about and George was banging the table.

Ness appeared in the living room. 'What's going on here? What are you all laughing about?'

'It's ... it's ... nothing,' Tommy could barely get the words out.

'We just began laughing and it turned into something silly, I don't even know what we're laughing about now,' said George.

Mary wiped her eyes on her apron and stood up. Ness thought she hadn't seen her laugh like that for ages.

'Do you think you should be up and about?' said Mary. 'I was thinking of calling the doctor out – you had a nasty bump on the head. George said you were out for the count. I think that's what he said.'

'I'm fine now, honestly. A little bit of rest and a cup of tea have set me right. I'm fighting fit now. I think it was the thunder clap, or the lightning striking the tree, that gave me the biggest shock.'

'Not coming round and seeing my face, then?'

'No, George, I'm sorry, I was rubbish at getting up the bank in the rain. Thank you for being such a gent and helping me.'

'It was nothing, honest. Do you remember much about the tumble?' George looked a bit uncomfortable, and Ness wondered why. He'd not been at all shy during their picnic or in the car on the way there.

'I remember we had a nice picnic and that it was interrupted by a storm, which we thought might be the Germans coming to bomb us.' But she couldn't remember much after the fall or about the trip back.

George laughed, and the moment was over. When she saw him to the door later he reminded her they hadn't posted the letter to Robert.

'Yes, I know. I'll have to dry it out before I can send it. Thanks again for today. I hope I didn't spoil it too much for you.'

George looked directly at her, 'Not a bit, Ness. Not at all. Please, if you need anything, you can ask me. I don't care what it is.' He gave her arm a meaningful squeeze and went out to return the car to its owner.

***

That night Ness went to bed early. It was still light and as the storm had cleared the air the evening was fresh. She had nothing planned for Sunday, but hoped she and her mum could have a little time alone again and she would get the opportunity to talk in practical terms about what to do. She might have to move out of the house, go to another area. Maybe the family could say she'd married Robert when he'd last been here on leave. That way, the neighbours would be helpful rather than self-righteous busybodies stirring things up. The trouble was that Eileen knew it wasn't the case, and George knew she hadn't married anyone. George, poor old George ... She felt mean treating him with indifference the way she did. He didn't deserve that. He was like a faithful puppy, wishing to please all the time.

Sleep came at last, but in the morning nothing had changed. She was still pregnant, she was still in Ridley, and she still had no idea who the father was.

Twenty-two

Monday 13th July 1942

Robert looked at his watch. Ten thirty at night. He was off duty and had an hour or so to spare. He thought he'd write to Ness while he had the time.

July 13th 1942

Dearest Ness,

I'm still missing you very much. I look at your photograph every day.

One thing about being here is that it's mostly calm seas. Until the bombs drop, of course. I've been lucky so far. Several escort ships have been hit. It's a terrible thing to see them go down and hear and see the panic. We've picked up survivors in the past. Just like I was rescued.

Robert wondered how much would be censored from his letter. He wanted so much to share everything with Ness and not write in some mundane fashion about nothing much at all.

I keep myself going thinking about you most of the time. Wondering what you're doing each day. I imagine you in the factory office typing away and can't wait to whisk you away from all that. One of the other POs on board comes from Leeds. He was telling me all about the city.

He knew of Ridley but said he'd not been there for years. I don't think I'd like to live in the north of England. Would you be prepared to move south with me?

Morale is very high among the crew at the moment. It's amazing how it spreads through everyone when there's a good feeling. Probably because it's been a quiet few days at sea. It won't be the same from tomorrow, though. Can't tell you why – they'd only cross it all out. Give my regards to everyone, and write soon, my darling.

I miss you and think of you all the time.

With much love

Robert xxxx

Robert folded the letter. No point in sealing it, because the censors would be opening it anyway. There'd been no action all day. Robert's ship had passed through the Strait of Gibraltar a couple of nights before, and they'd rendezvoused with the convoy carrying oil and other essential supplies to Malta. It was moving along well without too much interference from the enemy. This was his fourth trip from Scapa Flow down to Malta, and since the sinking he'd been lucky, but he'd seen a few other ships sunk by bombs or torpedoes and he didn't want to repeat the experience.

The night passed without incident, but during the morning there were reports of enemy aircraft, and their aircraft carrier was sending up its Spitfires. As Robert climbed up the ladder to the bridge, he heard, then swivelled his head to see – as if from nowhere – a bunch of torpedo bombers heading straight for him. He shouted to the bridge, but they didn't respond. As he ran to action stations he thought of Ness.

Twenty-three

Thursday 16th July 1942

Ness fiddled with her ring as she sat in the doctor's waiting room. It had been agreed she'd say she'd married Robert in April, before he'd gone back to sea. There had been a family discussion about it.

'Our Ness with a baby!' said Tommy. 'I'm going to be an uncle, then? When can I tell everyone?'

'With luck, she'll not show properly until September, and she's good at sewing so nobody needs to know anything for a while.' Mary, tight-lipped, was barely speaking to Ness. 'But if you want something to talk about, Tommy, it's best you spread the rumour about the wedding, then there won't be too many tongues wagging when you tell.'

'Is George in on this?'

'I'll tell him,' said Ness. 'It's only fair he knows. He's been a good friend up to now, as good as Eileen.'

'He'd like to be more than a friend.'

'I know, Tommy – but it just can't be.'

Jack was angry. His little girl had let him down. The only good thing about it was that he liked Robert and thought he'd stand by Ness. He didn't talk much about the pregnancy or the baby, of course – it wasn't his business. If she needed a bit of money he'd see what he could do. But he didn't think he could offer much else. When Ness hugged him in thanks, she could tell he felt uneasy. Only time would change that, she thought.

***

The doctor's waiting room was drab. Just a few wooden chairs around the wall of the room, which had been the entrance hall of a large Edwardian house. Ness had a twenty-minute walk to get there from the shop. She didn't mind; walking was good for her. Her usual doctor had gone – either called up or volunteered – so this Dr Browning was someone she didn't know. Ness waited for her name to be called. There were six other people there, but she was the next to go in. An old woman hobbled out of the surgery door, helped by a young woman, who tried to hurry the older woman along as she muttered, 'Does he know what he's talking about? Never can trust these doctors. They're all so young these days.'

'He was kind and helpful, Mother. Come on, let's get home and get that medicine down you.' They struggled with the front door and when nobody else moved, Ness got up and opened it for them.

'Thank you, dear,' said the old woman. 'Good luck with the baby.'

Ness, surprised, blushed.

'It's the look of you,' said the woman. 'You'll have a bonny boy, I reckon.'

Ness didn't think she looked the least bit pregnant, but you got these women who could tell you everything. She wondered if it was just a Yorkshire thing or whether there was one in every county.

The bell from the surgery rang and the receptionist beckoned to Ness. 'Your turn, Mrs Proctor. In you go.'

Doctor Browning was sitting behind his desk. He was reading something – her notes, she thought – from a brown open-ended envelope. She couldn't imagine what would be in her notes; she was hardly ever ill and had visited the doctor on very few occasions. She didn't think he was young at all – late fifties, perhaps – but he looked kindly enough. He sported a grey moustache and his hair was longer than the usual short back and sides. Perhaps he'd been so busy he hadn't had time to visit the barber.

He didn't say anything, so Ness sat down on the chair opposite him. It was uncomfortable, probably so patients wouldn't outstay their welcome. For a second, she thought about the old lady before her. There was only that one chair, so he must have made the daughter stand.

'Now then,' said the doctor. 'What can I do for you?'

Ness told him what she knew, about being pregnant, dates and other things.

'And are you feeling well?'

'Yes, I was feeling a bit sick, but it's better now.'

'Well, let's take a look at you then. Just hop up on the couch behind the curtain, please.'

'Should I take anything off?'

'No, no, I just need to feel your tummy. If I need to do anything else I'll tell you.'

Ness lay on the couch behind the curtain. It was hard to climb up onto it and even though it had a sheet on it, it was the most uncomfortable piece of furniture. The doctor came in her, felt her abdomen, took her blood pressure and listened to the baby's heart.

'That'll do for today. Come back in around a month's time.'

When Ness sat down again in front of him, he was writing on a piece of paper. He glanced up and smiled.

'Well now. You're most definitely pregnant, and having looked at the dates I calculate that the baby will be born around the beginning of January, let's say the sixth. How does that suit you?'

Ness didn't answer.

'Now then, where's the father in all this?'

'He's away at sea. I don't know when he'll be back.'

'You are married, I take it? Because I only have your maiden name on my notes.'

'Yes, on his last leave ... in April ... that's when it happened. I've not been able to change everything yet.' Ness hated lying.

'So, where are you living?'

'At home, with my parents. The address on the notes.'

'And where will you live when your husband comes home?'

Ness didn't know what to answer. She was digging a hole for herself with all this lying. 'I suppose we'll stay with my parents until we find our own place.'

Ness wasn't sure what the doctor made of her. He was kind enough. But she felt sure he saw right through her. He went on to tell her she should be able to give birth at home and the midwife would come around near the due date to see the situation in the house. She told him she had her own bedroom, the parents ran the shop which the house was attached to, and they had an inside bathroom.

'All good, all good,' he said. 'Well, the government will be pleased with you boosting the population.' He smiled.

'That's what my friend said,' Ness replied weakly. It hadn't been a comfort when Eileen said it, and it sounded worse coming from the doctor. And she felt pretty sure he didn't believe she was married any more than a lot of other people would.

Twenty-four

Saturday 8th August 1942

T he summer was warm – loose clothing was just about acceptable for Ness, as for anyone – and she avoided meeting others as much as possible.

'Hello, it's me!' Eileen called out as she came through the house to find Ness sitting at the table in the back room. 'Here, this is for you, I think.'

Eileen held out a letter and Ness immediately jumped up to take it.

'I met the postman on my way in,' she hesitated, 'I don't think it's from Robert, though. It's got a London postmark.'

'London?'

'Well, it's no good looking at it. You've got to open it, then you'll find out who it's from. Mind if I make a cuppa?'

Ness didn't answer, but on beginning to read the letter let out a gasp and slumped back on the chair. Eileen, sensing trouble, took another cup from the shelf, 'I'll make a couple of strong sweet teas, shall I?'

'Yes.'

'Who's the letter from?'

'Robert's sister, Rose.'

Ness handed the letter to Eileen in exchange for a cup of tea, which she put on the table and stared over the top of it into nothing. Her eyes were dry but a horrible sound came from her throat and she put her head in her hands with her elbows on the table.

Eileen took the letter and read,

4th August

Dear Ness,

I am Robert Granger's sister, Rose. I am afraid I am writing to you with some awfully bad news. There is no easy way to tell you, but Robert was killed in action during one of the runs to Malta. We have not been told exactly what happened, but his ship was hit and there were several fatalities. We do not know if there was a body recovered, but if there was, he would have been buried at sea. I don't know what else to tell you. One can only imagine the details.

He wrote to tell me about you before he left Liverpool in April and asked me to let you know if anything happened to him. I wish I had written to you before now, but I have been rather busy. I left Devon for London in June, and I am now working for the Air Ministry and I am a member of the WRVS, driving ambulances and fire engines. As you can imagine, I am devastated to lose my brother, and so soon after my father passed away too. I have visited my mother but I could not stay for too long. She has taken it rather badly, but her sister, Florence, has gone to stay with her for a while.

It is a shame we have not met. I don't know what else to write.

My mother will put an announcement in the local paper and in The Times next week. I will make sure I keep a copy for you and send a cutting as soon as I can.

I am so sorry to be writing with such dreadful news. Please write back when you feel up to it, and let me know how you are keeping. I believe Robert gave you our Devon telephone number and address but you can contact me at work in London on Kingsway 2386. If you're in London you dial KIN and then the number, unless coming through the exchange, when you ask for the whole thing. Sorry, I'm making it sound as though you have no idea about these things, but Robert said you didn't have a telephone, so I'm thinking you might not use one that often.

Please do not hesitate to call me between 9 and 5 weekdays. Gosh, that all sounds very formal.

I do hope to hear from you soon.

With kindest regards

Rose Granger

PS There will be a memorial service, but we have not arranged the date yet. I will let you know.

Ness spread her arms across the table, knocking the tea over, 'I don't know whether to cry or be angry. I don't know how I'll cope.' Her voice was quiet. She pushed Eileen's hand away as it came to rest on her shoulder, then stood up and glared at her friend.

'What have I done to deserve this? It's so *unfair*. Why should Robert go? I *hate* this war.' She almost screamed the words.

'Ness, calm down, it won't be good for the baby.' Eileen was frightened of her friend's sudden erratic behaviour. 'Where's your mum, where's Tommy?

'I don't care, I do-not-care! I ... I ...'

She collapsed into Eileen's arms and let the sobs come, at first loud and uncontrolled, and then, as Eileen held her tight, they began to subside.

Eileen cleared up the tea and made some more, trying to behave as normally as possible.

Ness looked at the letter. 'It was a nice letter, wasn't it?' she said.

'It must have been difficult for her to write. I mean, she's obviously very upset too.' Eileen kept her voice light.

'I'd better write back, so she knows that I know – I mean, that I've received her letter, don't you think?'

'There's no rush,' said Eileen. 'What time will your mum be home?'

'She's gone to the market, and Tommy's out with the Home Guard again. He's spending more time with them than in the factory these days.'

'I'm not going to leave you until someone's back. I haven't got anything planned today. Do you want to me call your dad in from the shop?'

'I don't want to risk seeing anyone. I was going to tell them all at work on Monday, about the baby, although I think most people have guessed. Now I'll have to tell them I'm a widow. I'll feel such a fraud. I wish it had been me that had been killed. Me and the baby.'

Eileen shook her hand at Ness and told her she had no right to think like that, especially wishing the unborn child dead. What would Robert think of her reacting in this way?

'I don't even know if Robert got my last letter. He might not have even known anything about the baby.'

'I know you've had a terrible shock, but you must try and get things sorted in your head. You've lost Robert, but you owe it to him and that baby of his to be strong. What do you think he'd want you to do in the circumstances? Look, shall we go out for a walk, get some fresh air, clear your head? We probably won't see anyone.'

Ness sat, silent. The thoughts racing around inside her head were making it throb. That Saturday in April she'd been so happy for a brief moment, so blissfully happy. She tried to remember the feeling of his body next to hers. She closed her eyes and tried to bring his face into view. His smiling face. His hands holding her head, his dark eyes soaking her up. Then she remembered Alf and what else had happened in April. More than anything she wanted to tell Eileen about Alf. This made the whole baby situation different. It meant she'd never have to lie to Robert. But she'd have to lie to his sister by pretending the baby was definitely his.In her heart, though, she was certain it was Robert's. She had talked to herself so many times about it. It had to be Robert's. He was her first, it just had to be his. The situation was out of her control – she didn't want to go on with anything. But then she put her hands on her tummy. She had no choice.

'You're right, Eileen, let's get some fresh air,' she said.

***

Later that afternoon Ness looked at Eileen and, with a nod of her head and a lifting of her eyes, signalled that it was time to be getting back home. They'd been out for well over an hour and not spoken a word. They'd walked around and then sat in the park for a while. Ness was slow to rise and moved as though walking through sludge. Her head had not cleared, and she was no closer to knowing what to do, or how to do anything.

'Where's the letter?' she asked.

'I left it where it was, on the table back at the house,' said Eileen.

Ness's face drained of colour: 'We need to get back. They'll all be home by now.' She took Eileen's arm as they made slow progress down the street. When they entered the house, Ness knew the others were back. She could hear muffled voices and things banging about in the kitchen, and she knew she was too late.

When she heard Tommy's heated voice she panicked. She couldn't hear exactly what he was saying but she knew he wasn't being sympathetic.

Eileen opened the door and they could see her parents and Tommy standing by the range. Mary was holding the letter.

'You know, then,' said Ness, 'and I expect you're all full of good advice and helpful suggestions for me.'

Tommy looked aghast, 'Well, I—'

'Yes, I've got a good idea what you think right now, Tommy, and it's not very brotherly. You're—'

'Ness,' said Mary. 'Stop that right now. You're not the only person to lose somebody in this war, not by a long shot. The first thing you can do is stop feeling sorry for yourself and start planning what you're going to do about this mess.' She waved the letter around. 'I don't know who you are any more. What's happened to the lovely girl I knew a few years ago? It's not that I don't feel for you, but you've only known the chap five minutes – it's not like you've been together for years. Not like that poor woman down the road, she's been left with three kids to bring up after ten years of marriage—'

'Mrs Proctor, *please*,' said Eileen, 'Ness has been through a lot. Let her have time to think about things; I'm sure she'll sort everything out for the best.'

'*You* can talk! It's *you* who started it. If you hadn't put our address in those pockets in the first place, none of this would've happened. I don't know, it's enough to drive me to an early grave.'

'Stop that *now*,' said Jack. 'All this shouting don't help nobody. It's a mess alright, but nowt'll be fixed by arguing,'. He looked across at Ness with ready sympathy.

'Typical bloody man,' said Mary. '*You* won't have to look after the bairn when it's here. All chance of our lass getting any support now has flown out the window.'

The atmosphere was tense. Ness looked from her parents to Tommy and back in surprise. Why were they all being so negative and nasty? It didn't help at all. She began to cry.

'Come on, Ness,' said Eileen. 'Come back with me for the night. You can stay for as long as you like. Come on, right now.' Then over her shoulder, 'I'll drop by for some extra things later.'

Ness snatched the letter, and Eileen took hold of her shoulder and guided her to the front door.

***

Ness and Eileen shared Eileen's room for the week – Ness sleeping in the bed and Eileen on the floor with some pillows and rugs – and Eileen went to work each day, leaving Ness to sit and brood. She'd not been back home, and she'd not seen her parents or Tommy. She was upset they hadn't come round to find out if she was okay. But her mother was stubborn, her father wouldn't go against Mary, and she herself had probably scared Tommy off.

Eileen had told the office about Ness losing Robert, and they'd given her time off. 'Of course they think you've been widowed. All a bit of a mess really, isn't it? They're all being very sympathetic, especially when I told them you were expecting a baby. A couple of them had guessed already. I'm not altogether sure they believe you got married.'

'A lot of wagging tongues, that's all it is. Anyway, I've made up my mind,' said Ness.

'Am I going to like this or not?'

Ness smiled, something she hadn't done since she'd had the news from Rose. 'I've decided to go and see Rose in London. I've got a bit of money put by. Enough for the train fare and to keep myself for a couple of weeks. I went to the telephone box and rang her, just to thank her for letting me know what had happened, and she suggested I should stay with her for a few nights,' Ness stared at Eileen, who stood with her mouth open, 'Don't look so shocked.'

'But you don't *know* her. Ness, you've got to get on with things, it's just you now and the baby – you need to get it clear. Don't expect his family to have anything to do with you.'

Ness's moment of slight heart-lift was almost dashed, but she looked at her friend with a new determination and told her she wouldn't be put off. She'd hand in her notice at work and think about what to do when she got back.

'I'm not expecting great things. I don't want to face people at the office. I want an end to it, that's all. Rose'll tell me everything she knows, face to face. I don't want to write a letter. I'll go to London on Monday.' Ness was tempted once again to tell Eileen about Alf, but this didn't seem the right time. Maybe when she got back from her trip ...

After a moment of quiet, Eileen stepped forward and hugged Ness. 'Yes, I get it. It's all a bit of a mess, isn't it, and nobody can really help you. Perhaps by the time you get back your mum and dad'll have cooled off and they'll be happy to have you home. What'll you do for work when you get back, though?'

'I'll get some outwork from the factory. I'll have to do sewing at home for a while, until I can think of something better.'

Ness gave Eileen a note of the addresses and telephone numbers she'd been given by Robert and Rose. The two women hugged, and Eileen wished Ness all the luck in the world.

Twenty-five

Monday 17th August 1942 London

A man stood up to give Ness his seat; the train was busy. Looking around at the people's faces she could see some smiling, some laughing, hardly anybody looking sad. It was hard to believe there was a war on, except the carriages were crammed with people in uniform. Ness wondered where they might be going; home on leave or off to some ghastly place to fight for their country.

She wished so much that Robert was somewhere amongst them. She could see his handsome, clean-shaven face; the way he looked intently at her; she could almost feel and smell him. But how long would that image last for? It wouldn't be possible to remember for ever. They hadn't taken any photographs, and there were few memories. She almost let her guard drop, but swallowed hard. Of course, she'd have something very special to remind her of Robert. Would it be a boy or a girl? That old lady at the doctor's had said a boy, but what did she know? Right now, Ness just wanted it all to go away, turn the clock back eighteen months, and stop Eileen from putting those addresses in the pockets. But that was impossible. What had happened couldn't be undone.

**

At last the train pulled into King's Cross and Ness stayed in her seat, allowing everyone else to get off ahead of her. She was beginning to feel the weight of pregnancy and her bump was showing a little, but she was still able to make clothes to help disguise things a bit. She got her case down from the rack and made her way down the corridor and onto the platform. There were crowds buzzing around all over the place. Ness handed her ticket in at the barrier then she was on the main concourse. She wondered how on earth she was going to recognise Rose. They'd arranged to meet under the clock – it sounded a bit clandestine, something Ness thought Rose must have read in an Agatha Christie story. She looked around – people were milling about – and then one woman caught her eye. Ness moved forward and the woman smiled, raised her eyebrows and waved. 'You must be Ness,' she said.

'Rose?'

'Of course – who else would you be meeting under the clock at King's Cross?'

Ness hesitated, as did Rose, neither of them quite sure how they should greet each other.

'Pleased to meet you,' said Ness, putting out her hand.

'I think we can do better than that.' Rose put both her arms around Ness and gave her a solid hug. 'We're meeting in a time of war and tragedy, and I hope we'll be good friends, if not sisters. Now then, first things first; I think we should go somewhere and get a drink and a bite to eat. Shall I take your bag?'

Ness refused the offer and followed Rose out of the station.

'Let's get on a bus and go to Tottenham Court Road; we can go to the Lyons Corner House. It's quite comfy, and we can have a good chat.'

Ness was happy to go along with anything Rose suggested. On the bus she took the opportunity to look a little closer at her new friend. She was attractive, of medium height and build, and wore fashionable but sensible clothing. Ness thought that when they had hugged Rose had smelt of her name – it must be scent or talcum powder. She wore her shoulder-length brown hair pinned up at each side, showing off her high cheekbones and good jawline. There was definitely a likeness between her and Robert, particularly in the eyes.

'You're staring at me,' said Rose.

Ness flinched, but Rose laughed.

'I'm sorry,' said Ness, 'but you remind me so much of Robert, and I can't stop myself.' She looked through the window at the devastation in London. So many buildings damaged, and rubble all over the place.

'The Blitz has done a *lot* of damage,' she said.

'It was bad, but I wasn't here then – I was in Devon, missing it all. We've been busy since I arrived, but it's worse down by the docks.

Once at their table, Ness realised how hungry she was and looked at the menu, wondering if she could take a full lunch, and then Rose spoke: 'I'm going to make the most of this and have some liver and onions and probably a dessert.'

'In that case I'll join you, but not liver, I'll take the omelette with chips and peas, I think. I expect the eggs are dried, though.'

'I think you need to eat a good meal, don't you?'

'Yes, it's been a while since I left home. The journey was quite long on the train. Everything takes so much longer at the moment.'

'I meant ... because of your condition,' said Rose.

Ness blushed. Of course she should have realised Rose would notice straight away. It had been too hot to wear a big jumper or a coat, and she had fooled herself about her bump not showing in the dress she had chosen, even though its style was loose. She hesitated before answering.

'I ... erm ...'

'It's all right,' said Rose, 'I understand. You and my brother just fell for each other, and there's a war on. You're not the only ones to have acted quickly. So many of our men are going off to fight. I know it's not like the last time, but it's bad enough. You were unlucky to get caught, though.' She took Ness's hand, 'I've lost my brother and you've lost your true love. There's nothing we can do about that now – but you and I can make sure his child is given the best chance.'

'I don't even know what Robert would have thought about it. I wrote to tell him, but I have no idea if he ever received my letter. He might have died without knowing anything. I can't stop thinking about it.'

'I'm sure Robert loved you. He would have married you and been delighted about the baby ... I'm not sure what my mother will say, but there's only one way to find out. Would you like to come down to Devon with me? I plan to go home and stay for a few days. After you phoned last Friday, my mother rang to say she had arranged the memorial service for Robert for Friday. It'd be the perfect opportunity to introduce you. You don't have to get back to Ridley just yet, do you?'

'No, not at all. I've stopped working, and I have a bit of money saved up. My mother's not really speaking to me at the moment but I think she'll come around – so, no, I don't have to go back yet. I'll send a telegram to my friend Eileen, though, to tell her what's happening.'

'That's decided, then. We'll have a couple of days in London, and on Thursday we'll catch the train down to Totnes. Eat up, and then we can go back to my place. Is there anything you want to do while you're in London?'

'I'm not sure. I can't imagine doing any sightseeing ... I don't suppose. I mean ... couldn't we go to Robert's flat?'

'Oh, didn't I explain? That's where I'm living. He thought it'd be a good base for me, and as he was away for most of the time it seemed like a good idea. Then when he died. . . well, he already told me the flat would come to me if anything happened to him. . .' There was a slight pause while both women thought about Robert. Then Rose carried on, 'Do you feel strong enough to walk? It's about a mile from here, quite close to Regent's Park.'

Ness thought the walk was a good idea and they made their way towards Oxford Street, then across to Cavendish Square, where the railings around the garden had been removed. Ness was struck by the normality of London. She'd expected the streets to be empty, and was surprised to see children playing, running, riding bicycles.

'Everyone's carrying on here, too, as if there's no war going on.'

'It looks like that on the surface, but underneath people are watching, listening and aware that at any moment things could become frantic again. At night outside it's completely black, no lights anywhere. But inside the theatres and cinemas, it's all going on as before. Isn't it the same in Ridley?'

Ness laughed, and told Rose that Ridley was a pretty quiet town but yes, the cinemas were open and the dance hall, and Leeds was carrying on as normally as possible. She said they had to stick to the blackouts, same as everywhere.

They had walked for well over forty minutes when Rose stopped outside a large double-fronted townhouse.

It was a lot grander than Ness had expected. It was a row of terraced houses, too – but nothing like the street she lived in. These were large elegant-looking places with big black front doors and brass knockers.

The entrance hall was communal and had a large chest on one side with letters and notices for the other flats.

'This floor must take a bit of cleaning,' said Ness, tapping her foot on the black and white tiles.

Rose laughed, 'I don't have to worry about that.'

There was a central staircase leading up to other floors, but Rose led Ness to a door on the left. It was white with a number one on it and Ness stared for a moment, wondering how many times Robert had put his key in this lock on returning from work or a night out with friends. Had he brought any women home here with him? She told herself to stop it, and walked in.

Rose showed her around the whole flat, just as though she were a prospective tenant. There was a large sitting/dining room with a small round table and chairs set beside a window, which looked out onto the garden. There was only one bedroom, but it was big enough for a large double bed, a dressing table and wardrobe. The kitchen was tiny but modern with a small gas cooker and a larder. A polished wooden work surface surrounded the sink, and Ness imagined Robert washing up his cups and plates after a meal. She idly wondered what kind of cook he might have been. The bathroom was also tiny but rather sweet. The towels on the rail were pink. Ness supposed Rose had made some changes here, and probably in the whole place. Ness was sure she could still sense Robert everywhere, but thought it must be her imagination, as Rose had said she had packed up all of his belongings and taken them down to Devon.

'I found it just too difficult living here with all his stuff around me. I didn't like it even for a couple of days, not once I'd heard the news. I don't mind the books, though – but his clothes, shoes, toiletries and some of his personal things ... I couldn't bear to have them here. I left the paintings up, and obviously didn't worry about kitchen utensils, pots and pans, but you know the sort of thing I mean.'

'I was hoping there might be something here of Robert's which I could take away with me.'

Ness was close to tears and felt such a strong need for Robert. She was near him, here in his home – but he wasn't here, he was dead. Gone, never coming back. It was overwhelming, and she felt herself sway ...

'Here, sit down,' said Rose, 'I'll get some water for you. It's all too much, isn't it?'

As Rose went into the kitchen, Ness allowed her eyes to walk around the room. The shelves to the side of the fireplace were full of novels and books about the sea. There were some ornaments, but she could see they belonged to Rose; some china horses and birds, a glass bowl, and a small crystal vase, big enough for a single flower, probably a rose. The furniture must have been Robert's, though. The sofa was brown, velvet and leather, a matching chair with a rug thrown over the back of it. On the mantelpiece she saw a pipe, sitting as though it had been placed there carefully before its owner had gone to bed. She was still looking at it when Rose came back in with the water.

'Something I missed. I don't know why I didn't put it in the box with everything else. When I got back from Devon and saw it I hadn't the heart to throw it away. I think it was his spare one – I'm not sure he even used it.'

'Could I have it?' Ness was desperate to have something of Robert.

Rose handed it over. 'I'll leave you on your own for a while. I'm going to get some bedding out to make up the sofa, I'll sleep on it, I'm used to it. That is, unless you don't want to sleep in Robert's bed. I hadn't really thought about that. But the sheets are clean, and they're my sheets, not his. I brought them up with me from home. Robert's were a bit worn. Men don't seem to care about that sort of thing.'

After a while, Ness got up and moved around the room. Looking at it carefully, she thought about how far apart she and Robert really were on the social scale. In truth, they had hardly known each other. He came from a different background to hers – far superior. And now the idea of returning to Ridley felt physical, like a ball stuck in her throat. She'd been in London less than twelve hours and at this flat for only an hour or so, yet in that short time Ness could see that her future lay outside Ridley. She didn't want this baby to grow up there, to have to go to school there, and end up working there. If Robert had lived, then his child would have had the education and the chances Robert had been given. Even though she'd only just met Rose, she thought they would become good friends. She thought Rose might help her. Ness was determined to make a good life for herself and the baby.

Once in bed Ness buried her face in the pillow, but she didn't cry. Crying wasn't going to help anything – she had to draw strength from simply being here in Robert's bed. In what had been his flat. The bed didn't smell of Robert, it smelt like Rose, but she still drew comfort from it. She felt at ease. She was exhausted too, though; when she thought about the last few weeks of emotional ups and downs she felt drained.

Sleep came easily, and she woke early feeling better. As she lay there, she took in all that surrounded her. The bedroom had a dressing table – new, Ness suspected. She imagined Robert would have just had the oak chest of drawers and wardrobe. She wondered about the upholstered chair in the corner where she had left her clothes. Would that have been Robert's? And the curtains; his choice or Rose's?

She knew that one of her main problems in life now would be gaining acceptance of her as a single woman with a child. She thought that perhaps in London it wouldn't be so difficult. There must be many mothers who were managing on their own because their husbands were either away at the war, or had not returned from it. Ness had placed Robert's pipe on the bedside table. An extraordinary keepsake, she thought. It would be of no use to her, but she'd never let it go. She looked at her watch and saw it was just past seven o'clock. She got up quietly and went to the bathroom, then back into the bedroom to wait for sounds of Rose moving about.

It was after eight before Rose called her, 'Ness, I've made some tea. Are you up yet?'

'Yes, and I've brought my ration book with me if you need it,' said Ness.

'We'll certainly need coupons at some point, but for now we have some bread and margarine and some home-made jam from my mother's pantry in Devon. She makes a lot of stuff – or rather she did, but since my father died she hasn't made quite as much. Maybe now Robert's gone too, the supplies'll dry up altogether. I hope not, because along with our gardener, she's grown a lot of stuff and it'll soon be blackberrying time to go with our cookers.'

'It sounds idyllic,' said Ness. In her mind's eye she could see an orchard overlooking the sea, and beautiful meadows with wildflowers. She sighed and wondered if it would be at all like she'd thought it might be. At the end of this week she'd find out.

They took their breakfast into the sitting room and sat at the table, looking out into the garden. There were a few broken pots and weeds, not much more. Nobody had time for the garden, thought Ness. It was a shame. She didn't know anything about it, but surely a few vegetables could be grown, or maybe even a couple of chickens kept. What a waste. She'd noticed that some of the parks, when they'd walked from Tottenham Court Road the day before, had vast swathes turned over to vegetable growing.

'Where's the nearest shelter?' she asked.

'There's an Anderson in the local park, big enough for a couple of families, but most people go to the underground stations. Baker Street's the closest to here.'

'Aren't you afraid, living in the centre of London?'

'It's no more dangerous than any other town, really. The Germans could decide to hit anywhere at any time. The sirens go off and we shelter until the all clear. Sometimes it's a false alarm and nothing happens.'

'Do you have any friends here?'

'Yes, and some relatives just outside. My mother's family come from Leytonstone – they are quite well off. Her sister, our aunt, has a property there, well it's her husband's I suppose – but Robert wanted to be in the centre of London. I go to the cinema quite often, and the theatre, usually with friends from work. I'm happy enough.'

Ness sat finishing her bread and jam. Her resolve to get on with things and improve her life was slipping away with each mouthful. It was all very well thinking about it when lying in bed, but the reality was different. She changed her mind every ten minutes. *Go back to Ridley, don't bother with Robert's family, they're not the same as us. ... Don't be silly, you can do anything you want if you put your mind to it.*

Rose had told her about her job in the Air Ministry. It sounded very important. 'I'm just a shorthand typist really. It was exciting when I first came up to London to work. I was given an identity pass to get into the office and I felt very important. But now I take it all in my stride.'

Rose cleared away the breakfast things and wouldn't allow Ness to wash up or do anything, then asked, 'Is there anything in particular you'd like to do today?'

'Not really. I thought I might go to a museum or perhaps just wander around. Or go and look in a big department store and get some ideas for making clothes. It's something I do all the time – make clothes, I mean. I love sewing, and I'm getting pretty good at it. I made this blouse and trousers. I hoped they'd disguise my situation.'

Rose looked Ness up and down, and turned her round, admiring the outfit as she did.

'I must admit, you look good this morning. Are you telling me you made all this?'

Ness explained how much she enjoyed sewing and how one of the perks of working at Brodericks meant that she could go down to the shop floor and take offcuts home for very little money, sometimes for nothing at all.

'I'm also good at altering old clothes and making something different from them. You know, a skirt from a pair of a man's trousers, a blouse from an old dress.'

Rose had nothing but admiration for her and told her she was wasted working as a typist and ought to be designing and making clothes for the London fashion industry.'

'Don't be silly – I could never do that and especially not at the moment with all the restrictions on clothing.'

'Well, you can begin by making me some of those slacks, they're amazing. Where did you get the idea?'

'I saw it in a copy of Vogue magazine. Women are wearing slacks and siren suits nowadays which they'd never have done before the war. I could make some for you easily but how can we get cloth?'

'You would really make some for me?' said Rose. 'I love the idea. I think I have enough coupons in my ration book for some material, if I gave the book to you with some money could you get what you need from the shops today and make some for me please?'

Twenty-six

Tuesday 18th August 1942

Rose and Ness left the house together, Rose pushing her bicycle and Ness walking beside her. They parted company when they reached Oxford Circus, Rose continuing to Kingsway on her bike. Ness went to Selfridges first, but it wasn't what she'd expected. She hadn't realised that the building had been hit during the Blitz, and its windows were all boarded up. But all the same, she went inside and looked around at all the different designs. It was amazing that so many clothes were still being made, especially when there was so little material around. She noticed that some of the clothing styles and colours were a little drab, skirts shorter and fewer buttons, collars or embellishments. She longed for a time when she could visit when the war was over and the racks were bursting with glorious dresses again.

After Selfridges she walked down to Piccadilly Circus, where she found Swan & Edgar, another huge store with a restaurant inside it. She went to its fabric department and searched until she found a roll of cotton drill. There wasn't much choice of shade and she chose a cream colour. She thought the neutral shade would go with anything.

After paying with Rose's and some money, she headed straight back to the flat. She would be able to cut them out and have them sewn before Rose came home.

When she got back to the flat Ness was grateful for something to keep her busy. She put the material and the pattern, which she had made herself from newspaper, onto the table and began cutting. She'd taken all the measurements she needed and the two women had laughed a lot. Rose said she'd never had a single item of clothing made for her before, but Ness didn't believe her. She pinned all the seams and then sat in a comfortable chair sewing while listening to the radio. Ness loved hand sewing and thought she'd make a good enough job of making the trousers, but it would have been so much quicker, even with her hand machine. She just hoped they'd fit without any alterations. She began to feel quite at home sitting and sewing.

When the trousers were finished Ness was fairly pleased with the result, and when Rose arrived home she tried them on straight away.

'These are brilliant! You're so clever. I mean, they're really professional-looking – they don't look home-made at all. If you can do this by hand, how amazing you must be with a sewing machine.'

'It's very kind of you to say, but loads of people make their own clothes and they're just as good as me.'

'No, they're not – that's where you're wrong. I have friends in Devon who think they can sew, but honestly, their stuff turns out looking awful.'

'Would you like me to make a blouse for you tomorrow? It's the least I can do. I know where to go to get the material now, and I can do it easily while you're at work tomorrow. Then you'll be able to take it and the trousers to Devon.'

'That'd be wonderful, thank you. Are there enough coupons left?' asked Rose.

'Yes, you've hardly used any.'

'I was well set up before the war. I've got a lot of stuff I don't wear at all. Maybe you could alter them for me? I could pay you?'

'I'm sure I could but let's talk about that later. Are there any more old newspapers around? I used up the whole of the one you gave me yesterday.'

'There's a box under the stairs. I'll get it out for you tonight.'

***

The next morning they walked together again, but this time a little further before parting company at Piccadilly Circus. Ness was able to go back to Swan & Edgar and buy the material for the blouse. It was a lightweight cotton, the end of a roll, she was surprised it hadn't been snapped up earlier, it must have been hidden underneath other rolls for a few years.

Once she was. back at the flat, Ness pulled out a couple of old newspapers from the box Rose had left out for her. There didn't seem to be any hurry to get on with the blouse, it was a simple sleeveless pattern with no buttons, loose fitting, it pulled on over the head with a V-neck, open collar, but the facings might be fiddly. Ness began to leaf through an Evening Standard from back in May. It was the usual thin edition of course, only four pages. She glossed over the adverts for men's hair oil and cocoa powder – the news in it was mostly about the war. She thought of Robert and realised she didn't even know what kind of things he would have reported or which paper he had worked for. She must ask Rose. She turned the page and saw a list of casualties and those who had died in service recently. She looked down the Navy listings, and the blood seemed to leave the whole of her body, as with horror she read the name – Alfred James Taylor, Southall, listed under the ship *Caspia,* the date, 20th April, in the Mediterranean.

It had to be him. It had to be *the* Alf Taylor. This was unbelievable. She read it over and over again. She couldn't decide if it was a relief or not. Now, whoever the father of her child was, he was dead. Did it make any difference to how she felt? She pulled the page out of the paper, folded it up and put it in her handbag. Her life was becoming full of bits of paper with addresses or announcements written on them. It was almost a joke. No, it wasn't funny at all – it was mad, absolutely bloody mad. Her hands were shaking, then she tasted the metallic tang of blood. She put her finger to her mouth, then looked at the red liquid on the tip. She must have bitten her lip. Taking a hanky from her pocket she went to the sink and, dampening the hanky, held it against the wound until the flow stopped. She drank some water, then tried to think logically and sensibly.

She wondered how Alf had died. Did she care? The very fact he was dead should have made her jump for joy, but she had an uneasy feeling about it. What difference would this make to her unborn child? She thought about it and made up her mind that she really could believe that the baby was Robert's now, because as Alf was no longer around there would be no reason to think anything else. This thought comforted her a little. She would put the incident with Alf behind her. She would shed the guilt – he'd got his punishment. If there was a god, then he'd well and truly sorted Alf out. The news of his death could only be a good thing.

'Onwards and upwards!' she shouted and pulled herself together. She picked up another newspaper and spread it on the table, ready to draw the pattern for the blouse. It was hard to concentrate, but this was her way forward. Get on with things. Get on with her life. Have the baby and take care of it. Everyone, including the child, would be told that Robert was the father.

She hoped she'd make a good job of the blouse. It took her quite a few hours, and her fingers were sore by the time Rose came home.

'You've done a wonderful job. You wait until my colleagues see this! They're going to want to put an order in.'

'I'm pleased you're pleased – but I'm not sure I could even think about making more. It's not the right time at the moment.'

'But you are so clever. Maybe you could use your skills by offering to alter people's cast-off garments. I know a lot of people who can't sew, they'd be glad of your help.'

Ness listened to what Rose said and thought it might not be a bad idea. She needed to make some money now, and when the baby came she'd be able to sew from home. Her sewing machine wasn't much good – but good enough to make a lot of things. She would give it some serious thought.

'Maybe I could do *something*,' said Ness.

'Well, we can talk about it on the train tomorrow. You still want to come down with me, don't you?'

'Yes, of course – although I'm a bit nervous about meeting your mother.'

'Mmm yes, she can be a bit daunting,' said Rose. 'But I'll be there. Anyhow, I'm hungry. What'll we eat tonight?'

Ness's stomach reminded her she'd not eaten all day. 'Is there a fish and chip shop anywhere near here?'

Twenty-seven

Thursday 20th August 1942 Dittisham, Devon

It was late afternoon when they arrived at Totnes, and Jim was at the station to meet them with the car. Rose introduced Ness to him as her friend, as the two had agreed that for the time being they would not mention her connection to Robert. They'd break the news to Rose's mother when the time was right.

'Your mother said you were bringing someone with you, Miss,' said Jim. 'Mrs Leach has made up the bed in the spare room for her.'

Rose had explained to Ness who Jim and Mrs Leach were, and that nobody called Mrs Leach by her first name – not even Jim, her husband. 'In fact I didn't know for a long time what her name was until my mother wrote her a birthday card one year and asked me to sign it, to Kathleen. I was most impressed. It seemed a very posh name for our cook-housekeeper.'

Ness thought she could never get used to having people in her house to do the domestic work. Anyhow, her own family would be hard pushed to fit anyone else into their tiny box of a home. She supposed you were born to it. Eileen would be appalled – she couldn't stand posh people at all. Ness had been thinking a lot about Eileen lately and wondering if she'd approve of Rose. Ness didn't find Rose at all posh, though, just friendly.

When they got to the house, Rose jumped out of the car to swing open the gate, and Jim waited while she closed it behind them.

'Don't worry, Jim, I'll run up,' she shouted, and raced ahead to bang on the front door.

Ness knew it was Mrs Leach who opened it, because she was stout and wore an apron – the epitome of a cook. This made Ness smile in spite of the fact that she was in awe of what she was experiencing. The sweeping gravel driveway up to the house with lawns on either side, the beautiful country residence with big green bushes – rhododendrons, she thought – it was all way beyond anything she'd imagined. It felt like her first day at school. She was apprehensive but excited.

As soon as they got into the house Rose called to her mother.

'It's no good, Miss,' said Mrs Leach. 'She won't come down yet. She stays up in her room most of the time. On top of burying her husband in March, she has to accept that Master Robert's gone too. She's not looking forward to the church service tomorrow, neither, but perhaps now you're here she'll perk up a bit.'

'Thanks, Mrs Leach. We won't bother her yet, but we'll take our things up and then come into the kitchen for a cup of tea with you.' Rose turned to Ness. 'I don't know about you, but I'm dying for a cup and I'd rather sit in the kitchen than in the drawing room right now. I'll show you round afterwards.'

Later, for the second time in a few days Ness was being shown around a home by Rose, and again she felt as though she were a prospective buyer or tenant. She loved the house – it was impossible not to – and the views down to the Dart from Rose's bedroom were beautiful. It looked still and calm – nothing like Ness felt at the time – but she could see why Robert had loved it all so much.

'The view from my parents' room is even better, but we can't go in there right now.'

'How old is the house?'

'It was built around 1890, so not that old, but I think a cottage stood on the site for a long time before that. It's called Field House, and I imagine before it would have been Field Cottage. Robert and I loved it as soon as we moved here. We were at the surgery in Dartmouth for a while – I don't remember being there, I was just a baby – but when we came here Robert was eight and I was six. Couldn't have had a better childhood. We know we were lucky. Robert spent all his holiday time down by the river, and I spent my time hanging around the local farm.'

The drawing room was enormous, big enough for two Chesterfield sofas and a comfortable-looking armchair, which had a rug thrown over it. Although the room was elegant, it was obviously lived in: newspapers on the coffee table, and a writing desk with a massive bookshelf behind it. Many country paintings on the walls. A dog bed close to the open fireplace. The gold-coloured curtains hanging at the big bay window, heavy and long to the floor, and the dining room beyond.

'We eat in here most of the time, except I have my breakfast in the kitchen. Since father died, things have gone a bit awry. His study's through the door over there, but my mother doesn't like me to go in there at the moment. I don't know why that is, but I feel we should respect her wishes. I'm sure she'll recover from all this. But it is hard for her.

***

After a restless night, Ness came down to breakfast. She still hadn't met Rose's mother. It seemed strange thinking of her as Rose's mother rather than Robert's, but nothing was running as normal. The evening before, Rose and Ness had eaten alone in the dining room. Rose hadn't been keen; she'd said she would rather have eaten in the kitchen, and what was the point of laying the table in the dining room and pretending things were as normal? But Mrs Leach had thought it best, so Rose and Ness had gone along with it. Now they sat here again, but this time for breakfast. There was a sideboard laid with cereal, bread and boiled eggs, homemade jams and some real butter. 'We get it from the local farm, the one I used to hang out at when I was a child. They still have cattle; the pasture here is still plentiful even though most of the farmers have been instructed to grow grain for the war effort. Oh, those words, 'war effort', how I hate them!'

At that point the door opened and Mrs Granger came in. She looked from Rose to Ness and back again. 'So, who have we here?'

'This is Ness, Mother; she's a friend of mine, and she's staying with me at the flat in London.'

Ness stood up. 'Good morning, Mrs Granger. Thank you for having me here.'

'Well – *you're* not a Londoner with an accent like that.'

'No ... I'm from Yorkshire ...' Ness struggled to think of something to say, some reason why she might be in London. 'I'm a secretary and also a bit of a seamstress ... and I'm thinking of moving to London. A mutual friend put me in touch with Rose.'

'Well, you're welcome, I suppose – but your timing isn't good. We have to remember my son Robert, Rose's brother, today at a memorial service. I suppose you'll have to join us.'

'I would be ...' Ness struggled for the right word, 'honoured.'

The rest of breakfast was taken in silence.

As they got up, Rose said, 'Let's take the dog down to The Ham, shall we, Ness?'

'That's a good idea,' said Mrs Granger. 'Paddy hasn't had anywhere near enough exercise since ...'

Twenty-eight

Friday 21st August 1942

It was a surreal service. There were few people of Robert's age attending. Ness looked around at the faces, and most of them were her parents' age. A couple of Rose's friends had turned up, though. One of them, a pretty girl, was visibly upset, a handkerchief held to her face throughout the service. Ness decided she must be an old flame – or at the very least a girl who had strong feelings for Robert. She would find out afterwards when they had tea at The Red Lion. There were no contemporaries to give a eulogy or speeches. Rose read a poem; it was one about the sea, which Ness didn't know. She thought back to when her mother had begun to quote the poem 'Sea Fever', and how she'd become interested in poetry because of Robert. She'd hoped he'd be able to introduce her to more poets and poetry – but now that would never happen.

To Ness it was unbelievable. She couldn't help thinking perhaps Robert hadn't died and he'd be rescued and come home after all. How awful it would be to arrive in this little village and see your grave in the churchyard. His mother had organised a headstone, something which to remember him by. It was almost macabre, though – no body, no coffin, just a lump of cold rock with an inscription. Ness shed not a single a tear, and she couldn't understand her own feelings. His mother sobbed and Rose wept silently – but Ness was numb. It was as though the whole thing was happening to someone else. Like watching herself in a show or a film. What a good film it'd make. She smiled inwardly.

But there was no happy ending. Not now – and maybe there never would be.

The congregation moved out to the churchyard. They had put Robert's stone next to his father's grave, even though his headstone had not yet been erected.

'We have to wait six months before we can put up the stone for father. Not long now,' said Rose, 'It's strange that Robert's stone's here first – but there's no body, no grave as such.' Rose placed some flowers on the ground and waited for Ness to put some down too. Ness knew that people hadn't a clue about the real reason she was there, so she didn't make too much of a fuss about it, but stopped just long enough to read the inscription,

Robert Charles Granger
20 June 1916 – 13 July 1942
Beloved son and brother
who gave his life for his country

She hadn't realised the exact date he'd died until that moment. Robert was already dead when she'd had her first doctor's appointment. Her thoughts turned to the baby – it should say 'beloved father' on there too.

The Red Lion was a short walk from St George's church. Although it was a beautiful sunny day, the last thing Ness felt like doing was talking to people she didn't know. Especially as all the guests were thinking she was just a friend of Rose's and was there in that capacity. Rose introduced her to aunt Florence, who lived in Leytonstone. She seemed friendlier than Mrs Granger and asked Ness a few questions about where she came from and how she met Rose. It was a little awkward but she mumbled the same story about a mutual friend and staying in London with Rose to see if she liked it. She knew it sounded a bit iffy.

After half an hour, Ness was ready to leave. She sought out Rose, and told her she was going to take a walk around the village and not to worry about her – she couldn't possibly get lost, and she'd find her own way back to Field House.

Instead of walking back along Higher Street, which she knew led to the house, Ness walked down Manor Street and followed the road down towards the river. She'd been this way when they'd walked Paddy, down a small lane and onto The Ham where he'd run about like a mad thing. This time, instead of turning off along the lane, Ness kept on walking down the steep road to the river, where she stood on the edge of the pontoon which stretched out towards the centre of the flow. She stood there for a while and watched a little boat come over from the other side carrying a few passengers with it, then leave again with a few people. Backwards and forwards it went. After a while she walked to the end of the pontoon, and the next time the boat came in she asked the ferryman what was on the other side. He had a strong Devon accent, ' 'Tes Greenaway, Miss. Did 'ee want to go over?'

'Is there anything to see?'

'Well, Mrs Christie's house is where they all want to go – but you can't see nothing. Just the gates.'

Ness remembered Robert's letter when he'd told her how much he read, including Agatha Christie novels. She thought about his books in London, his flat, and his home here in Dittisham. She was getting to know him, but all too late.

'Well? Do 'ee want to go over?'

'No, sorry, thanks – another time perhaps.'

She'd been away for a good hour and a half, and thought it was time to go back to the house. The tide was out and she could see it was possible to walk along the shingle beach, beside the tiny cottages which fronted the river. It would take her to The Ham, and then she could walk up from there along Riverside Road, which would take her back past the church, then she would find her way back to the house.

It was gone four o'clock when she arrived at the gate. As she walked up the driveway she looked again at the house where Robert had been a boy, and tried to imagine him running around on the grass and playing football. She let herself in by the back door. Mrs Leach was nowhere to be seen; she and Jim must have gone home to their cottage next door, in a row with three others. She wondered if they rented it or if the Grangers rented it for them or even owned it. She had no idea how these things worked.

As she walked into the hallway, she could hear raised voices in the room at the front of the house. She moved a little closer and stood by the door, and could hear clearly what was being discussed with such rancour.

'But, Mother, she's a *lovely* girl and Robert obviously loved her.' Rose's voice.

'I don't believe it! Robert would never have fallen for a girl of *her* class. He had far too much sense. As for the pregnancy, how can we be sure it's Robert's?'

Ness blanched when she heard this, her guilt catching at the back of her throat.

'Oh, how could you *say* that? I've spent the last few days with Ness and there's no way she's *that* sort of girl. Robert spoke to me before he left and told me all about her. He even wrote to me and said he'd been to see her and they had "sealed their relationship". I'm sure Robert would want us to help her.'

'How can we help her? Pay her off perhaps? How much would it take for her to leave us alone and take the brat away somewhere we'll never see it?'

'You're talking about your *grandchild!*'

'So you say – but we've no proof.' Mrs Granger blew her nose loudly, but from the other side of the door Ness couldn't make out if she was crying. Should she go into the room – or would it make things worse? She felt a tightening in her throat, and her arms and legs were drained of blood. How awful it was to overhear people talking about you when they didn't know you were there. Rose was standing up for her – how kind! But she didn't like the image Mrs Granger was painting of her. It wasn't right – but then she didn't realise how close it came to the truth. She didn't for one minute consider she was '*that* kind of girl' – but she *had* been with more than one man, even though not by choice.

'Please, Mother, think about it. Ness might have a boy and then you would have a little piece of Robert still living.'

'I can't begin to even think like that. Robert should've been more careful. Son of a doctor, he should've known better. He's let us down. Let the whole *family* down – thank God his father isn't here to witness it. They could have only known each other five minutes. How on earth did he meet her? How did he come to be *mixing* with people like her?' Mrs Granger's voice was reaching an ever higher pitch.

'We're at war, Mother. People are changing; they live differently from when you were a girl.'

'You're correct in *that* assumption. I lived through the last war, and people didn't lose their heads then.'

'It makes me so sad to think you're reacting like this. Robert would be devastated.'

It was obvious to Ness that Mrs Granger had the same ideas as her own mother. Older people thought they were better than today's generation. It's probably always been the same. She was surprised, though, that Rose had chosen this afternoon to tell her mother about Ness, and that she hadn't waited for her to come back to the house so they could do it together. Perhaps, though, she'd known what the reaction would be, and had thought Ness wouldn't be able to cope.

It was time to show her face. She took a deep breath and knocked on the door. Not waiting for a reply, she walked in.

There was a horrible silence. Mrs Granger turned away and walked towards the window to look out across the garden. Rose looked shocked and embarrassed.

Ness spoke first. 'I didn't mean to listen outside but your voices were very loud and I couldn't help hearing. I'm so sorry you feel the way you do, Mrs Granger. You're right – Robert and I didn't know each other well, but what we had was special. I've only ever loved one man, and it was him. We went together somehow. It's not fair we didn't have more time. It's not fair he won't be here to be with me and his child. We didn't plan this. In the short time we had together, we spoke about marriage after the war. We discussed coming down here to Devon, to meet you all and then perhaps living in London. He would have done well, and I would've helped him. But now ... now I don't know what I'll do.'

'I'm sorry for your situation,' said Mrs Granger, 'but I *cannot* bring myself to accept that Robert would have fallen for a girl ... not of his class. I thought it was strange that Rose should have made your acquaintance, but I was happy to put up with it – at least for the duration of her stay at this time. But when you leave this house I do not wish to have any further knowledge of you or the child. Is that clear? Now, if you don't mind, I'm going upstairs to lie down. I may not be down for supper.' She walked steadily out of the room and as Ness went to speak once more, Rose shook her head and took hold of her shoulder to stop her moving towards her mother.

Both girls sat down, one on each sofa. Ness was quiet, thinking about what to do next. She wasn't welcome here. She didn't want to go back to Ridley. She could go back to London with Rose, but that was neither practical nor sensible. No room in the flat for a permanent lodger, She didn't have a job in London, and she'd given up her job in Ridley.

'I'm sorry about my mother,' said Rose. 'I don't know what Robert would think of her behaviour. They didn't get on too well, you know. I know Robert felt he'd let our father down by joining the Navy, and he never felt close to my mother. He was packed off to boarding school when he was seven, and although he loved coming home for the holidays I know he didn't love coming home to mother. She isn't exactly tactile. Goodness knows how she and my father managed to produce two children.'

The women fell quiet, lost in their own thoughts. Crashing into the silence, the telephone rang in the hall. They jumped. Rose got up to answer it. It was only a moment before she came back into the drawing room.

'It's for you, Ness – it's your friend Eileen. She didn't say what she wanted, but she said it's urgent.'

Twenty-nine

Saturday 22nd August 1942

It was getting dark when Ness stepped off the train at Ridley and began to head towards home, but then she saw George standing beside a car and waving.

'Hello, stranger,' he said. 'I've borrowed the car again, thought you might like a lift home.' Ness was surprised how relieved she was to see him, and got in the passenger seat without hesitation.

'Thank you, George, that's kind of you. I could've walked easily – it's not that far.'

'I'm so sorry to hear about your dad. It was a shock for everyone.'

'Yes, Eileen said when she rang me. Stupid accident.'

'You hear about people falling off ladders. Mostly they just break something, but your dad hit the back of his head on the counter. I don't think he knew anything about it.'

Ness didn't want to think too much about how it had happened. A stupid, avoidable accident. The worst of it was that Ness had not spoken to, or seen, her father since she'd left the house with Eileen after the letter incident.

She sighed, 'How did you know which train I'd be on?'

'I just guessed – but I did come and go a couple of times.' George took his hand off the steering wheel for a moment and patted her on the knee. It was a friendly pat of support and encouragement, and Ness appreciated it.

'You've been through a lot, I know,' he said. 'It must be difficult, in your *situation*.'

'What about my situation? Did Tommy tell you something?'

'Tommy didn't need to tell me.' George took his time taking a corner and after he'd straightened the car up he continued: 'I should've said before. You know that time when we went on the picnic? You blurted it out – you thought I was Robert, and you said something about hoping the baby was okay. Anyway, it's obvious now, just to look at you. I don't think any the less of you by the way. Just wish it had been *me*.' George laughed, but Ness, embarrassed, felt her neck go red.

The rest of the journey passed in silence. Ness looked around the familiar – but now, to her, unattractive – streets. The greyness of the place was so different from the greenness of Devon and the buzz of London. She saw how there were fewer trees here. Even though it was a warm day many of what trees there were had lost most of their leaves already, and instead of the smell of the countryside there was a faint smell of the local foundry gases.

At Ness's house George left her on the doorstep. 'I don't want to be in the way. It's late anyway, I'll call back tomorrow, or I'll go and see Eileen to find out how you are.' Ness gave him a quick peck on the cheek, saying once more what a good friend he was and how much she appreciated it.

There was a sign on the shop door. She didn't bother to read it, but she guessed it said something about her father's death and the shop being closed for a few days. She idly wondered what'd happen to the place now. She thought she might have to work there for the time being, at least help her mum out for a few weeks. It wouldn't be a bad thing, but the last thing she needed was to be trapped in Ridley working in a corner shop. *Another nail in my coffin* she thought.

Inside the house it was eerily quiet. No Tommy, no kettle on the stove, the radio silent. As she walked past the front room the door was ajar. She dropped her bag on the hall floor and took off her jacket and shoes. She couldn't see her slippers anywhere, but remembered she'd left them at Eileen's. They had been too embarrassing to take to Rose's. She opened the door tentatively – she knew what would be in there.

The open coffin lay across three chairs. Ness didn't recognise them, so assumed they'd been brought in by the undertakers. She wasn't keen on viewing the dead body, but she'd had to do it from a very young age. There was no one here at the moment, not even her mother. Ness padded to the side of the coffin. Her father looked peaceful, much as the other corpses she'd looked at in the past – but this time it was different. It was her own father. She hesitated before putting her hand on his forehead. It was cold. She didn't know what she'd expected. He didn't look real. She could see it was her dad, but it was just an empty shell. Everything about his personality had gone.

She spoke to him anyway: 'Dad, you stupid, lovely man. What did you have to go and do that for? Too old for climbing ladders. You should've got Tommy to do it for you, whatever it was you were trying to do. I haven't got to the bottom of it yet, but I will. You know we'll be okay. I'm so sorry you won't get to meet your grandchild. Not this one, or any Tommy might have. You're going to miss out on so much. Mum'll be lost without you, but we'll do our best to help her through. I've lost Robert and now you. There are people dying all over the world in this war, but it doesn't make it any easier when it's one of your own. Sleep well, Dad. I'll do my best for you. I'll make something of myself, you'll see. I love you and I'm going to miss you.' Ness bent down and kissed his forehead. It felt weird and she didn't like it, but she had to do it. 'And another thing – I'm so, so sorry about the last time I saw you. You were the only one of the family who seemed to sympathise with me after Robert's death. You were looking out for me even though I'd let you down.'

'Ness.' Her mother was in the doorway.

She walked towards her mother, put her arms around her neck and began to cry. All the pent-up emotions came out. Anger, sadness, hopelessness. She was at a low ebb.

'What next?' asked her mother. 'We've had a fair share of badness over the last couple of months.' She pulled away from Ness and stood looking at her. 'You're looking bonny, lass. That baby's growing, and you're carrying it well.'

Ness realised that this was her mother's way of telling her she was sorry she'd reacted so badly about the baby and about Robert's death.

'Thanks, Mum.'

'We'll just have to get on with things now. Manage the best we can. Now get yourself ready for bed and I'll make a cup of tea for you to take up. We've told the neighbours they can pay their respects between three and five each day. It'll be good to have your support now. Tommy went to work, he's on a late shift today. He's taking Monday off for the funeral. I'm glad you came home. You can tell me tomorrow all about where you've been and what you've been up to over the last couple of weeks. Eileen was a bit cagey about the whole thing.'

'I will, Mum, I will. Let's get the next few days over first.'

Thirty

Monday 24th August 1942

The cemetery was a desolate place on the outskirts of Ridley. The wind had skittered the litter as they'd walked behind the hearse, past the terraced houses with their blackened brick fronts. Ness looked at them with a feeling of dread. They weren't much different from their house in North Street, but the graveyard would be a grim view. The service at St Paul's had been quick, attended by a few neighbours and some of her dad's friends. Tommy and Ness had stayed with their mother, one on each side of her, supporting her throughout the ordeal. This last bit of the day was proving exhausting for them all, but particularly for Ness who had not slept well for the last couple of nights, even though she was back in her own bed.

They stood beside the gaping hole while the coffin was lowered into it and the vicar said a few words, then they threw some flowers in. But then the reality of her father dying suddenly hit her hard, and she cried for him and what he'd miss. She cried for Robert, too, and for the unborn child whose future was so uncertain, and she cried for herself.

Two funerals in less than a week, Ness hoped she wouldn't have to attend another for many years.

The wake was held at the church hall not far from the cemetery. They only had tea and a few sandwiches and cakes, but Ness thought she and Eileen had laid everything out nicely.

'The neighbours gave a lot, didn't they?' said Eileen. 'But rationing makes it difficult. I thought there might be some extra coupons allowed for a funeral, but it seems not. Still, Sid got a bottle of whisky. We've not brought it here, but I thought your mum might like to have it at the house, to drink herself or offer visitors. She's sure to get a lot in the next few weeks.'

'You've been great,' said Ness, glad of the support.

'What are you going to do after this is over?' asked Eileen.

Ness thought before answering. She'd done nothing but think since she'd got back from Devon. She longed to leave Ridley and go to London, but it didn't seem a practical thing to do at the moment – or a particularly kind one, either. How could she turn her back on her mother now? Tommy was out of the house more than ever. If he wasn't working, then he was with the Home Guard, and on top of that he had a girlfriend. She was here in the hall now. Ness looked across to where they were standing. She'd been so wrapped up in her own life that she hadn't taken that much notice of Tommy and his girlfriend, Emma. They caught sight of her watching them, and Tommy took the girl by the hand and dragged her over to Ness and Eileen.

'Emma's coming back to the house after – aren't you?' said Tommy.

'If that's all right with the family. I spent a bit of time at your place while you were away.' Emma looked at Ness. 'I mean, when you were at Eileen's and all, then when you went to the other places.' It sounded as though she felt Ness had been away for months.

'Mum's fond of Emma – so that's nice, isn't it?' said Tommy.

'I'm sure it's all lovely for everyone. But I'm back now, at least for the time being, and I've got a bairn on the way, in case you hadn't noticed.' Ness knew she was speaking out of character but couldn't help herself. They were treating her as thought she'd already left Ridley and wasn't a part of anything anymore.

They looked embarrassed. Tommy coughed and looked around for somebody else to speak to. 'Look, there's George. Hey, George! Come on, Emma – let's go and say hello.'

Eileen manoeuvred Ness into a corner where there were a couple of chairs. 'Sit down and listen,' she said. 'We've been friends for a long time. I can tell you're unsettled and it's not just because your dad's died. I don't know what happened while you've been away, but you're back now and you need to think about the future. What're you going to do about everything?'

Ness grasped Eileen's hand. 'I'm grateful to you, honestly I am. It's been a strange couple of weeks and I've seen another side of life – one I want to live. I know I'm going to have to help Mum in the shop for the next few weeks, but I'm thinking about a way of making money for myself and the baby. It won't be easy, but I'm making plans.'

'When you're ready to share them let me know,' said Eileen and she gave a weak smile. 'Look, George is coming over.'

Eileen stood up to let George sit down, then turned to go and talk to Mary.

George took Ness's hand. 'I've missed you while you've been away. I've been worried about, you know.'

Ness looked down at their hands and tried to control the swell of emotion which jumped into her throat …

'I know you only think of me as a friend, but I could be more than that, Ness. You need someone to take care of you and the baby. Would you consider marrying me? I'd be good to you.'

Ness didn't answer. She could never love George and she'd have to tell him so. Choosing her words with care, she looked directly at him. 'George, you're a good man, there's no doubt about it, and marrying you would solve a lot of problems for me. But I can't do it. I just can't. I know you think a lot of me, but please, I have to say no, and I don't ever want you to ask me again. It's final. You have to move on with your life and meet someone. There are lots of girls out there who'll make you very happy. I'll be fine. I'll go it alone if I have to. I'm sorry, really I'm sorry.'

She took her hand back and placed it in her lap.

'But—'

'No George. It isn't going to happen.'

She stood up and went to join her mum and Eileen, and when she turned back to look, George had gone. Ness knew that this time he'd accepted what she'd said.

Thirty-one

Wednesday 30th September 1942

It was over a month since her father's funeral and things were settling into a routine. Ness was working in the shop, and to make some extra money she'd been taking in some home sewing from the factory. Not a job she enjoyed, but she had to keep some money coming in somehow, as typing at home didn't work. An outworker for Brodericks was not what she'd imagined she'd be.

She emptied the box of shirts Tommy had picked up for her that morning. One needed hand-sewn buttonholes and buttons, and the other two just the buttons – she'd already done the buttonholes. The shirts were fancy ones for evening or special occasions. The factory hardly turned out any of those these days, and even though the material was delicate and lovely to work with it was still a tedious job. Every now and then she stood up and walked around the table, stretching her back and arms. She thought back to making the blouse and trousers for Rose and how much she'd enjoyed it. But since being back she'd done nothing about trying to either make new things for people or to alter old clothes. The war made it all so difficult.

She'd had a letter from Rose, telling her that the office she worked in was moving from Kingsway to Oxford Street. She'd given Ness the new address and telephone number, and she'd also mentioned she'd only been back to Devon once – and that sadly her mother had not changed her mind about Ness. In a way, Ness wasn't bothered. Especially as there was no absolute guarantee that the baby was Robert's.

It was getting on towards evening now, and the nights were drawing in. This evening they were expecting Tommy's Emma to come round and join them for tea. She was a nice girl. Ness was a little jealous of her relationship with Tommy – it was uncomplicated. Ness began to clear away the mess on the table so they could get ready as soon as her mum came in from the shop.

She put the kettle on, then looked in the larder, to see that her mum had made a potato stew with carrots, and there was a tin of corned beef to go with it. Not much to offer everyone, but at least there was a fresh loaf and some marge to go on it. They wouldn't starve. Ness was happy to share the milk ration she'd been given because she was pregnant.

'At least that's one good thing about having the baby,' her mum had said. 'We get a few extra rations.'

'I *told* you,' Eileen had said, 'the government's encouraging women to have more babies for the war effort. You did the right thing after all!' Even Ness's mum had laughed.

Ness was pleased things were a bit lighter with her family, but she was not enjoying living in Ridley. She'd had a taste of life outside the area and she preferred it. Perhaps when the war was over …

The evening was going along just fine when Tommy took Emma's hand in his and made an announcement. 'I've asked Emma to marry me and she's agreed.'

Ness looked at her mum and waited for her to say something, but there was a long silence.

'Aren't you pleased?' Tommy looked at both of them and squeezed Emma's hand.

'That's great, Tommy,' said Ness, 'Isn't that lovely, Mum? A wedding to look forward to.'

'Yes ... I suppose it is ... It just seems a bit quick. You hardly know each other, and so soon after your dad and all.'

'I know,' said Tommy. 'But Emma and I don't really want to wait – there's a war on y'know.'

'Yes,' Ness said, thinking of Robert; they hadn't had a chance to get married. Better for Emma she ties the knot before there's another one in the family way. She wanted to say it out loud but thought better of it. Instead she said, 'Lots of people are getting married at very short notice these days, Mum.'

'Yes, I suppose that's right – well, it'll be nice to have something to look forward to. We'd better drink a toast. Pop down to the pub, Tommy, and get a bottle of sherry or something,' said Mary, tipping some money out of the pot on the mantelpiece.

Later in evening, after they'd had a few glasses of sherry – Ness too, with the rest of them – they felt a lot more relaxed. Ness liked Emma; she was young but quite mature. She'd got two brothers and a sister at home. Four of them altogether. The talk moved around to where Tommy and she were going to live.

'There's no room in our house,' Emma giggled.

'Looks like it'll have to be here, then. Will you be wanting me to move out of my bed for you youngsters?' said Mary.

There was a pause in the conversation, then Tommy said, 'It would be difficult for Emma and me to be in my bed, Mum.' He beamed at her. He knew exactly how to get round her.

'I suppose I could think about it.'

Tommy jumped up and hugged his mum. 'Thanks! It'll work out fine, you'll see. Emma and I'll be no trouble to you at all. She can even help out when the baby comes, Ness.'

'Well, she's not moved in yet so you'd better walk her home. It's getting late and it's a devil of a job to see your way round these streets with a blackout and not that much of a moon.' Ness and her mum saw them off and set about clearing up.

'I don't know what your dad'd say – Tommy getting married and not nineteen until next month, and Emma's even younger. But,' Mary sighed, 'they seem to know what they're doing, and at least they'll be doing it the right way round.'

Ness flinched at the dig but she let it go. Her mum had been less antagonistic since Jack had died.

'We've both suffered a loss, Mum, I've lost my dad and before that I lost the man I'd fallen in love with. It's not easy for any of us.'

'Look, lass, I wouldn't have wanted it this way, but I can't change it. We'll make the best of it.'

Ness hugged her mother and felt a wave of emotion sweep through her body. It wasn't what she wanted, to stay in Ridley, but perhaps it wouldn't be quite as bad as she'd thought.

'I think we should agree to Emma and Tommy living here,' said Mary. 'Not sure about him having my bedroom, though – it'd make more sense for you and the baby to have it.'

'No mum, that'd be unfair. I don't need a double bed, and the baby'll sleep in a cot for a couple of years. Give your room to Tommy and Emma. It's not really the right time to buy furniture and stuff, so we'll have to make do and mend. I can make some new curtains and a bedcover for them.'

'With another one in the house, I think we might have to start using the front room a bit more, don't you?'

'We never bothered when *Dad* was here, and we'll be the same number.'

'I know – but, you know, Emma's not family – not yet – and they might need somewhere to sit in the evenings, or you and I might, or you might. Did they mention a date? I can't remember.'

'Maybe they'll do it on Tommy's birthday.'

'But that's only three weeks away!'

'Time enough,' said Ness.

Thirty-two

Thursday 1st October 1942

'Morning, Sis,' Tommy came into the kitchen. 'Pinch and a punch and all that.'

'You're bright today. Wedding excitement, is it? Have you set the date? Mum and I were wondering last night if you might do it on your birthday.'

'Nice idea. But we'd like to do it on a Saturday, so maybe a bit later, at the end of the month. Thirty-first perhaps?'

'That gives you a bit more time to get organised. Would Emma like me to make her dress for her?'

'That'd be great! I'll let her know. Thanks. We'll have to do the whole thing on the cheap. Just a few mates down the pub afterwards, you know. There won't be a honeymoon – but maybe one night in Leeds – in a *hotel!*'

'Have you ... I mean are you ... waiting for the day then?'

'Ness, honestly – that's for me to know, and for you to never find out.'

They heard a hammering on the door.

'I'll go,' said Tommy. 'I've got to get off to work now, anyway.'

'It's a delivery for you, Ness,' called Tommy from the hallway. 'I'll bring it through – it's too heavy for you to carry.'

Tommy put a heavy wooden crate on the table. 'Here you go, then. I'd like to see what it is, but if I do I'll be late.'

Ness waited until the front door had slammed before she began to open the crate. There was an envelope stuffed securely under the slats, and she had a bit of trouble getting it out. As soon as it was in her hand she recognised the handwriting as Rose's. She could barely contain her excitement – perhaps Rose hadn't forgotten after all ...

25th September 1942

My dear Ness,

I hope now a little time has passed since your father died, that you are feeling better. I wanted to come up and visit you, to deliver this myself, but I wasn't able to get enough time off. I visit Devon as often as I can and that has to be my priority for the moment.

I went to see my mother a week ago, and I believe she's not feeling quite so much animosity towards you as she felt in August. Perhaps if we wait a little while, she will come to accept your relationship with Robert, and even wish to see the baby when it comes.

Ness didn't know what to make of that. She was just getting used to casting off Mrs Granger.

I have sent you this gift for a good reason. You are to start sewing as many things as you can. Perhaps begin with the trousers and the blouse. You can maybe ask around if people have coupons for cloth and you can make up the items for them, the way you did for me. Just charge a small amount for your services. I know I could get some orders from my colleagues at work but the practicality of delivering them would probably make it too difficult and you wouldn't make any money. I realise you will need some money to start off with, and I have put a little something inside the parcel. Robert had some savings and they were passed on to me. As you know, he made a will before he went off to sea but sadly he didn't know you at the time. I'm sure he would have changed it, given the chance, and left you well provided for. I know you are proud so you can call it a loan if you won't accept it as a gift. But I think Robert would like you just to take it. Like I said, he never had a chance to provide for you, but I'm certain he would have done the right thing, so even if you don't get into sewing things, please use the money for the baby. We can call the machine an early birthday present for you. It's next month, isn't it? So only a month early.

It's not a new machine, I'm afraid. The company are not making any right now, as they have to make weapons for the government instead. But it's a good one – it's only had one owner for the last five years, and she hardly used it. I got it through a friend at work.

Take care and write soon.

With fondest love,

Rose.

Ness opened the crate with care. She had to wrench the slats off to get to the box inside. A wooden handle was poking through a crack in the cardboard, and as she pulled the sides of the card apart she found masses of screwed-up newspaper. She pulled up on the handle to lift the wooden case; it was heavy, but not too difficult. She unlatched the catches on each side and lifted off the cover, revealing the sewing machine. She was thrilled. It was a Singer – and it was electric! It was a beautiful black metal machine and she fell in love with it instantly. She scrabbled around the bottom of the box in amongst the papers and found another envelope, which contained a bundle of banknotes – £25! It was incredibly generous.

She went to get some paper and a pen, and sat down to write back to Rose immediately.

1st October 1942

Dear Rose,

I cannot tell you how grateful and excited I am. Your gift is wonderful, and I'm sure it will be a big help to me. I'll be happy to make a few things and maybe a few pence. As for the money, £25 is a fortune, but you're right, it will help with the baby. It's lovely and I agree that Robert would be pleased you are helping me.

I've had an idea, and I'm going to see if we can change the store room around at the back of the shop so maybe I can set the machine up in there. It has a lot of wasted space right now. It's always been bigger than we needed, but since the war started we've been storing less and less stuff in there. The machine has arrived in time for me to make Emma (Tommy's wife-to-be) her wedding dress. I'm making it from her mother's. The wedding will be at the end of this month, and this machine changes everything. I'll let you know how I get on.

Thank you, thank you, so, so much.

I hope Robert is looking down and seeing that you and I are friends.

Much love

Ness

The machine could not have arrived at a better time. At last Ness felt that things were turning around.

Thirty-three

Tommy and Emma's wedding was planned for Saturday 31st October. They were to be married in St Paul's – the church where only a couple of months before the funeral service of Ness's father had taken place. Ness wondered if her mum would be able to cope, but it seemed that the wedding and the idea of becoming a grandmother had just become two of the most important things in her life. They were all she talked about. And Mary and Emma's mother between them were adamant that there was no way it was just going to be a 'few mates down the pub'.

Ness was in the store room. She and Tommy had cleared it out and cleaned it. He was a lot more helpful than Ness had ever expected, but she thought it might be because she was making Emma's wedding dress. The room had a window which was high up, but it did let a decent bit of light in. Its two doorways were a bit annoying, though, as they took up space; one led into the rear of the shop and the other out to the back yard, which was where some of the stock was brought through. The yard door made it cold, and the winter hadn't even got going yet. So Ness kept the door to the shop open, which helped a bit, and she kept warm by wearing plenty of clothes including woolly socks and gloves; Tommy had got her a pair of fingerless mittens which worked quite well. She had used some of Rose's money to buy a paraffin heater, but as paraffin was rationed she was holding off using it for as long as possible. Any hand-sewing she took back into the house, and sat at the kitchen table near the stove. Her stuff took up a bit of room, strewn about the place. She tried to keep it tidy, but now that they were using the front room more often to listen to the wireless or play games, she could often get on undisturbed in the back room.

She had been sewing all day, altering Emma's mother's wedding dress to update it and make it fit Emma. At first, she'd tried just altering it, but as Emma was petite and her mother had obviously been quite a bit bigger, it turned out to be simpler to deconstruct it completely and start again. Emma's parents were an odd couple – they'd broken the mould, thought Ness: her dad was little and mouselike, and her mum was large and dominating, in a pleasant way. Nothing too dramatic, but pleasantly yet firmly taking charge of everything. She adored Tommy, and as far as Ness could see he could do no wrong in her eyes. Ness imagined that must irritate Emma's brothers no end.

The dress was ivory lace over white satin, made in 1920. Ness wondered if Emma's mother might have been pregnant at the time with the first of her five children, as the dress was gathered under the bust and fell away fully to the floor. There was plenty of material to play with. She'd drawn a picture of what the finished gown would look like; it had a boat-shaped neck with scalloped edge and long lace sleeves, and its silk-lined body hung in a straight A-line to the floor with a layer of lace covering the whole. There was plenty of lace left over for a train, which Emma had insisted she wanted; this was attached to a coronet made of lace flowers on her head, and fell down her back onto the floor. With only two weeks to go, Ness had to work fast to finish it all in time.

'I've shed a few tears into this material,' she told her mum.

'I expect you have, but it'll be worth it.' Mary hadn't understood the real reason Ness had been crying. The thing was, she didn't ever want to get married – she'd got used to the idea of being on her own and bringing up her child. She'd cried because everything was pretend. Pretend widow. Pretend father. Pretend no Alf having his way. She longed to open up and speak to Eileen. She'd nearly said something last week, but Eileen was going on about some interesting Americans she'd met at a dance at the Empire.

'I didn't invite you – I didn't think you'd be up for jigging about now you're getting so big. I went with a couple of girls from the factory floor. We had a good laugh. I didn't tell Sid. The Americans gave us a good time. Look here.' Eileen pulled out some chewing gum from her handbag. 'Do you want to try it?'

Ness turned up her nose.

'Sid's getting too involved in stuff he doesn't want to tell me about. He's always off for the night somewhere. That's where he was when I went to the dance. Well, I don't actually know where he was – he didn't tell me – but I reckon he's up to no good.'

Eileen carried on about the Americans and what fun they were, and Ness's chance to tell her about Alf vanished once again.

***

Emma came to try the dress on for the last time before the wedding. As it was a cold day Ness lit the heater before helping her into the dress. They both stood admiring it.

'I'm so excited,' said Emma, 'I've never had a dress made properly for me before, and you've done a wonderful job on it. My mum won't recognise it!'

She stood in front of the full-length mirror Ness had bought for this specific reason; she knew that her clients would want to see themselves in their reconstructed outfits. Admittedly there weren't any actual customers knocking on the door at the moment. Business was a bit slow to get off the ground.

'You wait until everyone sees this dress. Everyone'll want *you* to make their wedding outfit,' said Emma.

'I hope you're right. Things're a bit slow at the moment, though. It's not really the wedding season. Which reminds me – I thought you might be a little cold on the day, so I made this cape from some left-over silk and I've lined it with Winceyette. It'll keep off the worst of the chill.'

'That's lovely, thank you. I hope the church isn't too cold. Although we're only going to have to walk next door to the hall afterwards, this'll be just the thing.'

'How are you getting to the church?'

'George is borrowing a car for me and my dad.'

'Good old George,' said Ness.

'I think he's got himself a girl at last,' said Emma.

Ness suddenly felt cold. She hadn't seen George since the funeral, and she'd felt bad about putting him straight. It had been the right thing to do, though. She hoped that if he'd really found a girl she'd be good to him. She missed him calling round all the time, but she wouldn't have it any other way.

'Well, that's good news indeed. I'm glad George has found some-one. Now, give me a final twirl before you take this off and I'll pack it up for you to take home. We can't risk Tommy getting sight of it now, so close to the day. I've managed to avoid that so far by keeping it here most of the time – but we can't take any more risks.'

Later, in the kitchen, Ness thought again about George. She was surprised that Emma's news had upset her so much. She was being selfish and a miserable spoilsport. She didn't like the idea that Eileen was having fun mixing with the Americans, and that George had moved on while she was not moving on fast enough.

***

The wedding went well and the dress was admired by all. Ness hoped that in the New Year she'd get some more clients. The food for the reception was plain but plentiful. It was amazing what some people could produce with the rationing – they'd brought sandwiches and cakes and all sorts. There had even been a proper tiered wedding cake, although only one tier had been edible and that was not iced – the bottom two tiers had been made from white cardboard – loaned to them by the local baker. He'd got a couple of them always on hand so people could have a photo taken with a cake.

Ness met George's new girlfriend, Sarah. She thought George had made a wise choice, and she wished him luck.

Ness had also spoken to an older woman – in her late fifties, Ness thought – a relative of Emma's family, who had moved from Ridley to London some years earlier but returned to Yorkshire to live in the countryside for the duration of the war.

'I'm very impressed by your handiwork' the woman had said. 'You're wasted here in Ridley; you should get out and go to Leeds, or even London, where people would appreciate your work – but I suppose that's difficult in your situation. Widowed, you say? So many of us are these days, but not as bad as the last war yet – that's when I lost my husband. Could you turn your hand to making or altering anything, do you think?'

'I think so. What are you thinking of?' said Ness.

'I'd like a suit for the spring. Something in tweed that I can wear with a jumper or a blouse. You know the sort of thing – suitable for church, lunches or coffee mornings.'

'Yes, I know exactly,' said Ness, thinking how different this woman was from the other people at the wedding. 'As long as you can get the material with your coupons, then I can make something for you.'

When Ness was chatting with Emma later, she asked who the woman was.

'Pauline Meadows. My mum's cousin — I think. She married above herself, but never had any children, which was a shame as she's been alone for a long time. We didn't think she'd even come to the wedding – thought it would be beneath her – but perhaps she was being nosy.'

'She's going to come here after Christmas,' said Ness, 'to put in a proper order, be measured and everything. I don't know what she'll think of our house and my attempt at a dressmaking business in the store. It's a while away yet, though, so I'm not holding my breath.'

'She could introduce you to lots more customers,' said Emma.

It was a comforting thought, but right now Ness had to get through the next ten weeks. She was managing the finances. Her new book-keeping skills came in handy, and she was able to add up without using her fingers – well, most of the time, anyway. The trouble was that she could see she wasn't making any money. She still did some out-sewing from the factory, and she worked three afternoons a week in the shop, which relieved her mother. She wasn't paid for that, but then she didn't have to contribute to the family budget. She did do the books for the shop, though, and those were a lot healthier than her own.

Thirty-four

Ness's birthday was on 7th November. She didn't welcome turning twenty-two. Her life was not turning out the way she'd planned it. She'd managed her pregnancy well, but she knew that there was still a long way to go, and her bulge never stopped wriggling. She hoped it would be a girl. She thought a girl would be less trouble and grow into a nice woman. Ness was right off men in every way. She still missed Robert – or at least the idea of Robert and a life with him – but because they'd spent so little time together the memory of him was fading. As for the other one, she'd relegated him to the bin of bad experiences to be buried where nobody would find it. Ironic, really. She'd never wanted a man – not yet anyway – but then two had come along and now they were both dead. She was strong. She was tough. She'd survive and she'd succeed. At least that's what she told herself every day, especially when there were only a few pence in the tin.

Tommy and Emma living in the house was turning out to be a blessing. Emma was good at helping in the kitchen. And she worked in the shop on Saturdays, giving Mary the day off. As long as she didn't fall pregnant just yet, there was plenty of room for them all. Emma and Tommy went out nearly every Friday and Saturday night to the pub, the pictures or a dance.

Ness joined them less and less frequently. The days were short and the evenings dark. Business was slow. She had done a bit of work for local women, alterations or reworking an old dress into something else, and the customer was always delighted with the result. It didn't produce the money she needed, but for now she would have to accept that the people from Ridley, at this time, only needed help with alterations and repairs and so many women could do that themselves. She would have to rely on the Pauline Meadows of this world who had a bit of money and either weren't able or couldn't be bothered to sew themselves.

***

Christmas Eve. Presents were few, and everyone did their best with the rationing to prepare what they could. The Proctors had joined a local pig club and got two joints for themselves from what was left after selling half the pig to the government. Ness was sitting in the back room with a box of Christmas decorations from past years. There were a few glass baubles and old paper chains that were definitely past their best. She didn't feel enthusiastic as she sat cutting up strips of newspaper to make more 'bits' to hang around the house. She'd read that if you dipped holly into a solution of Epsom salts, when they dried they'd look frosty. Ness looked at the ones she'd already dipped; they were sitting on top of the stove. She didn't think it had worked. Perhaps her solution was too weak.

As she stood up from her chair to take another look at the holly a wave of nausea swept over her and a rush of warm water gushed down her legs onto the floor. She gasped, and without knowing whether to laugh or cry, she knew this was the beginning of labour ...

**

Ness was amazed at how heavy he felt in her arms. Even though he was three weeks early he was still a good size. The midwife folded a sheet around him, knotted it and hung him on the weighing machine. 'Six pounds thirteen ounces – a good'un!' she announced proudly.

There was no doubt as to the father. He had the same dark hair, and the shape of his face resembled Robert's. Ness shed a tear with relief.

'He'll lose all the fluff on his head,' her mum said, 'babies always look like their fathers when they're born, but believe me he'll be different in a few weeks.'

'Now then, young lady,' said the midwife. 'I'm going to leave you in the capable hands of your mother. I've got another birth to attend to. You should be fine. No getting up and running about, now. Plenty of rest, and you should be back on your feet in no time. I'll look in again at the end of the week.' She turned to Mary. 'Make sure she drinks plenty and gets enough to eat. Her milk'll be in soon. Well, I don't need to tell you that – you've had a couple yourself.'

After she left, Mary brought in some tea and sat on a chair next to the bed. 'I'm proud of you, lass. You did so well – but you were lucky, a short labour for a first baby. Blimey, you practically shot him out after only a few hours. It's only just gone nine now and the first shout you gave me was about four, wasn't it?'

Ness smiled, and the baby wriggled and looked right at her as though noticing her for the first time. His tiny hand was grabbing at nothing, so she took it in hers.

'Have you thought of a name for him? How about Richard? Or Jack, after your dad?' Mary ventured.

Ness supposed a name would just come into her head and although she didn't want it as his first name, she knew Robert should feature somewhere – but she didn't like Richard.

'I'm going to call him Raymond Robert Proctor. I think it rolls off the tongue nicely.'

'Shouldn't you give him Robert's surname?'

'I don't think I'm going to carry on lying about being married. It's stupid. I'll put Robert's name on the birth certificate, but Raymond will have my surname. That's how it should be.'

'Well, that's what it'll be, then. Why Raymond, by the way?'

'I like the name, and he's my little ray of sunshine in this war and the winter,' said Ness.

Her mum laughed, 'Well, Ray's going to need something to sleep in this evening. I'll take the bottom drawer out of the chest in my room and we can make him comfy for the time being. We should have been more prepared for his arrival – but no worries, the neighbours will soon rally round. I'll stick an old pillow in to make it more comfortable, and I've already cut down a sheet or two to make some smaller ones for him. I should have done more knitting. We'll not be able to get much other baby stuff until after Christmas.

'There's some money in the tin in the top of the wardrobe, Mum. Part of it is the money Rose sent and I've been putting a bit aside for him for a while. If we need anything we can use that.'

'Righto. I'm going to organise the crib for Ray, and you should sleep for a while if you can.'

'I can't believe it's almost Christmas Day,' said Ness to her baby. 'You're the best Christmas present I could ever have had.'

But later, she couldn't stop the tears. Ray was asleep in the drawer beside her and everyone else in the house was asleep. She'd wanted a girl but as soon as she saw him it didn't matter that he was a boy. She cried into her pillow, stifling the sobs. She cried for many things. Her body was sore. She cried with relief. Ray resembled Robert, assuaging her fears that he might have been fathered by the other man. She cried for the war and the way they were all living. What kind of world had she brought this baby into? She cried for a dad who would never meet his grandson. Exhausted, she cried herself to sleep.

The night passed quickly. Ness's mum came in twice to make sure all was well. The baby fed a few times and slept well.

'Don't expect it to go on like this – he's just tired from the birth,' said Mary, dashing any illusions Ness might have about a perfect baby. 'He'll soon be bellowing every five bloody minutes to drain you. You'll feel like a cow, that's for sure. Make the most of the next couple of days.'

Tommy came in to meet his nephew. 'He's right bonny, Sis. Well done.' He didn't stay long, and Ness didn't want to keep him. 'I've got to pop down the shops, Mum's given me a list and I need to get to the bakery quick to beat the queue. She says there's always a queue on Christmas morning.'

Ness smiled at him and thought he seemed glad to have an excuse not to hang around.

Emma wandered into the bedroom bleary-eyed and looked at Ray sleeping in the drawer. 'He's gorgeous, Ness,' she whispered. 'I won't disturb him now, but I can't wait for a cuddle.' With that she left the room and Ness was left in peace.

Thirty-five

Saturday 30th January 1943

January had been cold and damp, and for Ness, an exhausted new mother, the prospect of going to London had slipped further away. But she'd managed to make a start on sewing the suit for Mrs Meadows, and she was rather pleased with the result; she was expecting her to arrive for a fitting this afternoon.

Eileen had arrived to help with Ray. 'He's a lovely boy, Ness,' she said, rocking the baby in her arms. 'He's grown so much already, and only a month old. Look how he holds his head up!'

Eileen told Ness she missed seeing her during the day and when walking home after work. It wasn't the same without her. 'The girls are either really old or very young. The old ones talk about nothing but the war and what they're getting up to while their husbands are away, and the young ones talk about the lack of boyfriends.'

'You haven't suggested that any of them should put their address in a shirt pocket, have you?'

Eileen laughed at the idea.

'Ray's the best thing,' said Ness, 'that's come out of this, and I want to do right by him.'

London was an impossible mission now. She'd spoken to Eileen about it only the other day. It was obvious, though, that Eileen didn't approve of the idea, and she'd made a good argument for Ness staying put in Ridley – at least while the war continued: 'What would you do with Ray while you worked? Your mother wouldn't be there with you, and neither would I. Please, Ness, give it a few months. See how it goes.'

Ray began to cry, and Eileen was quick to hand him back to Ness.: 'Give him what he wants, and then I'll take him round to my place so you can see Mrs Meadows on your own. My mum dotes on him, and she'll be waiting a bloody long time for me to produce anything. Over the last few years I've realised that babies just aren't my thing – other people's babies are okay, especially Ray here, but that's where it ends. There'll be no little Eileens running around Ridley any time soon.'

The room was tidy, the suit was ready, the paraffin heater was alight and everything was in its place. With a bit of careful planning, the store room had been improved over the last few months, what with a lick of paint and some of her sketches of dress designs framed and hung on the walls. Ness placed a small bunch of flowers in a vase, then took a quick look around and decided the place was ready. She glanced at the clock on the wall – only five minutes until Mrs Meadows would arrive. She dashed through the shop, where Emma was working, then back into the house to see what her mother was doing, and was pleased to see she'd made up a tray with a pot of tea.

'Where did you get those fancy cups, Mum? They look really good.'

'I picked them up at a jumble sale in the hall the other day. I thought they'd look better than my ropey old things. This jug, though, I've had for ages, tucked away in a cupboard. It's not the sort of thing I often use. We've no sugar, though.'

'Let's hope she doesn't want any.'

Mrs Meadows arrived on time and – much to Ness's relief – didn't take sugar in her tea. Still, Ness was shaking when she handed over the suit for Mrs Meadows to try on. She paced up and down the room, waiting for her to come out from behind the curtain.

'It's lovely. I'm really delighted.' Mrs Meadows turned around to try and see the back. 'I love the way the pleat falls – and the length, just below the knee, is perfect. Thank you.'

'I'm so pleased you like it. If you'd like to change back, I'll pack it up for you.'

It was a shame she only had some brown paper to put it in, but she folded it carefully, placing between the layers some plain white sheets of paper that Eileen had smuggled from the factory, hoping that would help it travel better.

'You know, I have a couple of friends who'd probably like to order from you. In fact, they definitely will after they see this suit. Could we come over next Saturday? Or would a weekday suit you better? They could get the material before they came. And I know one of them would like an evening dress altered. She's had it years but hardly worn it. Do you think you could update it for her?'

'I'm sure I could, and next Saturday would be fine.' Ness felt a bit of panic setting in.

'I'd like a blouse, too; I've actually got the material already, It's a piece of beautiful silk. I've had it stashed in the top of my wardrobe for years. Always wanted to do something with it but just haven't got around to it ... until now.' Pauline Meadows smiled.

'Perhaps something like this?' Ness quickly drew a sketch on a blank page of her book. It was a fitted blouse with a peplum around the bottom. The sleeves were flared below the elbow.

'That looks wonderful! Could you make it by next Saturday if I drop the material off here on Monday?'

Ness said she could. Mrs Meadows thanked her profusely and left the shop with a smile on her face.

When Eileen came back with Ray about an hour later Ness was bursting with ideas.

'Slow down! – you've only got a couple of jobs.'

'But it's a start, isn't it? I think it could go really well. Are you around next Saturday to help again?'

'Yes, I will be. I'll help when I can, as long as it doesn't interfere with going to the pub and the pictures when I want to.' Eileen paused for a second, then said, 'Perhaps now you'll realise you can't go to London. You've got to stay here, where there's help for you. But do you think enough people will be able to buy new clothing while the war is on? I mean the clothing coupons go nowhere.'

'Exactly! What people want and need is a new look to their wardrobe. The ones who don't have coupons or much money might have old clothes that they can't alter themselves. And the ones who've got coupons and money – and who can't sew – can buy material and pay me to make something up. I don't mean the girls from the factories but women like Pauline Meadows and Rose – but she's in London, so that's complicated, but we might even be able to work something out there.

'Rose doesn't know everything – and besides, she's different from us. She and Robert had money before the war.'

Ness suspected that Eileen was jealous of Rose, and that was another reason why Eileen didn't want her to go to London. But Eileen didn't need to be upset about Rose and Ness being friends; even though Ness had kept in touch with Rose, and Rose had encouraged her to forge ahead with the dressmaking business, that was about it.

'Rose knows a thing or two,' said Ness, 'and she has good ideas – she's sensible.'

'I might not be sensible, but I can have good ideas too,' snapped Eileen.

***

On Sunday morning Ness wrapped a blanket around Ray and put him in the pram Tommy had got for him. Thank goodness for neighbours – they'd never stand back and watch anybody who needed help. Tommy thought some of them were too interfering and that they should mind their own business before poking their nose into others' – but this time, he told Ness, he was grateful: 'Can't have my nephew getting cold in his first winter.'

Ness made sure Ray was tucked in well, with his woollen bonnet firmly on his head, before she headed off down to the park, meeting Eileen on the way.

'You look a bit worse for wear this morning, Eileen. Good night, was it?'

'We went to the pub with some of Sid's friends from Leeds. There was a lot of drinking and talking going on. I don't know why they bother to come to Ridley – Leeds is a much better option for them for a night out. I reckon Sid's up to something, but I'm not sure what it is. I trust him, but last night's crowd were a rum lot.'

They walked on through the park. It wasn't a bad day; the sun was popping out every now and then from behind the clouds, and on the whole, it was pretty mild.

'Do you remember when we used to sit here on our lunch breaks? Seems a lifetime ago.'

'Well, it's *Ray's* lifetime ago, isn't it? Ness pulled back the cover to look at her sleeping baby. She hoped so much for a good life for him. Then she sighed.

'What's your problem now?' asked Eileen.

'I was just thinking about how different things might have been if Robert had lived.'

'Well, I hate to state the obvious, but he didn't. Things aren't so bad, Ness. Your sewing thing's doing all right and I've had an idea. I've been bursting to tell you. Let's sit down here and I'll explain.'

Eileen had dreamt up this plan that Ness could make up a selection of clothing from second-hand stuff – suits, skirts, blouses, dresses and anything else she thought would fit the bill – and they could hire the local theatre one Saturday afternoon, and put on a bit of a show. Ness could use some of the money Rose had sent to pay for the venue. Emma and Tommy could help on the day, and Emma could model some of the outfits. Maybe Rose would even come from London and bring a couple of friends. It was just the thing people needed to cheer them up.

'It's all very well supplying a couple of local people here who've got money, but even I have to stick to the government rules for them.

Not too many pockets – if any – no frills and fancy bits. That's hardly fashion, is it? And then there's the coupons ...'

'Well, nobody needs coupons for children's clothing. So you could run up a few of those if you can get the material. But you can make something new from something old. 'Make do and mend', right? That's the government's slogan – and you can do it in style!'

Ness was impressed, even keen, 'I could also show people how I can alter things and make them into something they can wear again. Old wedding dresses, men's suits cut up for women, old shirts for blouses ...'

'That's brilliant!'

'We should put an advertisement in the shop windows for second-hand wedding dresses. I could use Rose's money to pay for them. Then when I sell them on there's no need for ration books.'

'I need to think about it, Eileen. It's a good idea, but I'm not sure I'm up to it all yet.'

'It's not going to happen next week, is it? You'll have plenty of time to organise it. It's so exciting!'

'Let's think about the costs and dates then. Maybe we should go and see the manager at the theatre, to find out when it's available,' said Ness, her voice rising in enthusiasm.

'I knew you'd think it was a good idea.'

***

Mrs Meadows came back the following weekend with her friends and, as hoped, they brought material with them and put in a couple more orders, so Ness was kept busy through February.

Eileen came around every Saturday and some Sundays. Ness would do some drawings during the week, and although Eileen was hopeless at any kind of design she had a good eye for what looked good and what didn't, so they would sit down and go through everything, picking out the best. Emma said she'd be happy to be one of the models, and couldn't wait to take part in the show. A few orders trickled in by word of mouth, enough to keep Ness working and bring in a few shillings a week for the pot. She was covering her costs. Rose had been really enthusiastic about the show, and said she'd come up to Ridley for the event, and bring a friend with her.

Eileen and Ness wrote out little adverts asking people if they could give or sell their used wedding dresses, evening clothes or any other substantial item of clothing. They also mentioned that Ness could, for a small sum, alter clothing using 'Make do and mend' to encourage people. They asked for the articles to be brought to Proctor's corner shop where a price would be agreed. They posted leaflets through letterboxes in the better part of town and put notices in shop windows.

But to begin with nothing much happened; they got a couple of motheaten fur coats, which she could use to make hats – there was no rationing on hats – one wedding dress and two 1920s suits. Ness felt her confidence waning.

Thirty-six

Saturday 20th March 1943

Ness was in her workroom at the back of the shop. They'd stopped calling it the store room; 'workroom' sounded more professional. A few more orders had trickled in, but for the forthcoming show they hadn't nearly enough clothing which was either made or altered. Now there was only seven weeks to go before 1st May, the date they'd settled on with the manager of the theatre. He'd been surprisingly keen for them to put on a show. He suggested they perhaps did it to raise money for the war effort or for some other cause.

Back at home, Eileen wasn't happy with that idea. 'You need to make your own money,' she'd moaned. But Ness thought there was no reason they shouldn't make a collection for the Red Cross or something more local perhaps. They would think about it.

In the middle of their conversation Emma called out from the shop. 'Ness, there's a couple of young girls here who want to see you.'

'Come on through,' called Ness.

The two came into the workroom, one of them carrying a bag which she held up as they spoke to Ness. 'We're not sure if this is the sort of thing you do, but the notice in our local shop window said you can make something new out of an old dress. We decided to come over and see you, and we've brought this one in. It's a ball gown from the nineteen-twenties. Our mother had it hanging in one of her wardrobes, and we thought you might be able to make it more modern.'

'Let's have a look,' said Ness. 'I'm sure I can do something. I assume your mother knows you've taken it?'

'Of course! – we wouldn't take it without permission.'

The girls were well spoken and seemed nice enough, so she had no reason to doubt them. She pulled out the dress out. It was blue, with a satin underskirt covered with blue lace and costume jewellery. It had an expensive feel to it.

'How do you want the dress to end up? Is it for parties, dinner out or something else?' asked Ness.

'I think it'd be lovely to make it short, and perhaps change the sleeves so it doesn't have any. I've drawn a picture – look,' said the older girl, and motioned to her sister to give her a sketch from the bag.

'This is very good,' said Ness, 'but really I'd need to see your mother to know if it'd suit her.'

The girls looked at each other and the younger one burst into tears.

'It's all right Alison, don't worry.' The older girl put her arm around her sister.

'What is it?'

'We're sorry, we should have told you. It's just that ... well, it is our mother's dress, but she doesn't know we're here. We wanted to make it a surprise because she's been so unhappy since ... what happened to our father ...'

'What's your name?' asked Ness.

'I'm Jennifer.'

At that moment Eileen came wandering in. She came round most Saturdays at some point. She looked at the two girls. 'What have we got here, then?'

'This is Jennifer and her sister ... ?'

'Alison,' said the younger girl.

'They've brought a dress for me. Isn't that nice, Eileen?'

Eileen raised her eyebrows. 'You're not running a Help the Children shop here.'

Ness, putting her arm around Alison and guiding her to a chair, said to Jennifer, 'Now, tell us all about it.'

But she hesitated, an anxious look in her eyes.

'Take no notice of Eileen – she doesn't mean it,' said Ness.

Then Jennifer spoke with a more assured air: 'Our father, he was the owner of Tanner's Shirtings Factory over the other side of town. He and the other boss, his partner, had to go and work in the steel factory. They had to do the work of one worker between them, so they took it in turns to go there. They had no choice; they were ordered to do it, as well as still running their own business. Our father hated it – he wasn't cut out to be a factory worker.'

'You say "hated" it – so does he not have to do it now?'

The girls looked at each other again.

'No, there was an accident, you see, an explosion. Several people were burnt and five were killed. One of them was our father.'

'But that's terrible. Your poor mother – no wonder she's miserable – and you poor girls.' Ness was quiet for a moment, and Eileen put in her word. 'You know a pretty dress can't fix things.'

Ness glared at Eileen. She thought she was being unnecessarily hard.

'We're not stupid,' said Jennifer. 'We thought it might be a start. She's got nothing to do, no hobbies, and now that Uncle Bobby's taken over the business my mother doesn't even have to attend any social events, because he takes Auntie Jane to them.'

'Mother hardly does anything,' said Alison. 'She doesn't have any interest in seeing her friends, and although they were good at first, they seemed to have dropped off.'

'What about war work?' Eileen asked. 'She must be doing *something*.'

'She goes into the Community Feed Hall most days, but she doesn't like it. She hasn't made any new friends by going there, anyway.'

Ness looked at the girls and wondered how on earth she could help them. 'Perhaps you should bring your mother here in person?'

'I'm not sure she'd come,' said Alison.

They all sat silent for a few moments, wondering what to do about the situation.

'I've got an idea,' said Jennifer. 'Why don't you come over to our house for a visit?'

'But why would I do that?' Ness was puzzled.

'Well, you could say that we'd popped over to see you after we saw the leaflet and we started talking and I told you how much I liked fashion and sewing and stuff, and I invited you to come and meet my mother because I want to work in dressmaking.'

'Oh, you do, do you?' Eileen sounded sarcastic.

'Yes. I think I'd like to design clothes when I leave school and when the war's over.'

'There's no telling how long it'll be before *that* happens!'

'You're not helping, Eileen.'

The sisters were holding each other's hands and looking at Ness expectantly. 'Please say you'll come,' said Jennifer.

'You could come tomorrow – it's Sunday,' said Alison.

Ness hesitated, 'I'd have to bring my little boy with me. My mum has him a lot of the time but not on a Sunday.

'You could bring him with you.'

'Of course, Alison,' said Jennifer. 'That's a splendid idea.' She turned to Ness: 'Come for tea at three tomorrow, and you can meet our mother and talk about the dress and me helping with design and stuff.'

'Don't let's get too far ahead of ourselves. I'll come to tea, and then let's see what happens. All right?'

The girls thanked Ness and smiled at Eileen, who seemed to mellow a little, and they left the shop looking a little happier than when they'd entered.

'What's wrong with you, Eileen? Those poor girls and their mother – you were a bit harsh.'

'I just don't think you're a charity, and it all sounded to me like you were wanting to help the family out. But it's *you* who needs help.'

'Maybe you're right, but I've said I'll go, and I won't change that.'

Thirty-seven

Sunday 21st March 1943

E ileen thought Ness was mad and the whole episode was going to be a real mess. Mary thought Ness was being stupid by involving herself with two girls and a woman who was clearly not well.

But Ness thought differently. She felt an affinity with this woman, even though she'd not met her, probably because she, like Ness, had lost her husband and found herself in a difficult position. Ness had taken to Jennifer and Alison, too; they seemed lovely girls, and they'd obviously had their mother's welfare at the centre of their visit to the shop.

Once again, the early spring sun was shining and Ness left herself plenty of time for the long walk to the far side of the town, the south-west. She hardly ever ventured out that way – it was where the posh lot lived. Sid and Eileen had dropped some cards there.

If it weren't for the sandbags, soldiers, fire engines and Red Cross vans, it would have been easy to imagine it was a normal Sunday in August. Ness walked past the Ridley Baths, which had been turned into a hospital for servicemen, and a few of them were sitting outside smoking. She smiled as they called out to her, but she quickened her pace. She thought some of them were Americans – they were always more forward than the British boys. She'd propped up Ray on the pillow in his pram and he seemed interested in everyone and everything. She thought she should count her blessings, and Ray was the biggest of them.

She took out a piece of paper to check the address the girls had given her: Hill View, Churchfield Way. Now she had entered the posh part of town. The trees were green and the air smelt good. Most of the owners of the factories and mills lived up this way. The houses were large, detached Victorian mansions with grand entrances, surrounded by high hedges and mature trees. Even though they were closer to the Sheffield side of Ridley, they hadn't seen much bombing during the first part of the war. Ness had walked a good two miles from home. As she walked along looking for Hill View, she wondered idly which hill it would be that the family could see.

She approached the front door with some trepidation. Perhaps Eileen and her mum were right. A young woman answered the door – a maid, Ness thought. Not many people could afford to keep maids these days.

Ness introduced herself and the maid let her in, telling her that Mrs Arbuthnot and the girls were expecting her. Would she like help with the pram? Ness said she'd leave it outside if that was okay. It was a cumbersome thing. Ness took Ray in her arms and ventured into the house, following the maid as though she were a tour guide. The house seemed enormous to Ness as she looked around the large hallway, with a beautiful sweep of carpeted staircase on the right-hand side. They walked on along the tiled floor to a door at the end, which the maid opened, then quietly announced Ness's arrival. The room was light and airy with French windows out to the garden. Ness noticed there was a lot of furniture – two sofas, armchairs, side tables, lamps and a fireplace – but it didn't seem to be overcrowded. She felt as though she might be in a hotel lounge. The girls came running up to her and took Ray, laughing as they did so. He didn't seem to mind as they took him across the room to a rug and some toys that must have been put on the floor for him.

A woman in her late thirties or early forties, Ness thought, stood up from one of the armchairs and walked towards her. Although smart in her appearance there was something lacking – make-up, maybe – and her hair was tidy but uninspiring for a woman of her class. It didn't look as though she'd bothered too much with it.

'Hello, Ness. Jennifer and Alison have told me all about you and your little shop. A new venture, I understand. It's very good of you to come all this way and visit us.'

'Thank you, Mrs Arbuthnot, I hope you don't mind me coming. The girls asked me yesterday, and it seemed very short notice.'

'Please call me Elizabeth. We weren't doing anything today, so there's no problem. Jennifer told me she has an interest in making clothes. It's the first I've heard of it, but then young girls these days don't discuss anything with their parents ... mothers.'

'The girls have told me what happened to their father. It must be a terrible loss for all of you. I've suffered something similar – Ray's father was killed at sea, before he was born. I don't even know if Robert knew about his child.'

'Such a shame. The war's a terrible thing. It's good to keep busy, and you're obviously doing that. But I find it very difficult to settle to anything. I think the girls have despaired of me. They know other children who have lost their fathers, and the mothers seem to be doing fine. Some of them have even started seeing other men – but I could never do that. Anyhow, my two are determined I should get all my dresses altered and start going out and about town as though nothing has happened. But that's not going to happen. I'd be happy to burn the contents of my wardrobe.'

Ness could see she wasn't joking.

'Do you think we could take Ray around the block in his pram?' asked Jennifer. 'It's such a lovely afternoon. We'd be very careful with him.'

Ness said that would be fine.

'You girls go on out, then,' said Elizabeth. 'Don't be too long; we'll be having tea in half an hour.' To Ness she said, 'They'll take good care of Ray.'

After the girls had left with Ray, Ness and Elizabeth sat in silence for a while. Ness noticed photographs of a handsome couple, obviously Elizabeth and her husband. She looked glamorous, her hair and make-up immaculate. And there was a brightness to her eyes that was definitely missing now.

The silence between them wasn't exactly awkward, more a mutual agreement to just sit quietly and think about their situations, so similar to each other's in one important way. But Ness considered Elizabeth to be in a far better position than herself financially, and she didn't seem to have many friends or family around for support. She wondered if it'd be a good idea to draw her out about this, but before she could do that Elizabeth spoke.

'I may be financially stable, but I don't have any real friends. My parents are both dead and I was an only child. The girls mean the world to me, but somehow without Cyril the world's empty for me. '

'I do understand how you feel – but really, I do feel he'd want you to get on and live life as much as you can, surely? I know Robert would definitely not want me to sit about moping all the time.'

'You're probably right – but I don't have any interests. I used to enjoy buying clothes and things for the house, but now there doesn't seem any point.'

Ness then told her about Rose and the sewing machine and Eileen, and the hoped-for fashion show in Ridley.

Elizabeth showed a great deal of interest, and when Ness stopped to draw breath Elizabeth said: 'It's lovely to hear your story.' She laughed, then jumped up with a determined clap of her hands. 'Do you know? I have an idea, and I want you to come upstairs, have a look at something and tell me what you think.' She led the way out of the sitting room, up to the first floor where a long landing had several doors leading from it. Ness followed Elizabeth through one of them.

The bedroom was huge, as big as the ones at Field House. She thought she could have fitted Tommy and Emma's bedroom into it three times or more. There was a beautiful bay window looking out over the garden.

There were twin beds with fancy covers. Ness didn't like to ask if there had been a double bed there before Cyril's death. Considering the depth of Elizabeth's feelings for him, it seemed odd if they'd have slept in separate beds. But maybe that was how the other half did it.

Elizabeth had disappeared through an open door, which turned out to be a walk-in wardrobe. She turned back, flung the door wide, and asked, 'Do you think you could do anything with some of these clothes?

Ness was astonished at the amount and the quality of them. Evening dresses, suits, day dresses for winter or summer. Everything neatly hung up in order of style and colour.

'You have some beautiful items here, and some of them hardly worn. I'd love to get my hands on them.' Ness laughed at Elizabeth's expression. 'I'm sorry, that didn't sound good, did it? But I'd be honoured to take some of this clothing. How much do you want for it?'

'Oh, it's not for sale. I don't need the money, but I'm thinking a good clear-out would do me good. You can have lots of it with the greatest of pleasure. Many of the things are rather old-fashioned now, but they were all quite expensive in their day. The girls and I talked about it before you came. I think that's what they had in mind when they invited you to come and visit.'

Ness didn't mention the dress that the girls had brought into the shop. She supposed the story would come out sometime.

'It's very generous of you. I'm sure I can alter the dresses and bring them up to date. In return for your kindness, I'll make some special dresses for you, and I'm sure you'll love them.'

They discussed the logistics of the clothes being moved to Ness's workshop; it was decided that Elizabeth would choose the garments, then would get them all sent over to the shop.

Shortly afterwards, when they had returned downstairs, the maid came in to ask about tea. Elizabeth said they would take it outside, as it was unusually warm for the time of year. The rest of the afternoon was spent in the garden; the girls, having come back from their walk, played with Ray as he lay on a blanket on the grass. Ness hoped they'd be invited back soon; it was lovely for her and Ray to be out of their own little house where there was hardly any outside space for him.

At the end of the afternoon, Jennifer and Alison said they were sorry to see Ness leave, but delighted that she and their mother had come to an agreement about the clothes. They would be delivered by taxi, probably in the middle of the coming week, and Jennifer was to come to the shop next Saturday morning to help sort them all out. And the girls made their mother promise that Ness and Ray should could come again to visit.

***

When the clothing was delivered and Eileen saw its extent, she felt she had to apologise to Ness. They now had a large selection of materials, with haberdashery – buttons and trimmings and other adornments for dresses. There were chiffons, silks and satins as well as tweeds and linens, and loads of lining material. It was a massive hoard of treasure as far as Ness was concerned, and Eileen was happy to agree. It had all come just in time to save the show.

'There's enough stuff here for us to make a whole season of dresses, tops and skirts – and it hasn't cost us a penny!' said Eileen, impressed.

'Elizabeth said she'd recommend us to some of her friends, and suggest they should come to the theatre on the 1st May to see what we can do.'

'She wants nothing for all of this?'

'No, not exactly ...'

'What d'you mean?'

'I said Jennifer could come around occasionally and help with the design side of things.'

Eileen raised both hands, palms up, and shrugged: 'Seems fair enough'

Thirty-eight

April 1943

Time was moving fast and there was plenty to do in preparation for the show in May. Although Emma had said she'd be more than happy to oblige as a model, Ness had been concerned in case she might fall pregnant, so she'd made a back-up plan – to adapt old clothing for pregnant women – but it hadn't happened.

'Tommy and I aren't desperate for kids,' said Emma. 'Of course, it could happen, but we try to be careful.'

'It was all too easy for me,' said Ness, 'I wish *I'd* been careful.'

'Aw, you don't mean that – Ray's a gorgeous little chap, and so good.'

'He ought to be – he's got my mum running around in circles after him! Wait until he's a toddler. You and Tommy aren't much better, always spoiling him. He's a lucky little boy.'

Ness and Eileen had worked out that they'd need five models and twenty outfits. It was going to be a hard few weeks.

Ness was worried about the whole thing. Would they be able to get enough people to come? Could she think of enough ideas for outfits?

What if it all went terribly wrong? What if the Germans decided to have another go at Leeds on 1st May and a stray bomb hit Ridley?

'Now you're being silly,' said Eileen. 'Come on, first things first. Get down to drawing some clothes, and I'll tell you what I think of them.'

Ness sat down at the kitchen table with a pad of paper and a pencil.

'You're as good as Norman Hartnell, you are,' said Eileen as she glanced over Ness's shoulder. The famous designer had been asked by the government to come up with some good ideas for utility clothing for women, and Ness guessed it was to try and keep up the morale of the general public.

She'd seen some of his work and thought she could do just as well within the restrictions. 'But perhaps I'm getting above myself, if I'm going to start comparing myself to the likes of him,' she said. So she tried to think of something different. She rather liked Eileen's idea of something reversible, which would make two items out of one – but how to do that and make it look good? Siren suits, like the one Winston Churchill wore, had become popular. She wondered if she could fashion something out of parachute silk on one side and a pattern on the other. Food for thought.

'What are you planning now?' said Eileen as she saw the sketch Ness was drawing.

'I'm not sure, but I think it might be something quite special. If it works I'll have to give you some credit.'

As she doodled on the page another idea came – to sew some patterned headscarves together, making a blouse with a halter neck for the summer. Amongst the stuff that Elizabeth had sent there were loads of scarves. Ness wasn't at all sure if it would work, but Eileen was very enthusiastic: 'That'd make a great top for a cocktail dress, I saw one in a magazine a bit like it, but nowhere near as unusual as that one.'

'I'm not sure. I think it might be all right in London, but I don't think anyone around here would like it. I mean, Ridley's not really a cocktail *area*, is it?'

'I think you should work on it as your sort of centrepiece. At the end of the show we could make up a little group of the five girls, a picture, you know, like a ... what do they call it?'

'You mean a tableau? Like the church does at Christmas with the nativity? Mary, Joseph and the baby, the shepherds, the wise men and the animals?'

'Yes, that sort of thing, but a scene of ...' Eileen thought for a moment. 'A scene of people at a party or something.'

'Well, it's an idea, I suppose.'

'What about a wedding party? It could be the bride in her go-ing-away outfit!'

'A halter-neck cocktail dress in wartime?'

The two women began to laugh at the idea, but Ness had to admit it was a good one.

When they told Mary what they'd thought of she was surprisingly encouraging: 'Well, I never thought you two had it in you! How do you think of these things? You could use some props, too. Cups and saucers, wine glasses and maybe a wedding cake made of cardboard, the same as Emma and Tommy had for part of their cake. I'll see what I can dig out.'

Over the next few weeks it all began to come together. Eileen turned out to be far more of a help than Ness would ever have thought pos-sible. She proved to be really clever at ideas for promoting the event.

She prepared twenty posters by hand, and they stuck a few of them on the notice board in the factory, church halls and shop windows.

Then Eileen asked George to come over and bring Sarah with him. It was lovely that they could all be friends. Ness asked Sarah if she'd like to be involved in the show, and she jumped at the idea. 'Could I bring my mum's wedding dress over? Would you be able to alter it for me?'

They all laughed a lot about that, and teased George mercilessly.

'When's the day, then, George?'

'Sarah'd be a lucky girl to have you as a husband.'

And when Sid and Tommy joined in ....

'Hey – we've not been together that long.' George leapt to his feet.

'Come on, man! – there's no time like the present.'

George was going red and getting hot and bothered, so Sarah put her arms around him. 'Don't worry – I thought it'd be a nice idea to alter my mum's wedding dress so that I'd get a starring role in the show,' she said with a smile.

'It's a lovely idea,' said Ness. 'Bring it over as soon as you can.' She looked around the room, taking stock of the garments and the materials. Her sketch pad was full of completed patterns, now approved by Eileen and Mary. She had been able to use all the clothes that Elizabeth had given her. Many she'd completely unpicked, and then used the ironed material to make a new design altogether.

They had a meeting, and Ness delegated the various jobs. George would be in charge of getting Tommy, Sarah and Ness and all the outfits over to the theatre on the day. Sid would transport five of the models. There were now to be six in all, as Eileen, Emma and Sarah would be joined by Lorraine, Carol and Gayle from the factory.

'We'll need a man to be the groom in the final tableau,' said Eileen.

'George can do that,' Ness said with a smile. 'He and Sarah will make the perfect pair. George, have you got a really smart suit, or can you get one from somewhere?'

'Of course I can.'

This was greeted with a murmur of approval while George went even redder and Sarah looked pleased with herself.

Ness needed to get down to work. Now she only had about three weeks left to complete everything. It was going to be a push, but with the help of her friends she thought it could all be ready.

The days passed in a whirl of material, cotton, paper patterns and chaos. Ness had no time for outside activities, and wrote a very scrambled note to Rose, letting her know how things were going. They didn't know how many people to expect because they hadn't thought about selling tickets – the plan was for people to just drop in and view. Rose suggested they should charge for entry, but although Ness and Eileen thought this was a good idea they didn't really think they had the nerve to ask for money except for charity.

'What we really need are loads of orders for clothes.' She paused for a moment. 'Do you think we could sell the clothes after the event?'

'Good plan, Ness!'

So that was the decision. No entry fee, but the opportunity for people to buy items at the end.

'I doubt Sarah'll part with the wedding dress – have you seen it, Eileen? I'm really chuffed with the way it's worked out. I'm sure George won't hesitate to pop the question when he sees it.'

'But it would be unlucky for her to wear something he's seen, wouldn't it?'

'Hmm ... I could add something to make it a little different, I'm sure.'

Ness was up early every morning and worked late into the night. Her mum worried that she was doing too much, but had to agree with Eileen that Ness looked healthier and seemed happier than she'd been for a long time.

'Do you think she'll find somebody else?' asked Mary. 'Pity she didn't accept George – he's such a lovely chap.'

'I don't think she and George would ever have got together, not properly, said Eileen. 'But I was wondering about getting her along to one of the dances with the Americans.'

'Well don't you go meddling. You did enough in the first place.'

'Come on, Mrs Proctor, you wouldn't have Ray if I hadn't. He's been wonderful for you and the family. Especially since your Jack's gone. He would've loved him too, of course.'

'Yes, I'm sure he would. Once he'd got over the shock of his daughter's behaviour. Like I had to.'

Eileen was in charge of ironing and hanging up the clothing as well as sewing buttons on. She didn't mind doing it, even though she did a lot of it at work. There was a general shortage of buttons due to the war but somehow a few would end up in her pockets after the last shift each week. She felt a bit bad about it, but not for long.

'I seriously hope this business of yours takes off, Ness, and I can leave the bloody shirt factory behind.'

'I hope so, too. I think we make good partners. Fingers crossed that after 1st May I'm inundated with orders and we can set everything up properly. Proctor & White.'

'White & Proctor runs off the tongue better, I think,' said Eileen.

Thirty-nine

Saturday 1st May 1943

'Where's George? And where are the girls from the factory, and where's Sid? They should all be here by now.' Ness was getting into a panic. She'd given Ray his bottle and made sure everything was ready for her mum to look after him for the day.

'You're just getting yourself in a state over nothing. George'll be here in a minute with the van, and so will Sid. Everything's ready – you need to calm down.'

Ness took a deep breath and looked at herself in the mirror. She was wearing slacks and a blouse, and for the event she would put on a jacket and skirt she'd made from one of her dad's old suits. She'd managed to turn the trousers into a skirt, and she was really pleased with the result.

Tommy and Emma came into the back room to join the others.

'Where is everyone?' asked Emma.

'Surely,' said Tommy, 'they should all be here now and we should be leaving for the theatre.'

'What's happening?' Mary came in carrying Ray, who bawled for attention as soon as he saw Ness. Eileen was telling Tommy to collect the outfits from the front room, Emma wanted to know who had the make-up. Everyone was talking at once.

Then Sidney walked in the door, and he could barely make his voice heard over the mayhem: 'Hey everyone. Listen to me! Nobody's going anywhere today.'

There was total silence.

Then Ness spoke. 'What on earth do you mean?'

'I mean nobody's going anywhere. You can't even get out of the end of the road. I had to leave my car on the other side of town and walk here the long way round. There are police, ARP wardens, Home Guard and anyone else they can drag in. They're telling everyone to go home and stay inside. We were lucky to get through, but I saw George on duty and he let me – they'll be calling for you soon, Tommy.'

Tommy rushed upstairs to change into his Home Guard uniform.

'There was no air raid warning,' said Ness. 'Nothing! What on earth's happened?'

'Go on, Sid,' said Eileen. 'We're all desperate to hear what you know.'

'Word has it an aircraft came down beside the brickworks. It's taken part of the railway line out. The Railway Hotel's been evacuated, and the town centre's closed off. I think the plane came down in the early hours of this morning.'

They were interrupted by a knock on the door.

'That'll be for me. See you all when I get back,' said Tommy as he rushed down the stairs and out of the door without stopping.

Ness was getting very frustrated with all the coming and going. 'But what about the theatre?' she asked.

'All shops and public buildings are shut for the day. Sorry Ness. I think it's going to take all day to clear the wreckage, and they don't want anybody out and about. Only in an emergency.'

'But this is an emergency!' Ness stormed out of the door and ran down to the end of the road where several of the neighbours were wandering about.

'I'm sorry, Miss, but you can't pass here. The whole town's cordoned off. Go home.'

Ness didn't know whether to laugh or cry. She looked at the warden in disbelief. 'What am I going to do? I have to get to the theatre.'

'Well, the place won't be back to normal until tomorrow, probably. They're waiting for the experts to come in. I can't tell you more than that.'

'But I have to get through to the theatre – it's really important!' She could feel her voice rising and panic taking over. Eileen and the others, now standing behind her, began to beg the warden, but he was having none of it.

'If you lot don't calm down I'll have to call the police and get you forcibly removed.'

'But people will be arriving at the station and wanting to get to our show!' Eileen was furious.

'Look, lady, the station's closed and there are no trains in or out. Now *if* you don't mind, I think you should clear off and let those who need to work get on with their jobs. There's a war on, you know!'

'Bloody hell, If I had ten bob for every time someone said that I'd be a rich woman,' said Eileen. 'Let's go back to the house. We can have a rethink,' and she took Ness by the shoulders and turned her around to go home.

'I knew something was going to happen to ruin today – I just *knew* it,' said Ness.

'Come on now, Ness,' said Sid. 'It's not the end of everything, just a setback.'

'A *massive* setback – and why did it have to happen *today*? And what about the girls from the factory? They'll wonder what's going on.'

'Don't worry about them,' said Sid. 'They'll have found out what's happened. They'll likely be disappointed, but they've got a morning off anyway.'

Back at the house, with them all sitting around the kitchen table, Ness began to laugh.

'Are you getting hysterical now, then?' asked Eileen, but began to laugh with her. It was all so ridiculous.

'What am I going to do with all the stuff we've made? What am I going to say to Rose? I feel such a fool. Whose idea was this, anyway? And what about the money we've lost?'

'Maybe the theatre will give you a refund, as it's something beyond anyone's control,' said Mary.

They all began to speak at once: 'It was a good idea ... You can do it another time ... Don't worry, something'll turn up ... It's not the end of the world ... Have you thought of taking the stuff to the market?'

'Wait a minute – *that's* not a bad idea!' said Eileen.

'The market's a great place to sell stuff,' said Emma. 'Not sure how you go about it, though.'

'Well, it's certainly something to think about,' said Ness. 'We wouldn't put on a fashion show, but I've got the racks to hang it all up, and I'll want a table of some kind. Will I need a licence?'

'Sid'll help you out there,' said Eileen. 'Won't you?' And Sid nodded in agreement.

'Do you think it could be organised by next market day?' asked Ness. 'That's a week today, isn't it? I mean, it's not as though there's a lot to get ready. All the clothes are ready. Anyone up for giving a hand?'

There was a general agreement; if Ness could sort it in time they'd be there. George would help with the transport and setting up, providing Ness got her licence from the council. Mary would look after Ray again, and this time for the whole day, she hoped.

The mood became a little more buoyant, but Ness still felt the day was a disaster.

***

Ness and Eileen took the wicker basket full of clothes back to the storeroom. They had thought it would be empty and waiting to be filled with loads more orders by the end of the day, but of course that wasn't the case now. And by now everyone would know the show had been cancelled. It was a big setback.

'Honestly Ness, don't worry. The market's a great idea. It's a shame that the theatre only had today free for the show, but maybe it'll turn out for the best.'

'I don't know how you can say that, but thanks,' said Ness.

Early that evening, Sid came back to collect Eileen, and he was able to give them more news of what had happened. 'People are saying that it was one of our planes that came down, but the government are trying to hush it all up so there aren't that many details. Not good for the morale of the country to hear about any losses of our own on the home turf.'

'How awful. Were there any survivors?' asked Ness.

'The pilot tried to miss the town but didn't quite get far enough. It happened in the early hours of the morning. Strange we didn't all hear it. It must have slid along the waste ground near the brickworks. I don't know any more details. I think the pilot was killed.'

'But what about the rest of the crew? Did they all die?' asked Ness.

I don't know. Tommy'll be able to tell you more. Like I said, it's all very hush-hush.'

'Those poor boys. The Air Force boys are always so young. I suppose it makes my disappointment for the day seem a bit insignificant. Think of those mums who've lost their sons.'

'Yes, you're right, said Eileen. 'We'll all help you, and in a few weeks you'll see this was just a little hiccup.'

Ness smiled, but she wasn't convinced.

Forty

Wednesday 5th May 1943

N ess was surprised to see George come into the back room; Ray was sitting propped up in his pram and she was sitting at the table.

'By yourself are you?' she said.

'Yes, I just came on my own to see you,' smiled George. 'But don't worry – I'm not expecting to light any old flame. Me and Sarah are very happy, thank you.'

'That's great. Now sit down and I'll get you a cup of tea.'

'No thanks, Ness. I'm fine without. Sid asked me to call on you, about the market, you know?'

'I thought he might have forgotten – it was all such a mess last Saturday.'

George told her that Sid had been to see the chap in charge of the market, who'd said there was a single pitch up for grabs. It was quite cheap, only five bob for the morning, but it wouldn't be for long – just the rest of the summer. The chap who was usually on that stall had been taken into hospital, and none of his family were prepared to take it on while he was ill.

'What do you reckon, Ness? Worth giving it a go?'

'I don't know, George. I mean, how will people try things on? They won't buy if they can't try.'

George laughed, 'That sounds like a catchy phrase.'

'Perhaps I could rig up some curtains, in a square shape. It wouldn't need a roof, just enough room for one person and a mirror ... and a chair. Would that be possible, d'you think?'

'Either that – or what about the inside of a van?' suggested George. 'You'll need a van anyhow to get the clothes there, and then you could put a mirror inside and people could change in there.'

'That's sounds a bit difficult. I mean, how would they climb up into the back? And it might be dark in there. At least if it's the curtains it'll be light. And where am I going to get a van from, anyway? And I'll have to take Ray with me. Oh, it's all going to be ridiculous waste of time. Whatever made me think selling on the market was a good idea?'

'I wonder what that chap sold on his pitch? Sid never told me. Maybe he's got some transport he could lend us for an extra five bob a week. Do you want me to find out?'

'I don't know, George, I honestly don't. I'm beginning to wonder why I even started this venture.'

'Come on – that's not like you. At least let me find out. Give me the rest of today to see what I can organise. You need to be up and running by this Saturday.'

'What about you? Shouldn't you be working today?'

'Believe it or not, I've got three days off. Been ill since yesterday, and I think I'm still going to be ill tomorrow and the next day,' he smiled.

Ness didn't think George could afford to take time off. He wasn't like Sid, who always seemed to have an extra few quid in his pocket and didn't appear to ever actually work at all. But still … 'Thanks, George.'

'It's okay. Anyway, I've been running a few errands for Sid, so he owes me.'

'Please don't get into any trouble, especially not on my account.'

***

Ness was up by five the following Saturday morning. George was a miracle worker; everything had been sorted – van, pitch and curtain. The rails they'd had for the fashion show stood nicely in front, displaying the ready-made clothes, and they had a trestle table borrowed from the church hall. Eileen was there to help, and George was there with Sarah.

'We won't be able to come every Saturday,' said George.

'But George can drive you here first thing, and then get off to work and come back at the end of his morning shift,' said Sarah.

'Blimey, you've got some good friends,' said Eileen, 'me included!' She was holding Ray on her hip, 'I hope your mum can take him next week, though. He's getting too big for me to carry around. What are you feeding him on?'

The mood was good. All they needed now was for the clothes to be sold. A few people came and looked and asked where the usual man was. It turned out that he'd sold bric-à-brac and small items of furniture; wooden chairs and side tables and other bits of no use to anyone, so it became clear to Ness that his customers weren't going to be particularly interested in what she was selling.

'There's a war on, didn't you know?' asked one older woman, and she fingered the clothes and inspected them like some overseer looking for faults. 'Quite nicely stitched, though, but not really my style.'

Ness would like to have retorted that she didn't appear to have any style at all, but she smiled politely instead, and suggested perhaps she might be more interested in some of the scarves and hats on the table.

Eileen had taken Ray off for a walkabout, and George and Sarah had sneaked off somewhere. She couldn't blame them – nothing much was happening. A group of younger women came by and began looking quite interested in what was on the racks.

'Can I help you?'

'My sister told me about you; she works up at the shirt factory, said you'd got some nice stuff so we thought we'd take a look. It's really nice. Bit out of our price range, though.'

Ness was beginning to think the people who shopped in the market weren't really the sort of people who'd have the money to spend on her clothes, and she wasn't up to the market banter some of the other stallholders were spouting to get the punters to buy their wares. It had been a big mistake. First the fashion show and now the market. She'd probably have to pack it all in, go back to working in the factory office, still alter and remake clothes at home and sell by word of mouth. It was the only way.

Eileen and the others arrived back around three o'clock to find Ness sitting looking dejected.

'What's up? It can't have been that bad! Didn't you sell anything?' asked Eileen.

Ness had managed to get rid of a couple of collars and some gloves which she hadn't even made, and she'd sold three dresses at a completely knock-down price to some young girls who had come on a recommendation: 'They hardly had any money to spend, but I couldn't let them go away empty-handed.'

She decided, though not to speak of her worries about the market not being the right place to sell her things and her thoughts about going back to working from home and making things for people she knew.

***

In the evening after Ray was asleep, Ness sat in the workroom and pondered about the last week. She felt she'd let Rose down, and Robert would probably have thought she'd given in too easily. She'd tried to do too much too quickly and think herself bigger and more capable than she really was.

Rose had been understanding about the fashion show. These things happened – they were just a setback. But now the market had been a disaster, too. Ness didn't exactly feel like cutting her wrists, but all she could think about was the mess she'd got herself into. The more she tried to be positive the more she felt a complete failure. It was unfair to write to Rose and complain, but just putting pen to paper helped.

Saturday 8th May

Dear Rose,

Well, after the mess of the fashion show that never was I tried the market for a Saturday. But even though everyone was helpful, borrowing a van and getting me set up, it was hopeless. My mum thought we should give it another go, but my gut feeling's telling me it's just a waste of time, effort and money. I'm going to have to stick to altering and making things for a few people from home and not get ideas above my head.

Mrs Meadows is a good supporter and always sends people to me. I need more Mrs Meadowses. I've got quite a bit of stock now. Have you got any ideas? Perhaps I could traipse it all down to London and you could flog it at the Air Ministry. (Only joking.) Wouldn't it be wonderful to wave a magic wand and make things happen? I wouldn't magic Ray away, though. Not now. He's very important to me. My little bit of Robert. Do you think your mother might come round soon, and accept that she has a grandson? Not that I can see her getting on with my mum, not at all.

I'm rambling, aren't I? I don't know what I'm going to do, Rose. I'm thinking I'll have to get a job in the munitions factory and put Ray in the nursery. They're encouraging young mothers to do that round here, but he's still very young. Only five months.

How are you, Rose? Have you got yourself a man yet? There must be plenty of eligible chaps where you work. Did I tell you about George and Sarah? I think they make a lovely couple. She's very good for him. I wouldn't be a bit surprised if they got married. The dress is already made, after all!

I hope it won't be too long before we get to see you again. I'll write again soon. Please write back. It doesn't matter if you've got no news – a line or two would be wonderful.

Love from me and Ray,

Ness x

Ness posted the letter on Sunday morning, and on Tuesday she received a telegram:

GOT YOUR LETTER

DON'T YOU DARE GIVE UP
LOVE ROSE

Ness stared at the words. Rose was the only person who knew her worries about the market and that she'd wanted to abandon the whole thing. She'd not told the others how despondent she was. This telegram was all the encouragement she needed. Rose was right – perhaps she hadn't given the market enough time. She had the licence for another few months, until the end of August anyway. She should stick it out until then, at least.

***

For the next three Saturdays in May Ness stuck at it. She had nothing to lose, really. George didn't mind taking everything down there first thing and dropping her there. Her mum looked after Ray and Emma worked in the shop. Eileen came along as moral support and even began to drum up a bit of business. They made a sign to go above the stall, which read:

NEW CLOTHES FROM OLD
(Make Do and Mend)
No coupons needed!

They made a few little cards with Ness's name on, and handed them around to people in the market. Ness had the idea of giving 10 per cent off any item if the person showed the card when they came to the stall. It worked well. Things improved, and by the last Saturday in May most of the current stock was sold. It was a start, and people were beginning to talk about her. Quite a few brought in an old wedding dress or a man's suit for her to alter for a modest sum. Ness always quoted according to what she thought the client could pay.

'White & Proctor will be up and running before you know it,' said Eileen.

'I'm not sure that's the right thing to call us. If there is an us. Not enough work for both you and me at the moment.' Ness was fully aware of Eileen giving up her time for nothing. But the market had turned out to be a minor success.

On the first Saturday in June, Eileen turned up with an American GI, Larry, on her arm. He was stationed the other side of Manchester, and had come to Ridley before Christmas to visit relatives. He had stayed with them for his week's leave and had met Eileen at a dance back then. But he hadn't returned until now.

'We met up again last night. Remember, I told you I was going to the Empire again. I was really surprised to see Larry there.' Eileen smiled up at this handsome American. Ness didn't know what to say. She'd not seen much of Sid lately, not for the last few weeks. She'd asked Eileen a couple of times if all was well between her and Sid, but Eileen was reluctant to talk about it. And now this.

'Hello, pleased to meet you,' said Ness.

'I hear you're a pretty good dressmaker, and Eileen here helps you out. I'm impressed with what I see here. Perhaps I should buy something for my new girl, eh?' He gave Eileen an extra hug. It was all a bit soon for Ness to take in, and she wondered why George or Tommy hadn't said anything about Sid. Perhaps they didn't know anything. No doubt Ness would hear all about it over the coming days.

Larry did actually buy a summer dress for Eileen. Money didn't seem to be a problem, and he wasn't restricted by ration books and coupons. He pulled a roll of notes from his pocket and drew out £1. 'Keep the change,' he said, again smiling. 'If you need anything from the base, let me know. I can get most things – stockings, lipstick, sweets – you know what I mean? Just give me a list.' He winked at Ness, but it was a genuine friendly wink, nothing naughty about it.

'I'm guessing you'll be dragging Eileen off now, so I've lost my help for this morning.'

'I'll not be long. Larry has to get the train back today. It takes ages through Manchester.'

'I'll only keep her from you for an hour or two. And I'll be back another day, I hope. Don't forget to send me the list.' He smiled again at Ness and walked off down the road with Eileen hanging on his arm and on his every word.

Forty-one

Sunday 22nd May 1943

E ileen came around to see Ness at home. It was a beautiful morning and Ness suggested they should go out for a walk with the pram and sit in the park.

When they got there, Ness said she wanted to know all about Larry and what was happening with Sid: 'Spill the beans, then.'

'It's hard. I feel so ashamed.'

'You can tell me anything.'

'I'm not so sure you're going to like this.'

'Has Sid gone off with another woman?'

Eileen gave a weak laugh, 'Nothing as simple as that. Look, if I tell you, can you keep it to yourself? I know news spreads fast and I expect George knows, but he's not seen that much of Sidney lately.'

Eileen told Ness that Sidney had been dabbling too deep in the black market. She'd known from the start that he was a bit shady, selling stuff here, there and everywhere, but she'd always turned a blind eye – she'd liked the face cream, the meat and the other stuff that came her way. But now he'd gone too far and got mixed up with a bad lot from Leeds. They'd been dealing with some big stuff, stealing from shipments into Liverpool and the like. Anyway, one of the inside men had got caught and dropped the rest of the gang in it. It was possible that Sid would have to serve two years inside, but it hadn't got to court yet. They were being held on remand in Liverpool Prison.

Ness was shocked, but not surprised. She tried not to show it, and she put a comforting arm around Eileen's shoulders. 'Eileen, how have you kept all this to yourself? It must have been terrible! When did you first know, and why didn't you tell me?' As she said this, Ness was conscious of how much she had hidden from Eileen with the Alf incident. But yet again, this wasn't a good time to share that particular piece of news.

'You've got enough on your plate. I thought you might have guessed when you asked me a few awkward questions. I've known for ages he was doing something stupid, but I never imagined it was that bad. I suppose if I was a good girlfriend I'd stand by him – but I can't, Ness, I just can't. I'm not sure we ever had a great love for each other. I've been tagging along with him for a couple of years, and for the last few weeks I've been uncertain how I felt. When this happened it was the last straw. I didn't want anything more to do with him. Then yesterday Larry turned up again.'

'You have to do what you think is right, Eileen.'

'I feel so much better for telling you about it. My parents'd be horrified. I hope they don't find out – I've told them we've split up, and that's it. I'm just hoping it won't be in the local paper. If it is, I'm going to have to find a way to stop them reading it.'

'The trouble is Ridley's such a small town and people talk. Let's keep our fingers crossed that it only appears in the papers in Liverpool and doesn't get as far as Leeds and Ridley. Although, if all the gang are from Leeds, it'll make the news there too.'

Ness was glad that Tommy had settled down with Emma and not been dragged into anything with Sidney. She knew people talked about her being an unmarried mother, but they had come to accept the situation for what it was. Some of them still thought she'd been widowed, and even though she no longer stuck to that story she hadn't gone all out to tell everyone that she'd lied. She wasn't sure, though, what they'd make of Sid going to prison. Although maybe quite a few of them knew exactly what he'd been up to.

'Now you've gone all quiet,' said Eileen. 'Got anything you want to tell me?'

'No. I'm worried about you, that's all.'

'I'm fine. I've bounced back already. I should never've stayed with him as long as I did. He was a distant memory after a couple of port and lemons!' Eileen laughed. 'Now I've got Larry, and he's a good sort, I reckon. I know I've only seen him a couple of times, but I'm taking my lead from you and Robert.' She laughed again.

Eileen would never know for sure how pleased Ness was about her split with Sid.

Back at the house, Mary had put some food on the table. They didn't go in for Sunday lunch these days – it was corned beef, plus mash and cabbage from the allotment. After they'd eaten, the three women sat around the table while Ray played on the floor.

'I've got to decide what to do with the market stall. Should I take it over on a permanent basis?' said Ness, looking from Mary to Eileen.

Neither of them answered for a moment or two, then Eileen said, 'If it's making enough money for you to get by then I think you should carry on. It'll be tough in the winter months but if the weather's really bad then you could just stay in the workroom on those days.'

'I was thinking perhaps we could change the shop around so that you could have a corner in there,' said Mary. 'I mean, there's nothing to stop us putting up a rail of clothing by the shop window, is there? It'd be better than freezing to death in the market.'

'That's a brilliant idea,' said Eileen.

Ness agreed that it made sense. She'd be sewing out the back and then selling from the shop. It wasn't exactly the answer to her dreams but as long as she could keep going and bring in a few shillings each week she could manage. She would continue with the market until September. The war couldn't go on forever.

Forty-two

Saturday 8th April 1944

N ess was in her usual place sewing in the back of the shop. Ray was in the house with Mary, who had her hands full as these days he was all over the place and into everything. It was Easter Saturday, and Emma was working in the shop, but only a few people came and went throughout the morning.

Despite the fact there had been more heavy bombing, now mostly at nighttime, in London since January the news was that the Allies were gaining ground in the war, and the mood in the country was optimistic. People planned outings for Easter Sunday, to the races or out for a picnic. Rose had wanted Ness to go and visit her in London but they'd decided to leave it for the time being. Instead, Rose was coming up to Ridley and would arrive late that afternoon.

Ness was fully aware that it was two years to the day since she and Robert had slept together. She'd managed to take care of Ray and look after herself during those years but it hadn't been easy. She was sick of Make Do and Mend. While she worked with the WVS teaching other women how to make the most of the clothing they had in their wardrobe, she much preferred being paid to alter or make clothing. Thank goodness for the Pauline Meadowses of this world. They had saved her from being completely penniless. She had taken to making children's clothing from some of the items she'd been given by others. She could sell those for reasonable prices, and as there was no rationing for children she could make as many as she liked. She found the small sizes a bit fiddly and she didn't enjoy designing them, but if the parents had the money she was happy to take it.

'Hello Emma.' It was Eileen's voice from the shop. 'Is Ness out the back?'

Before Emma could answer Ness called Eileen through, then asked her, 'What are you doing here? Isn't Larry around this weekend?'

'He came on Friday night and we went out for dinner. Look what he gave me.' Eileen waved her left hand at Ness, who could see the ring on her third finger. 'Aren't I the lucky one?'

Ness was shocked but tried not to show it. She should have seen it coming, as Larry and Eileen were together as much as possible and if he couldn't get to Ridley he would organise for her to go off to Warrington whenever he could.

'Well, that's … that's such lovely news.' Ness stood up, walked around her sewing machine and gave Eileen a big hug. 'When's the day, then?'

'We'll have to fit in in around his leave and when he can get over to Ridley, but we're not hanging around. I'd like it to be soon. Can you run me up a wedding dress? Larry's given me this material. He got it sent over from America. I was lucky it didn't get torpedoed in the Atlantic!'

Eileen handed over the bag she was holding and Ness pulled out some beautiful oyster-coloured satin, a packet of pearl buttons and some cream lace.

'Can you do something with it?'

'Of course I can! It'll be wonderful to work with some *new* material. Let's do some designs now. I've got a couple of hours before Rose arrives.'

***

Later that day, after Tommy and Emma had gone out, Rose, Mary and Ness sat in the back room around the table. Ray was in his high chair. They all talked about Eileen and Larry's plans. There'd not been a wedding since George married Sarah at the end of '43. It was very exciting. This would be quite something, as they knew Larry would have access to all sorts of food that they couldn't get hold of in England. They might even be able to have proper icing on the cake – in fact, they might even have a proper cake!

Ray banged his fists on the high chair table and shouted words that only Ness and Mary could understand.

'He's talking nonsense,' said Ness.

'He wants more to eat,' said Mary.

'Don't we all!' said Rose.

'He wants to get down.' Ness set him down on the floor and he ran straight to Rose, pulling at her skirt so that she would lift him onto her lap.

She cuddled him and kissed his head. 'He looks so like Robert, he really does. I think it's time to take him down to Dittisham again and introduce him to his other granny.'

Ness looked at her mum and saw her raise her eyebrows. She wasn't keen on developing any kind of relationship with the Granger family; she'd accepted Rose and that would be that. But Ness felt differently.

'Why don't we both go down in June? I can pay your fare from London if you can make as far as there.'

Ness hesitated. What if Mrs Granger was horrible like the first time? What if she's nasty to Ray? ... 'I'm not sure,' she said.

Rose almost read her mind. 'She'll be fine. I think she's changed a lot over the last eighteen months. Being widowed and then losing Robert was a lot for her to deal with, and I think she has a few regrets. Please say you'll come.'

'Okay then. But it depends when Eileen's wedding is.'

'That's why I suggested June. From what you've said they'll be married by the end of May so you'll be free in June.'

Forty-three

Saturday 20th May 1944

Ness had made the most beautiful wedding dress for Eileen. She had cut the satin on the bias to make a three-quarter length skirt which had a wonderful swing to it as it fell from a tightly fitting bodice. She had made the dress sleeveless, but she had also made a matching short bolero jacket to cover Eileen's shoulders for the church part of the ceremony.

'Let's do your hair and make-up first, and then you can slip into the dress by stepping into it,' said Ness as she helped Eileen get ready. They were in Eileen's bedroom, and Ness thought about all the other times they'd been in here and all the things that had happened over the last few years.

'Don't be sad, Ness. I can tell you're thinking about us and what'll happen after I'm married. I'll still be living in Ridley with my parents for quite a while, I should think. Larry's bound to be off somewhere soon – but what'll happen when this bloody war's over? Who knows?'

'Yes, I was wondering how I'd get on without you.'

'You've got Rose now. She'll still be around.'

'D'you reckon you'll go to America with him after the war?'

'It'll break my parents' hearts – but yes, I can't imagine life without Larry.

Eileen stood up for Ness to help her on with the dress. It was hanging on the cupboard door and Ness took it down then put the bolero on the bed. Dropping the dress to the floor, she held its top open as wide as she could for Eileen to step into it. Pulling it up over Eileen's hips, she laced up the long back opening with a lovely set of silk cords she'd made.

'Pity they're at the back, said Eileen, twisting her head over her shoulder. 'I can't see what they look like.'

'The lacing looks lovely, and the point is that everyone else will see it when you walk down the aisle and stand in front of them.'

Eileen put on the bolero and Ness helped her on with the shoes that Larry had managed to get for her; they were gold satin with a high heel and a peep toe.

'I'll not be wearing these again. They look nice but they're not so comfy.' Eileen laughed loudly and then the two women embraced.

'You look lovely, really lovely,' said Ness.

'I don't know why you refused to be a bridesmaid.'

'It just didn't feel right, me being a mother and that. Anyway, I couldn't have made another dress! C'mon – George'll be here with the car any minute. Let's go down and show your mum'n'dad how their little girl looks, shall we?'

***

The reception was a small affair, but Larry had done his best to help with the catering. They had a fruit cake made from pooled ingredients from the neighbours and Larry's contacts on the base. Eileen's parents were delighted their daughter had made such a match, although her mother shed a tear or two and Ness thought they must have been apprehensive about the future, knowing that Eileen was planning to go away with Larry, wherever he went, after the war.

The best thing of all was that Larry brought with him four members of his company's band. One of them, a trumpet player, was a good friend and was the best man. Everyone danced, and for Ness it was a bittersweet experience. It was lovely to see Eileen looking so happy dancing with Larry but it brought about a jealousy she didn't like in herself. She bit her lip and swallowed hard. She would not spoil this day for her friend.

'Wanna quick dance, Sis?' Tommy broke into Ness's thoughts. 'I know dancing with your brother's not the best – but c'mon, I'll swing you round the floor a couple of times, and maybe one of Larry's mates'll take over.'

Ness laughed and let Tommy pull her up from where she sat and drag her off.

'But what about Ray?' she protested.

'Mum's got him – look, she's already picked him up.'

Ness could see Mary jigging about with Ray in her arms, so she threw herself into the foxtrot and then just about managed a swing dance, but drew the line at the Lindy Hop. She stood back and watched some of the GIs on the floor with the local girls, throwing them in the air, surrounded by other wedding guests who clapped and cheered. Ray was jumping up more or less in time to the music with

Mary holding his hands. It made Ness smile, and for a while she forgot about all the difficulties she was dealing with.

When it was time for the newly wedded couple to leave for their honeymoon – it would be just one night in a small hotel in the countryside just outside Ridley – Ness stood outside with everyone else and waved them off.

***

When Ness put Ray to bed that night she held him close. He was all she had, and all she wanted, right now. She lay in bed thinking about the day. Ness wanted Eileen to be happy, but she couldn't help thinking about the irony of the situation; here she was stuck in Ridley, and Eileen, married to a man with money and prospects, was probably going to travel to America. Yet it was Ness who was the one who'd wanted to leave. She looked down at Ray in his cot and smiled. He was a beautiful boy, and definitely had the look of Robert about him. She had so much to be thankful for, but inside her there was a lingering sadness that she thought she might never shake off.

Forty-four

Tuesday 4th July 1944

E ileen had come straight from work to see Ness, and they sat
with Mary in the front room. It seemed to Ness that life hadn't
changed much since Eileen's wedding. She was still in Ridley with her
parents and had seen very little of Larry, because two weeks after the
wedding he'd been transferred to London. Ness was quite happy that
things were carrying on as normal.

Ray was pushing a wooden lorry around that Tommy had made for
him, and he kept knocking into the furniture.

'Steady on, Ray – you're gonna cause more damage than the Jerries
at that rate,' said Mary.

'Well, they're causing plenty of damage down in London right
now,' said Eileen. 'I can't believe how they've upped their attacks since
the D-Day landings. I think it's likely Larry was involved in all that, but
I don't really understand what he does. He works in signals, and that's
all I know for sure. I wish he'd get sent back here. If he did, I could
maybe move over to Warrington with him. I don't like to think of him

down south, especially now they've started dropping them doodlebug things.'

'Well, Eileen, we're certainly a lot better off up here,' said Mary. 'And they're overworked there, too. When Ness was going to visit Rose last week, Rose put her off, saying she was so busy with work after D-Day that she wouldn't be able to spend any real time with Ness. I wasn't sorry.'

'What does Rose actually do?' asked Eileen.

'She's a secretary in the Air Ministry, but you knew that.'

'Yes, I'd forgotten. I wonder if she ever sees Larry?'

At this, Ness burst out laughing, saying it sounded as though she thought that Larry and Rose might have begun some sort of an affair.

'It's not impossible,' said Eileen. There was a moment's silence before they all began to laugh.

Eileen clapped her hands. 'It's American Independence Day today. I know I'm not American – but I am half, by marriage, so why don't we have a mini-celebration this evening?'

'I'm not bothered,' said Mary, but I don't mind looking after the lad while you two join Emma and Tommy and go to the pub.'

'That'd be lovely,' said Eileen. 'What about it, Ness? You never go out these days.'

'Neither do you now,' Ness retorted.

'Well let's change that tonight, then. A weekday outing! I'm going to pop home and doll meself up. I'll be back in a jiffy.' As Eileen stood up to leave there was a knock on the front door. 'I'll let them in on me way out.'

A few moments later, she came back into the room, holding a telegram.

'It's addressed to you, Ness. Can't think what it can be – no-one in this family fighting anywhere, is there?' She handed the envelope over. 'He's waiting for a reply.'

Ness stood up and took the telegram. She read it first to herself and then aloud.

SORRY TO INFORM YOU
ROSE KILLED AT WORK 30TH JUNE
CALL ME LEY 4206 FLORENCE AMBROSE

'Oh, my lord! What are you going to do?' asked Mary.

'Sit down, Ness, before you fall down,' said Eileen.

Ness's face turned grey as she slumped into the armchair. She didn't speak, but slowly she began to cry.

'Tell the telegram boy to go on. She'll phone this woman later, no need to spend money on a reply,' said Mary.

'I don't understand,' said Ness. 'I just don't understand at all. How can Rose be dead? What have I done? Everyone I love and need dies. First Robert, then Dad, now Rose. It's just not fair.'

'You've still got Ray and your mum and Tommy and me,' said Eileen, almost offended.

'Aye lass, we're all still here,' said Mary.

'I suppose we won't be out celebrating tonight now, then.'

'How can you even think about that now?' Ness was furious with Eileen and, galvanised into action, continued, 'I'll get down to the phone box right now and find out what all this is about. Don't wait for me to come back, Eileen, unless you change your tune.' She grabbed her bag, checked her purse for change and rushed out of the room and the house calling out as she left. 'Take care of Ray for me, Mum. I'll be as quick as I can.

***

When Ness got back to the house Eileen was still there, and she immediately apologised to Ness. She hadn't meant to be unkind. Ness sat down and told the two women what had happened.

'The Air Ministry was hit by one of those flying bomb things. The full details aren't known, or at least the government aren't telling everything. A couple of buses were blown to bits, lots of people dead, and Rose was on one of the upper floors of the building, She was killed along with other women who worked there. Florence didn't know anything more, but she wants me to go with her down to Devon for the funeral a week today. I'm to go to London on Sunday, stay the night with her, and then travel down on the Monday for the funeral on Tuesday.'

'Are you going to go?' asked Mary.

'I think so, yes, but ...'

'But what?' asked Eileen.

'She wants me to bring Ray with me. She'd like to meet him. She said that he doesn't have to go to the actual funeral and that he could stay with Mrs Leach.'

'But won't Mrs Leach want to be there?' said Mary.

'That's what I said, but Florence said no, she couldn't face it; she'd pay her respects in her own way and take care of the food for afterwards at the house.'

'How did you leave it with this Florence woman on the phone?' asked Mary.

'I said I'd go, but I wasn't sure I'd bring Ray.'

'Well, I don't think you should take him,' said Eileen.

Which helped Ness make up her mind.

Forty-five

Monday 10th July 1944

Florence Ambrose had arranged for a taxi to meet Ness at King's Cross. When Ness arrived at the house, a beautiful detached house on the outskirts of Leytonstone, she felt an immediate kinship with Florence, a tall handsome woman with style and a warmth that seemed to fill a room. When Ness had met Florence before, at Robert's memorial service, Ness had hardly taken any notice of her, except to note that she was friendlier towards her than Mrs Granger. Now, Ness discovered that Rose had told her aunt everything and that Florence had taken the opposite view to her sister. She welcomed Ness and Ray into her home.

'It might have been better to have met you in town and stayed at a hotel, but honestly the less time spent in London at the moment the better,' said Florence as she showed them to their room. 'Now, get as much rest as you can; we'll have plenty of time to talk on the train tomorrow.'

Now they were on the train to Totnes. Florence's husband hadn't come with them, and Ness had only briefly set eyes on him, as he had come home late and left very early in the morning. She didn't know what he did for a living, but whatever it was the Ambroses clearly had plenty of money.

As usual, the train was packed, but not so many servicemen this time. Ness thought they must all be out in France or Italy now. Ray slept for a lot of the way. The novelty of his first ever train ride, from Ridley to London the previous day, had kept him occupied and now he was exhausted. He sat on Ness's lap, and she leaned on the window and held him close, his head on her shoulder, her arms like a girdle around his waist. Florence sat opposite them and she couldn't take her eyes off Ray.

'He's absolutely gorgeous, Ness. He looks so like Robert it's painful. What a credit to you he is; so well behaved. Any other eighteen-month-old I've ever had anything to do with has been a complete nightmare.' She paused before continuing, 'I never had any of my own. I was close to Robert and Rose.' Florence looked out of the train window, obviously lost in thought for a moment, then said, 'Tell me about your sewing. I heard from Rose that you're very good at it.'

At the mention of Rose Ness had to swallow hard. It was so unfair that she was dead. It had been her idea about the sewing, and her money that had bought the machine – and now she was gone, just as their friendship was growing. We could have been like sisters. I might have really made something of the sewing business after the war. Anything could have happened, but now she's not here to share in anything. Ness looked at Florence, who was clearly waiting for her reply.

'I'm not sure there's that much to tell. At the moment I just alter clothes and sell them on. Sometimes, richer clients buy material with their clothing coupons and then pay me to make something. My business is quite successful in its own way, and keeps the wolf from the door, if you know what I mean.'

'That's admirable. I know the government have been pushing this make-do-and-mend thing. I've been lucky, I suppose, because I had a good, and full, wardrobe before the war, and most things have lasted well. I might still get you to make something for me at some point, though. You've clothed Ray well, too, I must say. Did you make all his things?'

'I try to keep him looking smart, but it's not easy. I make children's clothes that I can sell quite well, too, as there's no rationing on them.'

'I admire your strength to carry on fending for yourself and supporting Ray.'

'I couldn't have done it without Rose's help. She sent me the sewing machine and some money. It was really generous of her.'

'I expect she did it for Robert.' Florence sighed and looked out of the window as the two women fell silent while Ray slept on.

***

It was late afternoon when they arrived in Dittisham, with the summer sun still quite high in the sky. Robert's mother was still very frosty towards Ness and didn't take much notice of Ray. While Mrs Leach welcomed them all into the house, Mrs Granger spent most of the time talking to Florence.

As it was still light and quite warm, Ness took a walk down to the Ham with Ray. He ran about on the grass, falling over every now and then but jumping back up, chattering away to himself and the seagulls who landed on the boats pulled up on the foreshore. It was an effort for Ness to stay cheerful with him. She was confused by her emotions – sad, yet happy to see her son here on the shore where Robert would have played as a young boy. She wasn't looking forward to the funeral. It would be different from Robert's, as there was an actual body. Ness didn't allow herself to think what state it might be in. She'd heard awful stories about only body parts remaining after a blast, but she knew that although Rose hadn't been hit directly by the bomb, the building had collapsed around her and the other women.

The sun was dropping. It was time to go back up to the house, eat supper and get Ray into bed. Ness would excuse herself and go to bed early. She could not face an evening talking to Mrs Granger, and suspected Mrs Granger felt the same about her. She wondered why – or even if – she'd actually agreed to Florence bringing her here.

***

There were more people of Ness's age at the funeral than at Robert's. The church was filled with flowers that the locals had brought in. It looked almost wedding-like, but the congregation, all wearing black, sniffing and shedding tears into their hankies, soon put paid to that illusion.

When the coffin had been lowered into the ground and it was all over, everyone went back to the house for Mrs Leach's tea. A few of the guests had brought a little something with them, so the spread was quite adequate. Mrs Leach brought Ray into the sitting room to join Ness. He'd obviously had a lovely time helping to get everything ready, and Jim Leach had apparently taken him into the woods to look for squirrels and find sticks to play with. He was the only child present, and before long became the centre of attention. He was a happy little boy and his presence lifted the mood of the gathering. Even Mrs Granger began to take notice of him. Ness was relieved that nobody asked any questions about his father. Ness assumed that they accepted her as Rose's friend, and probably thought her husband was away at war or had died in action but were too tactful to say anything.

***

That evening, after everyone had gone home and Ray was in bed, the three women were left alone. Ness couldn't make her excuses and leave; she felt obliged to stay and sit with them, and somehow make polite conversation. She was pleasantly surprised when Florence began to sing her praises, telling Mrs Granger how wonderful she thought she was, making clothes and earning enough money to keep her and Ray fed and clothed – 'and in wartime, too' she added with enthusiasm. Then, without flinching, she said: 'The boy looks exactly like Robert when he was a toddler, don't you think, Vera?'

There was a pause, and Ness, her eyes on the ground, waited for Mrs Granger's reply.

'There is something about him, you're right. But his hair's not the right colour; it's fair, and Robert was always so dark.'

'But he gets that from his mother, doesn't he?' Her question was directed at Ness.

'Yes, I think he does,' Ness spoke quietly. 'My mother says his hair's just like mine. It has a bit of a bounce in it when I let it grow longer.'

'I know what you're trying to do, Florence. I'm not totally convinced, but I know what Rose thought, too, and I'll give the whole matter serious consideration. But today's not the day. We've just buried Rose, Robert's been gone nearly two years and his father, my husband, just over two years. I don't know what the future holds for me. I am bereft right now. The war's still going on, even though there's talk that the Allies are making progress. I just feel very sad and alone right now.'

'I'm sorry, Vera, I was trying to say the right thing, I meant to help you and to make you see that ... well, look, I don't have to go back to Leytonstone for a few days. What about you, Ness? Are you in a hurry to get back?'

Ness felt cornered. She wanted to leave but as she felt it would be rude to say that, she just agreed that a few days would make no difference. Perhaps Ray would enjoy some time in the countryside. He had certainly taken to the Leaches.

Forty-six

Saturday 15th July 1944

For the next few days Mrs Granger rarely showed her face, then on Saturday morning she came down to the dining room to breakfast holding a cardboard shoebox. She put it on the table beside her but didn't say anything. When they'd all finished eating she smiled quietly and spoke directly to Ness.

'I've been doing a great deal of thinking. I must apologise for mis-judging you and treating you unfairly. I'd felt so sure that Robert would not have ...' she lowered her voice, 'got a girl into trouble. I thought you'd brought this all on yourself, and that you'd perhaps briefly met Robert then used him because he seemed handsome and rich. You'll understand, now you have Ray, that it's difficult to be objective about your own children. But I trust Rose's judgement and my sister's, and both of them have taken the time to get to know you. Although to begin with Florence could only know what Rose had told her, she's been acquainted with you for a while now.'

'Goodness, Vera, get to the point, will you?' said Florence. 'Ray's itching to go out, and I'm getting fidgety listening to you,'

Mrs Granger rose from the table and, picking up the box, said, 'It's a lovely morning. Let's go into the garden where Ray can run about and we can look at this in peace.'

In the dappled shade of a beech tree, she opened the box. Old family photographs. They passed them from hand to hand around the table:

'Look at Robert! What a handsome boy!'

'He was such a wonderful older brother – here, he's holding Rose's hand.'

'Don't they look sweet!'

'Ray looks so *like* him in this picture,' said Florence.

Mrs Granger began to sob. Ness didn't know what to do, but Florence moved behind her sister and hugged her around the shoulders, telling her it was good for her to let it all out. 'It's okay, Vera, it's okay.'

'But I don't think Robert knew how much I loved him or Rose. I wasn't very good at being that kind of mother, and it's too late now, and I didn't want to admit that Ray could be my grandson.'

Ness didn't know what say, and stood up to leave the sisters alone, but Florence signalled for her to remain where she was.

'I'm sure they knew you cared about them and loved them,' said Florence, 'and now's your chance to show some love and affection for Robert's son. There's no doubt in my mind that he is your grandson.'

Ness was close to tears herself as she watched the two women. Ray came running up to the table and climbed up onto her lap, and she buried her face in his hair and wept quietly.

'Come on, everyone,' said Florence. 'It's a lovely day. Let's go down to the Ham, walk along the foreshore and let the breeze dry our eyes.'

'You're sounding far too poetic,' said Mrs Granger. 'But you're right. We all need some exercise.'

As she gathered up the photographs and put them back in the box, Ness hesitated then asked, 'Would you mind very much if I had a couple of those? Perhaps the one where Robert's much older? I've got nothing at the moment. Nothing of him at all.'

'Of course you can. Actually, many of these are of them both as young adults, too, but you can take a couple of the pictures, and I'll look for some more recent photographs of Robert for you.

During the next few days Ness couldn't believe how much the atmosphere changed. Mrs Granger was a different woman; friendlier towards her and more interested in Ray. She was still obviously sad for Rose and Robert, but she got through each day without so many tears. Although Ness imagined that when she was alone in her bed she probably soaked the pillow with grief every night.

They couldn't stay in Devon forever, though. Much as Ness would have liked that now, she had to get back to Ridley and her clothing business. Before she left with Mrs Ambrose for the trip back to London there were promises 'We'll keep in touch,' 'When the war is over,' 'If you need anything let me know', that sort of thing ... but Ness thought it was idle talk, and that it would all fizzle out as time went on.

Forty-seven

1944–1953

B ut things didn't fizzle out. Florence and Ness met often, in Leytonstone and in Ridley. They travelled down together to Devon and in the summers of '47 and '48 Florence took Ray down on his own, and he stayed with Mrs Granger for a two-week holiday.

Rose's flat, which had been rented out for a few years, was sold towards the end of 1948 and Mrs Granger, with Florence's encouragement, gave the money she received from the sale to Ness with the explanation that both Robert and Rose would undoubtedly have wanted to support Ness and Ray.

Clothes rationing was gradually brought to an end, and Ness was able to begin designing and making clothes to sell. Her business did well, but she was still working from the back of the workroom with one rail up in the front of the shop window.

In 1946, when Tommy and Emma had twin girls the house got overcrowded. While the girls had been babies they'd slept in the same room as their parents, but as they grew changes needed to be made. When Ness had received the money from the London flat, she had put it on one side, not knowing quite what she wanted to do with it, but now it was time for her to make some decisions. She knew she should move out and make more room in the house; Tommy was sick of factory work and Mary was getting too old to run the corner shop. Ness didn't want to take it over; she thought she'd be better off moving to Leytonstone. Florence and Mrs Granger had suggested this to her the last time they'd all been together, late in 1948.

In early 1949, Florence Ambrose and her husband Anthony offered to back Ness in her business. They found a premises in Leytonstone for her to use as a workshop-cum-studio and a small showroom in the West End of London. The decision to move was almost taken out of Ness's hands. She used the money from Rose's flat to buy a small house in Leytonstone and got Ray into the local school.

Ness was worried about upsetting her mother. She'd been such a big help with Ray, and Ness knew that taking him away was going to hurt. But now the twins had come along Mary had other grandchildren to focus her love and energy on. Although Mary was a little jealous of the attention Ness and Ray were getting from Vera and Florence she also recognised that one had lost both her son and her daughter during the war and the other had been childless. She knew she herself was lucky to still have Ray and Ness, and it wasn't as though they were moving to America. Unlike Eileen, who had sailed out to meet Larry after he was sent back there from Berlin in 1946.

In Leytonstone Ness grew her business steadily, but her talent soon became talked about and custom soon increased. The Ambroses knew a lot of influential people, too, which helped. Her company, Eunice&Co, specialised in wedding dresses, evening dresses and ball gowns, and she brought Jennifer down from Ridley to work in her London showroom.

In 1952 Larry was posted to the American base in West Ruislip, and he and Eileen came back to England with their daughter, Wendy. They rented a house in Eastcote. Even though Ness and Eileen were living on opposite sides of London, they picked up where they'd left off, meeting in the centre and spending the occasional weekend in each other's houses.

Ness was, for the most part, contented with the way things were going.

PART II

1953

Forty-eight

Thursday 17th September 1953 Leytonstone, London

A noise at the window made Ness look up. Her sewing machine fell silent as she peered through the net curtains to glimpse a figure she recognised. 'What on earth ...?' She froze. She'd thought he was dead. She *knew* he was dead. She'd read it in black and white. But now ...

He must have heard her machine whirring. He came closer and she held her breath as he stared at the window ... but the nets would obscure his view. She watched him move towards the front door.

His knock sounded demanding.

She pulled up the foot and slid out the material, a heavy blue satin for an evening gown she was making for herself. She stood up and draped the half-finished garment over the back of her chair. It fell in folds over the seat, like a girl in a faint. She could have followed it at any time.

He knocked again.

What to do? If she ignored him he'd just come back again and again, and then she'd have to explain him to Ray. That'd be unbearable. So, without rushing, she made her way from the workroom to the hall, then opened the door just a crack. He looked a little older – well, it'd been over ten years. He looked scruffy, too.

'Surprise, surprise! You look a bit peaky. What's your problem? Aren't I welcome?'

'Did you think you *would* be?' Ness tried to sound as though she didn't care, but she was shaking all over, so she leant on the door jamb.

'I was just in the area and I thought I would see how my Ness is doing.'

'I'm *not* your Ness. I *never* was. I've a good mind to call the police. I don't know how you've got the nerve to come anywhere near me after what you did.' She could feel herself getting redder and redder. She was angry and scared in equal measure.

He shoved his foot onto the sill, so she couldn't shut the door. He hadn't changed a bit. He had a stupid grin on his face. It made her feel sick. 'I'm really busy, Alf. If you don't remove your foot from my door and leave, I'll call the police.'

Instead of his foot he removed his battered trilby, revealing a head of curly, greasy fair hair.

'Come on, Ness. Don't be like that. A lot of time's passed since I last saw you. It was just a silly mistake. I was angry, my life was a mess and I wasn't myself. I'd never done anything like that before or since. I never meant to hurt you.'

What she really wanted was for him not to be here, for him to actually *be* dead. Her cheeks felt odd, shivering against her teeth – it wasn't nerves, though, it was a mixture of anger and anxiety. Even though she knew what she was dealing with, Ness knew she would have to face it.

'Take your foot out of the door, then. Give me a minute and I'll get my coat. We can go for a walk and you can tell me what you're really doing here. I will *not* let you in.' Her voice was raised but controlled.

There was a pause before he answered. He still left his foot in the door. 'Honest, Ness. I just wanted to see you. I want you to forgive me. It's plagued me ever since it happened.'

'I don't believe that for a minute – and I've told you, you can't come in.'

He stared at her. She looked down and noticed his shoes were worn and dull. Her eyes wandered back up his body. His collar was a bit scruffy and the knot in his tie shiny with use.

'Promise you'll come out if I let you shut the door?'

She thought about it for a minute. Some sort of curiosity seeded itself in her brain. 'Okay, then. Yes.'

'Say it properly, then.'

She scowled. 'I promise.'

He slid his foot slowly away and she shut the door. She didn't slam it, but closed it with a firm shove.

She ran to the back door to make sure it was locked. Then she ran upstairs to the bathroom. She'd stopped shaking, but all she could think of was what does he want? All she could remember was how she'd felt afterwards – and now, sitting on the toilet brought back the memories she wanted to forget. She pulled the chain, washed her hands and splashed water on her face. No need for scrubbing this time. She picked up her coat, hat and handbag, and went at a steady pace down the stairs to the front door, where Alf was waiting for her.

They walked down the path to the gate. He opened it and stood aside to let her through before him. She would rather he stayed in her sight the whole time. She didn't know whether to walk quickly to get it over with, or to slow her pace and appear casual.

'That's a nice coat you're wearing. I imagine you made it yourself.'

'Yes,' she said, 'I make all my own clothes. I always have.'

'I'd have thought with your success you would've got somebody beneath you to do all that.'

'I'm only a minor player in this game.'

'Well, you seem to be doing well. Nice house, nice front garden.'

'That's none of your business.' She was regretting not calling the police. She'd put herself in a vulnerable position just like the last time. They walked in silence for a while. Ness kept her distance from him, although the pavement wasn't wide. At the corner of her road they turned left; she didn't want to go anywhere near the school. The old worries about Ray's father's identity rumbled through the back of her mind. Suddenly, Alf's fair hair was significant, even though she knew that Ray had got his from her.

'There's a park just down here, about ten minutes away. We could go there if you like.' She caught herself sounding as though she really wanted to spend time with him. 'Or we could just keep walking.'

'Isn't there a caff somewhere? A place we can get a cup of tea and a bun?' he asked.

'I don't usually go to cafés, but there's one next to Leytonstone station. We could go there.'

They passed some Victorian terraced houses with their small front gardens. She liked to imagine what the neighbourhood had been like when they had first been built. Leytonstone was suburban with lots of parks, and the schools were nice. She particularly liked the way the trees grew on the pavements, and they had wonderful scented, pink blossoms in the spring. Many of the war-damaged areas had been rebuilt with modern houses.

The café was small with a lingering smell of old frying fat. They managed to find a seat by the steamed-up window. Ness didn't really want a cup of tea or a bun, but dared not refuse. There didn't seem to be waitress service, so Alf went up to the counter and she watched him from where she sat. He was a weasel of a man. He didn't stand tall with his shoulders squared, but stooped slightly as though trying to keep a low profile. Ness thought him despicable. A stupid little specimen of a man who she'd allowed to get the better of her once. She wasn't to blame, but when she saw him standing there she wondered how on earth she could ever have let him get away with it. She glanced away as he turned to come back to the table. She didn't want him to think she was at all interested in what he was doing.

Alf plonked the tea in front of her. A white cup with a thick rim. Ness looked at it with distaste – she liked a fine china cup these days. She sat back and allowed him to talk.

'It's nice to see you again. You're looking good, you know. London must suit you.'

She let his words hang in the air, then stared at him before saying, 'I thought you were dead.'

'So did everyone. Including me.' He sipped his tea and looked her straight in the eye. There was a bit of a smirk on his face. She waited for him to explain.

'The ship went down and it was reported that I'd died – but I was fine. There'd been another Alfred on board, and they'd mixed us up.

My poor old mum was most upset – first a telegram to say I'd gone and then another to say I was okay.' He laughed in the most unpleasant way, a sort of snigger.

Ness didn't find the story at all amusing. 'It must have been awful for her.'

'Did you ever get married? I mean did you see that other chap again?'

She didn't want to engage in any more conversation with him. 'Look, I don't really want to go over the past. I've moved on – and so have you, obviously. I don't know what you want from me, but this isn't going to work. I can't imagine you're one bit sorry for anything. I'm going home now.' She gathered up her belongings and made to stand up.

'Don't go, Ness. I've got a lot I want to say to you. I honestly didn't mean it to happen. I just got a bit carried away with the moment.' He grabbed her wrist and held onto it.

She looked directly at him and measured her words: 'It was rape, Alf. Rape.'

'C'mon, Ness. You must have realised I was drunk and didn't mean it.'

'You never bothered to find out if I was okay, did you? Let me go.' She glared at him.

'Only if you promise to meet me again. I won't do you any harm, honest. I just want to make amends. We could be friends. You know what I mean. There was a war on, and it was hard for everyone.'

She wanted to tell him to leave her alone, but she knew that now he'd found her he was not going to let things go. That little seed of curiosity grew into a shoot, and she couldn't help herself: 'How did you find me?'

'I went up to Ridley to look you up. Your mum was surprised to see me and she told me you'd come down here. I guess you never mentioned what happened with us to her. I don't think she was that keen on me but she was quite friendly, and we had a cup of tea just like the last time. Sorry your dad died. I saw the shop. It's a hardware shop now and your brother Tommy and his wife Emma running it. Nice tight little family. Your mum told me all about how you started your little business there and how you'd come down here after the war. She told me everything about you and her lovely grandson – Ray, isn't it?'

Ness was petrified. He must know when Ray had been born. He'd have put two and two together. She also realised that her mother *must* have told him that Robert had died. Alf twisted everything to suit himself. She wondered why her mother hadn't told her she'd seen Alf when she'd spoken to her on the telephone last week.

As though he could hear her thinking, Alf said, 'I asked your mum not to say anything, I said I wanted it to be nice surprise for you.'

'It's not a *nice* surprise at all. What is it you *really* want?' Ness guessed the answer would be money. He'd obviously not got a great deal of it himself.

'Look 'ere, Eunice. I've found you now, and I don't want to lose you again. I'd like to meet Ray. Know what I mean? I'm sure we can come to some agreement.'

Ness felt panic rising. She had to stay in control. She said the first thing she could think of to get rid of him for the time being. 'I'll be here, in this café same time next week. It's that or nothing, so let me go now. And you're not to show your face at my house again or I'll call the police. Understood?'

'Can't we meet sooner? A week's a long time.'

'Well, you've waited more than ten years, so you can wait another few days.'

He nodded and slackened his grip. 'It would be nice to see you sooner than that, but I'm a patient man. Next week'll do.'

Ness pulled her hand away. She had an urge to wipe it on her coat, and she could still feel the unwanted pressure of his hand around her wrist like a snake. She made for the exit at a suitably controlled pace. She wanted to run, but that would have given him too much satisfaction.

Her heart was bloody thumping as she walked back down the road. She was angry – no, *furious* – she'd thought he was dead ... it was a bombshell. She had no idea how she was going to deal with him or with the consequences of his arrival. She took a glance behind her. He'd either accepted she didn't want him to follow her or he was still in the café. Either way, it was unnerving.

She walked the long way home. Under her breath, and sometimes louder, she said all the worst swear words she could think of, cursing Alf, and cursing her own stupidity for not doing something about it back in 1942. She looked at her watch. It was coming up for twelve. She had a few hours before Ray would be home. Thank God for school lunches. He was in his last year of primary school; he'd be eleven at Christmas and this time next year he'd be at senior school. Ness hoped he'd pass the eleven plus and get into the grammar school. She was pinning a lot of hopes on that. And she didn't want to upset everything now. He'd been told from very early on that Robert was his father, and there had never been any need for Ness to say anything different.

Her first thought was to telephone her mother. Then she decided it wouldn't be right. Mary was getting on, even though she was still very active in the community. Ness was able to send her enough money to supplement her income. Tommy, meanwhile, had built up a good business; that little shop had served them all very well over the years. Ness just didn't want to share anything of what had happened with her mother.

She couldn't tell Florence either – that'd be the worst thing to do. Involving her in this would be devastating. There was no way she could let any of Robert's family know what happened in '42. There was only one person she could talk to.

As soon as she was in the house, she rang Eileen: 'You remember me telling you ages ago that another chap who found the note in his pocket turned up on the doorstep just after the last time Robert and I were together?'

Eileen said, 'Did you even tell me?'

'I'm pretty sure I did. Anyway, that man's turned up here today. I don't know what he wants and I'm scared.'

Eileen thought she was being ridiculous. 'He probably just wants to rekindle the friendship as he missed out the first time.'

Ness nearly choked, but stopped herself. She found she couldn't speak freely about it on the telephone.

'You're definitely coming over this weekend, aren't you?' she asked.

'Yes, Wendy and I'll be there tomorrow evening. It'll be after six though, by the time she finishes school and we get the train over. Why can't you tell me over the telephone?'

'I can't. I should have told you years ago but I thought he was dead. I was *sure* he was dead, but—'

'None of this is making any sense. I'll see you tomorrow.'

Forty-nine

Friday 18th September 1953

The next morning Ness made up the spare room for Eileen and Wendy. She had painted the walls of the room plain cream, and put matching beige candlewick bedspreads on the beds. There was a chest of drawers and a wardrobe. It was all rather utilitarian, as it had been hard to get anything else after the war. Ness planned to replace it all before Christmas this year, to cheer the room up a bit, but for now it was fine. A decent room for any family or friends to stay in when they visited. At least, there'd been no complaints so far.

Before she left the house, Ness went around closing all the curtains and making sure no-one could see inside. It felt like being back in the war days, putting up the blackout blinds. As she walked through the sitting room she saw Robert's pipe on the mantelpiece. She picked it up, and closing her eyes, clasped it close to her chest. After a moment, she replaced it and with renewed strength, she went to the back door, locked and bolted it, then left the house through the front door to walk to the library.

It wasn't unusual for her to visit the library, but she normally took Ray with her and went in the evenings or on a Saturday. It was a treat to be there on a weekday, on her own with time to look around. The building had a grand art deco entrance with steps up to the first floor where the library was situated. The ground floor housed offices and shops. It was quite famous, because during the war they had made propaganda films inside the building, showing local people reading the books and browsing the shelves, to make it clear how the British encouraged book reading rather than burning them like the Nazis. At one time Ness had wanted to work in a library, and this one would have been wonderful. She thought that perhaps one day she'd end up there if she ever gave up the fashion business. Maybe she'd write a book about being a dress designer ... *pigs might fly* she thought.

The library was her place of solace – somewhere she could relax and lose herself for a couple of hours browsing the shelves. She'd read all the P. G. Wodehouse books and the Agatha Christies. She looked for something different and found *The Beautiful View* by Elizabeth Jane Howard; she was a new author, and Ness liked the look of the story. Then she picked up an old favourite, *Gone with the Wind*. It had been a while since she'd read it, and right now she needed Melanie, Ashley, Rhett and Scarlett in her life again. While she was browsing she saw a business directory on a shelf with a variety of other reference books. She already had an idea in her head – a thought about how she might deal with Alf. There might be someone in the book who could help her.

Leafing through it, she pulled out a notebook and pencil from her bag, ready to write down names and addresses. There were none that seemed suitable in the local area, so she looked in the central

London section. It might be better to keep it well away from home, anyway. She made a note of the one she thought looked the best: King's Investigation Bureau, Chancery Lane. This one was in a little advert, which was probably why she'd picked it; it wasn't just a plain listing like the others. She would discuss it with Eileen this weekend.

When Ness left the library she felt more confident – she'd made a move in the right direction. She never wanted to involve the police, but this might be the next best thing. She had an idea about what Alf might be up to, and she wanted to be ready for his next move.

She walked round to the workshop in Norlington Road. The property was big enough for a cutting area, a sewing area for three machinists, a front office and a reception area. There was also a large storeroom full of material, with a smaller room off it housing haberdashery. It was in this room where anyone new to the company would begin. Ness was keen to ensure that everyone who worked for her would have a hand in each stage of the dressmaking. She wanted them to retain their interest in the job as a career and not be bored by sewing buttons or side seams all the time.

Ness divided her time between the Leytonstone workshop and the London showroom where Jennifer held the fort. Ness oversaw all the orders and along with her secretary Betty, dealt with all the paperwork.

Ness walked into the reception area, a large room where Betty sat at the front desk, 'I thought you weren't in today,' she said.

'I know – I just wanted to pop in to see if anyone had been around asking for me.'

'No. Nobody's been in at all today. Except the buyer from Ferguson's to see what the 1954 summer collection might be. I told him there'd be a show in London in a couple of weeks.'

'Well, if anybody does come around – specifically a man who calls himself Alf Taylor – please don't give him any information about me. If he does come, he'll likely be probing about the company and how successful we are, things like that.'

'That all sounds a bit shifty. He's a rival, is he? Is everything all right?'

'Yes, it'll be fine. I'm dealing with it.'

Ness took a stroll around the workshop; she liked to keep her hand in and be visible to the women and girls who worked for her. She wanted to be approachable. The despatch room was busy today – it was a Friday, and the Christmas orders were being sent out to the department stores. Ness hired a delivery company, but she knew that soon she'd have to have her own driver and van, just like Brodericks. Ness thought back to the time when Eileen had put her address into the pockets of those shirts. So much had come of her actions. Eileen wouldn't be happy with Ness's revelations tonight.

Once happy that Alf had not been snooping around and everything seemed to be going normally, Ness walked home.

***

There was a banging on the back door. Ness was almost sick. She thought he was going to knock the door down. But she ran towards the door and shouted through it, 'Who's there?'

'It's me, Mum!' came Ray's voice. 'Why's the door locked?'

Ness unlocked the key and the bolt. 'Sorry – I locked it when I went out this afternoon and forgot to open it when I came back in.'

'You're all red. Are you okay?'

'Yes I'm fine. Just a little hot – I rushed to open the door for you.'

'I'm starving! Can I have a snack before supper. please?'

Ray kicked off his shoes and dropped his coat and schoolbag on the floor, then they went into the kitchen.

'I'll pick them up in a minute,' said Ray.

'You certainly will. My, you're getting big. I'll have to watch, because soon you'll be taller than me and I won't be able to do this ...' Ness cuffed Ray gently round the ear. 'Would you like some milk and a biscuit?'

He was a good boy, and he looked a lot like her. Although at first she'd wished he'd been a girl that had only been for a moment. It had partly been because she wasn't sure about boys, even though she had a brother. She hadn't been sure about babies, either – that was more to the point – not sure at all.

Ray made a move towards the biscuit tin. He lifted the lid and poked his fingers in, stirring up the contents.

'Broken biscuits again,' he said. 'Be nice to have a proper packet to open.'

'Don't be cheeky. They end up broken as soon as they go in your mouth, anyway.'

'I know that, but the flavours are all mixed up. I'm starving. School lunch was yuk as usual, but I ate it because if I don't I get pangs in the afternoon.' Ray stuffed a handful of the biscuits into his mouth. 'I'll pick up my stuff and then do my homework.'

'You're keen. Did you remember that Auntie Eileen and Wendy are coming this evening? Is that why you want to get it done?'

'No, I'd forgotten – but that's an even better reason to be done with it soon. I've got football tomorrow morning and I really want to go.

I'm hoping to get into the school team when I go to big school, so I need to play as much as I can now, to get better.'

'If it's not raining we'll come with you to watch. Where's the practice – in Western Park? If it is, then Wendy can play on the swings. Then we can pick up some fish and chips for lunch on our way home.' *Always fish and chips in a crisis,* Ness thought. 'But if it's raining, we might have to let you go on your own.'

'Mum, you haven't stopped for me to answer *any* of those questions.' Ray stood with his hands on his hips and shook his head at her as though he were years older.

'Sorry – what do you say, then?'

'Yes, it's in the park, and yes we can all go because it's not going to rain according to Mr Braithwaite – he's the coach for the local team.'

'That's sorted, then.'

'Fish and chips'd be great for lunch.'

There were times when Ray reminded Ness of Tommy. His enthusiasm and happy nature for a start. There was no way he could ever be anything to do with Alf. She'd been happy until he turned up yesterday. She liked her house. It was comfortable and it wasn't too large, a semi-detached Edwardian property with three bedrooms and a bathroom upstairs, and kitchen and two rooms downstairs, one of them a home office and dressmaking room, and the other, at the back, with a dining table by the French windows looking onto the small garden. Her mother had worked on the garden when Ness first moved in. There had been a time when Ness had thought her mother would move down with her, but she soon realised that Mary would never move out of Ridley and she was needed for Tommy and Emma's twins.

Eileen and Wendy arrived and Eileen wanted to pack the children straight off to bed so that she and Ness could talk. But Ness insisted they had something to eat first. By seven-thirty both children were in bed reading and the two women went and sat in the front room. Ness's had barely got herself comfortable when Eileen spoke, 'Right, then. What's this all about?'

Ness began telling Eileen her story, starting back in April 1942, when Alf had knocked on the door. By the time she'd finished they'd drunk two full pots of tea and Eileen was wondering where the gin was kept.

'I'm shocked on so many fronts. I wish I'd never put those bloody addresses in the pockets. I certainly wish you'd told me about it at the time. Why *didn't* you tell me? We could have gone to the police together, or I could've got Sid to sort him out. He knew all the right people for that sort of thing. Anything slightly underhand was right up his street. Ness, Ness, I feel terrible. I can't imagine what you've gone through.' Eileen dropped her head and shook it slowly from side to side.

'It's not just the rape, Eileen – don't you see? He could be Ray's father.'

Eileen reeled, 'Oh no! No way is he Ray's father. Look at him – he's the image of you and Robert.' She sounded very sure.

'I didn't think so either. Then when I read that Alf was dead and I already knew Robert was dead it didn't seem to matter ... but now Alf's turned up ... it's ruined everything.'

'Can't you just go on as before?'

Ness said it was impossible now. She'd never dared speak to her mum about it – and now her mum had told him about Ray. Then Ness hesitated before saying, 'That's why I think Alf has come.'

'What? Why?'

'I think he's going to blackmail me. I think he wants to get money from me by threatening to tell everyone about what happened – omitting, of course, that he raped me, but just saying I was a willing participant. *And,* of course, that Ray's his son. It's all a dreadful mess again, and I'd thought I was home and dry. Can you imagine what Florence and Mrs Granger would say? It doesn't bear thinking about.'

'Absolutely right! It would ruin everything, they're all very proud of you now. What on earth are you going to do?'

Ness told Eileen about the private detectives she'd looked up.

'I'm going to see one in Chancery Lane. I rang them this afternoon and I've got an appointment on Monday to go and see a Mr Jeremy Harvey. His secretary sounded very nice.'

'What did you tell her it was about?'

'I just said a bad man from my past had turned up, and was bothering me again and I wanted to find out what he was up to. I truly think Alf's going to blackmail me, and I just want to be prepared.'

'For what it's worth, I think you're doing the right thing. Not that I know anything about private detectives. I hope he's not too seedy.'

'I've got a good feeling about it. I mean, he has a secretary for a start, so he must be sort of above board, if you know what I mean.'

'Do detectives have to be registered or have some kind of qualification, do you think?'

'Honestly, Eileen, I've no idea.' Ness began to laugh, because the whole situation seemed so preposterous. 'I'd like to think I'm worrying about nothing – but I'd do anything to protect Ray.'

'You're right. And you've got to protect yourself, too. But don't you think you should tell your mum now?'

'Maybe one day – but I don't want to spoil things for her right now. It wouldn't be fair. I don't need her help to sort this out, and now that I've told you everything I feel better about it than I have for years.'

'Well, I'm exhausted. Let's get up to bed. Those two'll have us up at the crack of dawn.'

Fifty

Saturday 19th September 1953

In the morning the weather wasn't too bad, so Ness and the others went with Ray to the park to watch him at football. Ness couldn't help thinking this was more Alf than Robert, because Robert had never shown any interest in football – he was more cricket and rugby, the result of boarding school. But then she felt cross with the way her brain was playing tricks on her. Loads of boys liked football – it was nothing to do with their dads.

The boys were playing as well as they could, all hoping they'd be spotted by the sports master from the senior school, who was watching from the sidelines. Their parents shouted encouragement when things were going well and bellowed their disproval when they weren't going quite so well. Ness thought it was a bit unfair. They were only young boys after all. Ray was above average height for his age and his build was stocky and strong. Robert had been tall and lanky, but at this stage there was no way of knowing how Ray would turn out. Ness had not bothered for years about Ray's paternity. She had managed to convince herself that Robert was his father. But now Alf turning up like this was making her question things all over again.

Who's that man on the other side of the pitch? He's staring at us,' asked Eileen.

Ness looked. The colour drained from her face and she swayed towards Eileen, turning her back on the pitch.

'It's *him*. I told him not to come anywhere near me. I've said I'll meet him next Thursday morning. What the hell's he doing here now?'

'It's okay. He knows you've seen him. Try not to look agitated. He just lifted his hat and gave me little smile and a cocky wave. Now he's moving.'

'No, no, no ... he's coming over, isn't he? ... What am I going to *do?*' Ness shook Eileen's coat sleeve.

'He's not coming over. Relax, he's walking towards the gate. I think he's leaving the park.'

A cheer went up. A goal had been scored by Ray's team. Not by Ray, but that didn't matter. Ness saw him jumping up and down with excitement and running back down the pitch with the other boys. He couldn't be Alf's, he just *couldn't*. Ness knew she had to remain calm and act as though nothing was bothering her. She shouted along with the rest of the spectators as Ray looked at her for recognition of his team's success. She had to bring her emotions under control – it was vital to stay level-headed. She needed to concentrate on Ray for the rest of the weekend. She would not let Alf get under her skin.

'Easier said than done,' she said under her breath.

'What's that?' asked Eileen. 'Hold back there, Wendy – it was only a goal. They haven't won the game yet!'

'I'm so glad not to be on my own this weekend, Eileen. Thank goodness you and Wendy are here.'

Eileen put her spare arm around Ness's shoulders. 'If you like, I could phone home and stay longer. Wendy can miss a couple of days of school – it won't hurt.'

'No, don't do that. It's not fair on either of you. I'll be fine. I don't think he'll do anything stupid. I've already threatened him with the police. I think he's just trying to scare me, and I will not let him. I just won't.'

Eileen gave Ness a squeeze. 'You're a brave woman. Look what you've done so far for yourself. You'll be fine.'

'I'll go and see that detective on Monday, and I'm sure I'll feel better about it all afterwards.'

***

That afternoon they all went to the matinée at the cinema on Saturday and saw Walt Disney's Peter Pan. Wendy, of course, was thrilled with the fact that the heroine had her name. When they got home Ray was very patient and played with her, pretending to be Peter Pan, and he never seemed to realise how stressed Ness was. Ness managed to forget about Alf for a short time and just enjoy Eileen's company and that of the children.

***

On Sunday morning they went for a walk. Ness was a little on edge but tried not to show it to anyone. After lunch, Ness and Ray walked with Eileen and Wendy to the station to catch the train back to Eastcote.

'Let me know how it goes tomorrow, won't you? said Eileen. 'You can ring me up in the evening. I'll be waiting. Make notes before you go up so you don't forget anything you want to ask. I'm sure everything'll work out fine. I'll see you soon.'

Ness gave her a hug and pushed her on her way. The children didn't hug each other – they were good friends but hugging wasn't in their repertoire. They grinned at each other and said their goodbyes with slight embarrassment. Ness smiled to herself, Eileen had remained a good friend, despite their differences. Their lives were very different now to the lives they'd lived when they were younger. Eileen didn't go to work and had become quite the model housewife and mother. Ness was self-supporting and quite the career girl. Ridley days seemed a long time ago.

Ness and Ray went back home. It looked no different from a week ago but so much had happened in the meantime. Ness was extra vigilant about locking the doors. The nights were drawing in, and the clocks would soon go back. But for now she concentrated on keeping Ray ignorant of how anxious she was. They ate their supper in the kitchen, listening to Sunday evening's episode of The Archers, then Ray had his weekly bath, got into his pyjamas and came downstairs for storytime, a ritual they did every Sunday evening whenever possible. Ray could read very well for himself, but he loved Ness to read to him. She turned to Chapter Ten of *Treasure Island* and read the title aloud: 'The Voyage'.

They settled down on the sofa for the next hour. Ness enjoyed the story too, but couldn't wait for him to be old enough for *Gone with the Wind.*

Fifty-one

Monday 21st September 1953, Morning

Much to Ray's mortification, Ness walked with him to school on Monday morning. 'I really don't want you to walk with me – I'm not a baby,' he moaned.

'I'm going your way this morning anyway, so I thought I'd accompany you for a change. Don't worry – I won't kiss you goodbye when we get there.'

'You certainly will *not*,' said Ray, and to make sure of it he ran ahead, then turned around and waved as he rushed through the school gates, meeting his mates in the playground. A quick glance around showed her that Alf was nowhere to be seen. Relieved, she made her way to Leytonstone station to catch the Central Line to Chancery Lane. She hurried past the café, praying he wasn't in there, but she didn't imagine he'd be up and around at this time of day. He struck her as a lazy individual.

It took under an hour on the tube. It was the line she took to the London showroom, so she knew every stop on the way. She arrived at just after ten, and as her appointment wasn't until eleven, she strolled around Lincolns Inn Fields. She loved the old buildings and the quietness of the lawns. She sat on one of the benches for a while. The buildings had been bombed, but little evidence of that remained by now and a great deal of rebuilding was going on. She looked at her watch – only ten minutes until the meeting. She should get going.

She found the entrance to the building that housed King's Investigation Bureau and, gingerly opening the main door, discovered herself in a small reception area. It wasn't seedy, how she'd feared it might be, but clean and bright. On the wall was a list of the businesses there, with the number of floor and office beside each name. The man on reception didn't say anything to her, Ness thought he was some sort of security person, as he was wearing a grey uniform, not unlike one of the services. He was reading a newspaper and hardly looked up as she stood searching the board. It took a few moments to find King's. Third floor, Office No. 320. She looked around to see if there was a lift, and the security man, who must have decided she'd stood there long enough and might need help, lowered his paper and smiled.

'Can't find who you want?' he asked without a shred of concern in his voice.

'No, I've found it. I just wondered if there was a lift.'

'Round to the right there. It doesn't always work, but you're in luck today. Which floor are you going to?'

'Three.'

'Ah.' He raised his eyebrows as though he guessed who she was visiting: 'Divorce, is it?'

Ness bristled, 'It's none of your business!'

She turned and walked in the direction he had indicated. The lift was an old-fashioned one with a metal expanding gate inside the door, which had to be pulled across before the lift would move. She slammed it hard against the catches and pressed the number three. The lift jerked into life and lumbered upwards. Ness felt a bit sorry for it, working hard every day, doing the same boring journey. This thought cheered her up and her body relaxed. After her encounter with the security man she had felt tense and cross. Not really the way she wanted to appear before Mr Jeremy Harvey. The lift bounced to a standstill and as she got out she remembered to shut the doors behind her; if she didn't, nobody would be able to call it.

She was faced with a small landing with two corridors from it. A sign indicated the office locations, 311–320 to the right. She had to walk to the end of the corridor, where she found door 320 facing her. It must be a corner office, she thought, although what relevance that could have to anything escaped her.

She wasn't sure whether to knock, but when she tried the handle the door opened easily. Inside there was a small reception area, with a couple of chairs and a desk, behind which sat a woman, presumably the one Ness had spoken to when she had rung for an appointment.

'Hello. You must be Mrs Eunice Proctor.'

Ness confirmed she was, and said she hoped she wasn't too early. The secretary, June Withers (her name was displayed on a plaque on her desk) said all was fine and Mr Harvey was not with anyone right now, but Mrs Proctor should take a seat until he buzzed through, and could she please fill in this form while she was waiting? 'It's just name and address et cetera, nothing too horrible. I'll let him know you're here.' She picked up her telephone and announced that Mrs Proctor was waiting.

Ness sat down and looked around. It wasn't anything like she'd imagined. She'd thought the office would be in a back street, the name of the company written in gold on the glass of a partially glazed dark wooden door. She'd obviously been reading too many detective stories. But this office was bright and there was a carpet on the floor, albeit a bit threadbare. There were a couple of framed prints on the wall, country scenes; it was all rather pleasant.

The telephone on June's desk buzzed. She said, 'Yes, Mr Harvey,' then stood up and asked Ness to follow her. Ness tried to hand her the piece of paper she'd filled in, but June told her to take it in with her. June opened the door and held it wide for Ness to go in.

Again, this was nothing like Ness had imagined. The desk was tidy, not covered in brown files or messy with sheets of paper all scribbled on. There was a telephone and a notepad. An ashtray at the front which held a couple of cigarette ends. Ness seriously hoped Mr Harvey wouldn't smoke while she was in there. In one corner of the room there was an easy chair with a standard lamp beside it, made of walnut, with an orange lampshade, plain except for the tassel around the bottom edge. It stood beside a bookshelf and there were two grey metal filing cabinets. In the other corner there was a coat stand with a brown trilby on the top and a suit jacket on a hanger below it.

Mr Harvey was standing behind his desk, 'Do come in, Mrs Proctor,' he said, 'and please take a seat.' He indicated the chair opposite him. She placed the form she'd completed on the desktop then smoothed her skirt underneath her as she sat down. She studied the man opposite her as he busied himself before sitting down. He fidgeted with the waistband on his trousers as though pulling them up, and at the same time screwed up his face a little bit. It was kind of endearing, Ness thought, perhaps a nervous tic of some sort? He was older than her, perhaps over forty, she thought. There were no photographs on his desk to indicate a wife or family.

'Now then, how can I help you?'

Ness began to tell him her story. It all came out in a bit of a rush. She found herself becoming a little emotional at one point and he urged her to take her time. She had made up her mind to tell him everything, right back to when Alf had come to see her in Ridley and sat in their back room being so rude to her parents. Having told Eileen the whole story only a couple of days before, she found it much easier to recount it to this stranger, especially as he seemed kind and interested. She left nothing out. In fact, she was more explicit than she'd been with Eileen.

Mr Harvey made notes as he listened, then sat quietly for a while. He got up and paced back and forth behind his desk, fidgeting with his waistband and twice putting his foot up on his chair and pulling his sock up for no apparent reason. Ness watched him while he walked and thought, her eyes following him backwards and forwards. He wore a shirt and tie, and his hair was brown, brushed back over his head with a parting on the left. She thought he was a little shorter than Robert. She wondered if he had been in the war, and if so, which service.

Eventually, he sat down again and began to speak. 'I take on very few personal jobs. In fact I mostly deal in commercial and industrial stuff, counterfeit and trademark queries, that sort of thing – but every now and then a case comes along when I want to help. I recently helped a man whose wife went missing for no apparent reason; they were a happily married couple, or so he'd thought, with two sons, but she just upped and completely disappeared one morning and didn't return.

After three days the man went to the police but they wouldn't help, so he came to me. I found her, of course, and when I did she said she'd just run away from the routine of everything, and found herself a job and a small bedsit to rent. She'd felt confined and seriously undervalued just being a housewife. However, I should add that she'd already decided to go back to her family but was too ... what's the word? Maybe too embarrassed and ashamed to go back. But happily it all ended well. I think her husband encouraged her to stay on in the job she'd found.'

'Well, that's wonderful and all very nice – but what about me? What can you do to help me? Or are you going to say you can't?'

He cleared his throat, 'Oh no, I'm absolutely determined to help you. I told you that story so you'd understand that I do more than just work for money. I can't stand any kind of bad behaviour towards women – sorry, 'bad behaviour' isn't really strong enough – but I'm shocked to hear your story and, like you, I'm convinced this man, Taylor, is going to be after money from you. What I need are as many details as possible about him – anything at all you can tell me. His date of birth, any addresses you know – but perhaps you don't have those, so anything you can tell me which might help me find him.'

'I have very little.' Ness looked down at her hands in her lap. 'I do have the newspaper cutting about him going down with the ship. I kept it. I'm not sure why.'

'Did you bring it with you today?'

Ness had it in her bag. She didn't know why she hadn't already given it to him.

'Right, thank you,' he said, and studied the cutting. 'And you said you'd offered to meet him again this Thursday, is that right?'

'Yes, at the café next to Leytonstone station at eleven.'

'Well, I'll be there too. I'll be discreet, I won't wear a disguise or anything like that,' he laughed, 'but I'll just sit quietly in a corner reading the paper and drinking coffee and observe. I'll ring you up the evening before to confirm.'

'What are your charges?' asked Ness.

'I'm rather expensive, but worth it,' he smiled. 'But I'll give you a discount, so don't let's worry about that right now. Like I said, I don't like women being taken advantage of. You seem to be a genuine and lovely person, and it upsets me to think a fellow man would behave so badly towards you. I'm also a huge believer in fairness, and I think this man needs to be taught a lesson. Within the law, of course.'

Ness could tell he was sincere, and relief washed over her. She'd been concerned about telling him of the rape – although it'd been a long time ago, she still felt a twinge of guilt when she talked about it. Jeremy had shown concern and understanding when she spoke, and some of the weight had lifted from her shoulders.

Ness looked at her watch; they'd been talking for over an hour. 'Everything you've said has helped me feel a lot better. Thank you so much for seeing me. I'm confident you'll solve things for me. But right now I should be going.' She began to stand up.

'Yes, well, wait a minute.' He lifted his telephone: 'June, have I got any more urgent appointments this morning? ... Very well, thank you.' He cleared his throat again and said to Ness. 'I'm about to go for a spot of coffee or tea and maybe a sandwich or a light lunch. I wondered, if you don't think it too forward of me, if you'd like to join me before you head back to Leytonstone. Perhaps we can discuss things further, but not on the clock, so to speak.' He smiled.

There was something about this man Ness really liked. She'd concentrated on her business for years, never thinking about any kind of social life. She went to meetings with clients which often included lunch or dinner and sometimes went to visit Florence and Anthony but as for anything else? There'd been nothing. She looked at his smiling face – a face willing her to say yes. The invitation to lunch was a bit sudden – they'd only just met – but she'd told him everything there was to know about her in that short time, and it appeared he wanted to spend more time with her.

And Ness realised that she too didn't want to say goodbye just yet.

***

They took a taxi to the Regent Palace Hotel. The girl on the door of the restaurant led them to a table for two in the corner. It was laid with a white linen tablecloth, cutlery and glasses for wine and water, and in the centre was an ashtray and a small vase containing a solitary flower. The girl gave them the lunch menu.

'Would you like a glass of wine?' Jeremy asked, but Ness declined. She didn't drink much, and certainly not in the middle of the day. 'We'll just have some water please,' he told the girl.

While she went for the water they studied the menus and Jeremy took out a silver cigarette case from his inside jacket pocket, 'Would you like one?' he asked Ness.

'No thank you, I don't smoke.'

'Do you mind if I do?'

Ness hesitated just long enough for him to guess that she'd rather he didn't.

'Dreadful habit anyway,' he said, and put the case away.

They ordered their food, Welsh rarebit for her and crab cakes for him. He poured the water and they said cheers, clinking their glasses.

'Here's to a job well done, I hope,' said Jeremy.

Ness smiled in return but couldn't think of an adequate response. They sat back and began to chat.

Jeremy told Ness that the hotel they were in, had quite a reputation during the war with the American, Canadian and probably English airmen spending time there, because it was considered a good place to meet young women.

'There's no doubt about it, the ladies were easily charmed by a man wearing wings.' He grinned and Ness smiled.

'Were you in the Air Force, then?'

'No, I wasn't – I was in the Navy. Just ordinary seaman Harvey. I was invalided out in July '44.'

'Did your ship go down?' Although the Navy was a very big service Ness couldn't help wondering which ship he'd been on and if there were any chance he might have come across Robert.

'Nothing like that. Actually I was involved in a fire in the docks at Portsmouth. The ship was in reserve waiting for orders, and there was a fire in one of the port warehouses. Me and two other chaps were sent to help fight it – we were holding onto a rope attached to the first man, who was aiming the high-pressure hose. All at once the main ceiling beam cracked and the lot collapsed, killing the first man and injuring me. The chap at the back got off scot-free. I had a bash on the head and a bad concussion. They sent me off to the hospital and then home. I'm not sure, to be honest, why I was never sent back – perhaps they thought I'd suffered a brain injury. But as you can see, I didn't. I wasn't going to complain, though – I was glad to be out of it. Still, I did my duty back here in London, fire watching and all that.'

'How did you become a private detective? Were you in the police?'

'I'd worked for another detective agency before the war; I'd started when I was sixteen and learnt the ropes with them. I never wanted to be in the police. I'd already decided to start up my own business before the war, so when I was invalided out with concussion, I didn't hesitate to set up here. Business was pretty slow to begin with, but since the war's finished it's really picked up. So much so that now I employ three other men and a lady to work for me, as well as June.'

'It all sounds very exciting.'

'You've done well too, it seems. Tell me about Eunice & Co. How did you choose the name?'

Ness gave him a brief run-down of her business, and told him everyone had a hand in what name she should use. She'd wanted to call it Grangers but everyone else thought it should be her name and that, even though she hated the name Eunice, it was a bit different and more memorable, so that's what she'd settled on.

'I think it was a very good choice,' he said.

Ness carried on to tell him about Robert's sister Rose being killed in June '44 and how after the funeral, she'd grown closer to Robert's family.

'I'm impressed with the way you struggled on through the war managing as best you could. How awful for the Grangers to lose both son *and* daughter, and *you* have lost Robert and a good friend in Rose. It's all been very difficult and I can't imagine how you have dealt with the paternity thing, not being 100 per cent sure who the father was. Such an awful thing to have happened to you.'

'That's kind of you to say. Time has passed on now, I have a lot to be grateful for...what about you? Are you on your own?' Ness asked with caution.

'Yes, I am. I was married before the war. But my wife was killed during the Blitz, and we didn't have any children.' He clearly didn't want to go into detail.

'I'm so sorry. The war was terrible – so many young people killed. And not just service people, thousands of civilians too.'

'Grace was just twenty-five,' he said.

'The same age as Rose.' said Ness.

When their food arrived they ate without too much talking. General chat about London and what was on at the theatre these days, what kind of music they liked and what books they'd read.

They discovered they had a few things in common – reading and walking in particular, although Ness admitted she hardly ever went walking these days. She was too busy with work, and then when the weekends came it was swimming or football or some other Ray activity. But during the summer they often caught the bus or the train over to Hackney Marshes. And she'd caught the train down to Southend a couple of times, but wasn't that keen on the place.

They ordered tea and sat quietly for a moment. Then, when Ness was just about to mention the time Jeremy looked at his watch and said, 'Gosh, I need to move, or my two o'clock appointment will be waiting for me. Come on, I'll get a taxi and drop you off at the station.'

'There's no need. I'm going to walk round to the London showroom in Great Marlborough Street – remember, I told you I go there a couple of times a week. It's not far from here.'

'Are you sure you'll be all right?'

'Of course, I'll be fine – I do it all the time.'

'Well, I'd better get a cab back now or I'm going to be late!'

As they parted company Jeremy said, 'I very much enjoyed your company today, Mrs Proctor, and I'll be at the café on Thursday. If you think of anything important in the meantime, please ring me up at the office, but remember I'll be phoning you on Wednesday evening, in any event.'

Ness shook his hand and said goodbye. His hand was warm and confident. She liked it, and they held on to each other for a moment longer than necessary. She was confident he would sort Alf out. She was also certain she'd see him again, and not just on Thursday.

Fify-two

Monday 21st September 1953, Afternoon

Jeremy made some initial enquiries about Alfred Taylor. He sent one of his men to Somerset House to check the births, deaths and marriages, and asked for his report to be on his desk by Tuesday evening. That should give him enough time; it was a bit late to expect results today.

At the end of the day he tidied up his office, as he always did. Emptied the ashtray – and decided there and then he'd give up smoking. He'd never liked it as a habit, and often found these days that the tail was wagging the dog – he was always wanting a cigarette and always waiting for an appropriate moment to give it up. Also, he thought, Mrs Proctor – Eunice – didn't like it, and that bothered him.

Jeremy couldn't get her out of his mind. He took a walk down Chancery Lane to the Temple and then to the river, where he walked along the embankment before catching the tube back to Harrow, where he lived in a rather smart flat in an Art Deco building. He'd shared the flat with his wife and since her death he'd had no interest in moving out. In fact he had no interest in anything much at all except work. He had built up his business by determination and hard work. June thought he overdid it. He knew she was fond of him, and she had on several occasions attempted to flirt with him, but he wasn't interested. He'd not bothered at all about being in a serious relationship. He didn't feel the need of it – Grace had been a wonderful wife, and he couldn't imagine sharing his life with any other woman. Until now. Eunice had lit the blue touch paper.

He opened his front door and realised for the first time in ages what a lonely existence he was leading. The place was a mausoleum, gravely quiet, except for the clock which chimed seven times, the last chime echoing slightly as it diminished. Today's newspaper was sitting on the coffee table alongside the book he was reading. Nothing had changed from this morning. But why would it? Nobody had been in the place. He employed a cleaning lady, but she'd not been today and even when she did come in she left everything exactly as she found it. The flat was verging on clinical. He had an urge to mess it up – he threw his briefcase onto the sofa and kicked his shoes off, leaving them on the rug, spread out like a couple of shot birds. He spun around to see what else he could do – lob the cushions onto the floor maybe? He was about to seize one when his eyes went to the walnut sideboard, where there was a photograph of him and Grace. The sight of it stopped his antics and his mood changed abruptly. The sensible Jeremy was back.

They had married in the church in Grace's village in Kent. It had been a small wedding, but he'd worn tails and she a long, lacy wedding dress. Her bouquet had been a large spray of roses and there had been two bridesmaids. It had been a lovely day. She'd looked beautiful, and they'd both been so happy. Jeremy felt ashamed that he'd not stayed in touch with her parents or any of her friends since her death. It wasn't like him – but he knew if he kept away from the life they'd had then he could stay close to her. Almost hold himself in stasis. He spoke to her all the time as though she were still in the flat.

He went into the bedroom and looked at the bed they'd shared. It was time to move on. It had been over ten years, but it felt like yesterday. *How clichéd,* he thought. It was ridiculous – he'd been living in the past, like a man obsessed with his own grief. He'd never get over losing Grace – but today at last the clouds, it seemed, were clearing.

Eunice had taken him by surprise. He'd fallen for her. He couldn't stop smiling when he thought about her. He stood in the bedroom and spoke aloud, 'I've met somebody, Grace – she's a little like you, but then on the other hand nothing like you. She has an accent from the North and I love it. I want her to keep on talking when I'm with her, and after I left her I could still hear her voice in my head. I only saw her for the first time today, which is mad, but honestly ... there was an immediate connection. I've met a lot of women over the last few years, even had a little dalliance, as you know, but I wasn't interested in any of them. I think you'd approve of her. I know you'd be glad that after all these years the wind has begun blowing again in the doldrums, and I'm feeling happier than I have for ages. I hope she feels the same way. It's been such a long time that I've forgotten how to flirt. I still love you and I'll never forget you – but it's time. Fingers crossed she feels the same.'

He took off his suit and hung it on the valet in the corner. He put his shirt into the laundry basket next to it, then put on corduroy trousers and a polo neck sweater before going into the kitchen to prepare some sardines on toast and a few tomatoes. While he ate he made up his mind to change things in the flat at the weekend. He would begin by buying a new bed, just in case ...

In the meantime, he'd get on with finding out about Alfred Taylor. He absolutely *hated* the fellow.

Fifty-three

Thursday 24th September 1953

On Thursday Ness woke with a headache. She didn't even feel like getting out of bed. The prospect of the morning terrified her.

She could hear Ray messing about in his room. She needed to be sensible for him and sort out this Alf business before Ray found out anything. He was a smart kid and she hated keeping things from him. She'd always been open about Robert being his father. But now she was afraid Alf would mess this up – claim he was the father, tell everyone she was living a lie ...

'Mum!' Ray shouted, 'Is it time to get up? My clock's stopped.' Ness had bought him an alarm clock last Christmas, but he was always forgetting to wind it up.

She went into his room. 'You could've come to my room instead of shouting. Honestly, did you think I'd shout back?'

Ray ducked back under his covers. 'Sorry.'

'It's seven o'clock. Your body must have told you to wake up, so you're not late – and yes, it *is* time to get up.'

Ness was a good mother, but there had been many times when she'd wished she could share the responsibility. When she'd been living in Ridley with her mother, things had been a little easier, and Tommy and George had been a good male influence in Ray's life.

Ness stood staring at the open wardrobe. She wanted to impress Jeremy, and she thought she might call him by his Christian name today and invite him to call her Ness; last time they'd been formal. And then, what might she wear to impress Jeremy but not encourage Alf? She decided on a plain dark blue wool skirt with a white blouse and cardigan. And the camel clutch coat she'd worn last time.

She sat in the kitchen with Ray as he ate his breakfast.

'Aren't you having anything today?' he asked.

'I'm not hungry. I'll have something later.'

'Are you going to the workshop today?'

'Yes ... I'll probably go later on this morning.'

'Are you all right, Mum? You seem very quiet today.'

It was hard for Ness not to tell Ray what was happening. She had to remind herself that he was still only ten. She often thought that over the years she'd told him too much. But being on her own it was hard not to. They would talk about current affairs, discuss books and talk about a great many things that most parents would discuss between themselves and keep from their children. She never burdened Ray with financial problems, though, or told him how lonely she was at times, but she did allow him to have a say in any decisions which affected them both. This time, however, she was not going to say a word about Alf or the private investigator, although she imagined that Ray would be fascinated by Jeremy.

'Yes, I'm fine. Come here and give me a big hug and a kiss.' She opened her arms wide, pursed her lips and moved towards Ray.

'No you don't!' He skirted under one of her arms and ran out into the hall laughing. She laughed too, and her mood lifted. He was about to leave when he came back to give Ness a quick kiss.

'Bye, Mum. See you later.' He smiled, and Ness saw Robert in his face and especially his eyes.

'Have a good day and work hard. It'll pay off in the end, you'll see.'

She went back into the kitchen and sat down. It was only a quarter to nine – over two hours before the café. She cleared away the breakfast things, tidied the sitting room, rearranged the books in the bookcase, looked through the magazines in the rack ... back in the kitchen she looked at the clock; nine-fifteen. This was unbearable. She didn't feel like starting any sewing or reading a book or anything at all. She began to think about what might happen this morning and decided to get a pencil and make a few notes. Thinking about them took her out of herself, and after much pencil-chewing and many crossings-out she ended up with:

1. Don't offer any information.

2. Don't show nervousness.

3. Don't let him get to you.

4. Find out about him.

5. Don't look at Jeremy.

6. Don't talk about Ray.

They were ridiculous, she thought, but she felt calmer for writing the list and it had passed a bit of time. It was ten-forty. Ness stuffed the note into her handbag and got ready to leave. Jeremy had called her the day before and told her he'd found some information about Alf. He wasn't going to share it with her yet, because he thought that the less she knew at this point the better. He'd tell her everything after the meeting. It was important for her to stay calm. If, or more likely when, Alf talked about money she was to go along with it and suggest a meeting place – but not the café; it was too open. Her office at the workshop in Leytonstone. And to make the appointment for 6pm on Tuesday, after all the staff had gone home. Jeremy had a foolproof plan and she wasn't to worry. He would fill her in with everything after she'd met Alf. He said he'd dealt with a lot of these blackmail cases and he knew exactly how to handle it. She only had to meet Alf, stay calm and not let him suspect that she'd told anyone what was happening.

The situation didn't exactly fill Ness with confidence, but she trusted Jeremy enough to do as he said. She was half-curious and half-terrified of what he might have found out. He'd only had a couple of days to dig about. And he'd been businesslike on the telephone, which was disappointing. She'd hoped for a little more.

The morning was autumnal; the early morning mist had cleared and the sun, though weak, felt warm. Any other day Ness would have enjoyed walking around the neighbourhood, to work or to the shops, but today there was an edge to her. She took her time, looking around as she passed side roads and alleyways – she'd been cautious of alleyways ever since that day. She never walked down them if she could avoid it.

She rounded the corner of Church Lane and walked past a row of shops towards the station. She looked at her watch; five past eleven. She'd intended to be late, and wasn't sure if this was late enough. It had taken her ages to decide whether she should try and get there before Alf and Jeremy, sitting waiting for them, or to get there a bit later so that she could walk in and find them. Anyhow, she was there now. She took a deep breath and walked through the café door. A quick glance around told her Alf wasn't there yet – and she couldn't see Jeremy, either. She went to the counter and ordered a cup of tea. She tried hard to act naturally, as though waiting for a potential blackmailer was the most common thing to be happening. Where was Jeremy? A frisson of panic slithered up her backbone – perhaps he'd decided not to come, maybe her case wasn't for him after all. She took her tea and looked around for somewhere to sit. The table over by the window where she and Alf had sat last time was available, so she sat there. It gave her a clear view of the whole place. Then the door opened and in came Alf. And at the same time she noticed Jeremy sitting in the corner, reading a newspaper and drinking a cup of something. He didn't look up. She wished he would, if only to give her reassuring eye contact, but he kept his head down obviously engrossed in the paper and making notes at the same time. Alf saw her and smiled at her. It turned her stomach. She had the feeling he'd been waiting around the corner watching for her to arrive and then followed her in after what he'd thought was an appropriate time interval.

'You got yourself something, then?' he asked.

'Yes.' Ness was determined not to be too chatty.

'Right, well I'll get a cuppa, then. Do you want a bun?'

'No.' She sounded rude but she didn't care. She wanted this to be over as soon as possible.

After he'd collected his cup he sat down opposite her like last time.

'I enjoyed watching your – or should I say *our*? – boy playing football last Saturday. He's a natural, isn't he? Must get it from me.'

Ness wanted to flee, but she knew that wouldn't be the right thing to do. She wanted to deny his parentage but thought that might lead to an argument. And she wanted to punch him.

She chose her words with care. 'You shouldn't have come. He's my boy. I'm all he has, and that's how it'll stay.'

'Fighting talk. Look Eunice, I'm a fair man. I don't want any trouble – but you know, times are a bit hard for me. I didn't do too well after the war. Our house was hit and my mother was in it. We lost everything and although she survived she was never the same again. I tried to care for her, but in the end she passed away and left me with nothing.'

It was a proper sob story, thought Ness, and she didn't believe a word of it. 'What do you want from me?'

'I thought you might want to help me out. For old time's sake, like ... and for the boy.'

'I'm sorry, Alf, I don't know what you mean.'

'Well, it's obvious to me that the boy's mine. According to your mother, though, you've told everyone it was that Robert chap that got you in the family way. Your so called *husband*.' He said it in a sarcastic voice. 'All nice and cosy like, happy little family. But I know better. I know what happened, and you put yourself about a bit. I reckon the fashion world would like to know what kind of woman you really are.' He leant in close to her, and she was reminded of that awful night. She wanted to recoil, but behind his back she could see Jeremy, who glanced up at her with a reassuring smile. So she didn't react. She hadn't realised what a good actress she could be. Alf's face screwed up as he spoke the words in a hushed and menacing voice, 'You're a whore, you are – a *whore* – and you know what the world thinks about *them*, don't you?'

'I'm asking you again, Alf, what do you want?'

He leant back in his chair and nonchalantly said, 'A little sweetener would go down well.'

'You mean blackmail?'

'Well, I wouldn't call it that. Just something to help me on my way. I don't want to rock the boat and mess up your life, but I need a bit of encouragement to stay away.'

'How much?'

'Let's say a nice round ton for starters, shall we?'

'A ton?'

'A hundred to you. But if you take too long to decide I'll be asking for a bit more.'

Ness didn't want to be too quick to agree, so she said, 'I'll need a couple of days, because I'll have to get it from my bank and they won't let me have it till Monday.'

Alf grabbed her arm, the way he'd done before, and pinned it onto the table. 'Listen to me, little lady,' he spoke through his teeth, 'don't you mess me around. I'm not giving you any time at all. I know you've got the money, I've done my homework. I want you to draw it from the bank and meet me here again *tomorrow*. Okay?'

Ness found she wasn't frightened of him any more. He was a pathetic example of a man. She eased her arm out his grip and said slowly and carefully, 'I'll get your money, Alf, but not tomorrow. You'll have to wait until next Tuesday. And you'll have to come to my office for it. After work, so it'll be private. If you've done your homework you'll know where that is.'

'Hmmm ... okay then, nice and cosy in your office. But don't get any ideas about calling the police or anything. That would be stupid, now, wouldn't it? You don't want all your dirty washing aired in public, now, do you?'

Ness smiled at him. 'No more threats, Alf. I'll pay you this one and only time. I'll see you next week. Come at six in the evening, after the staff have left. No earlier. And if you want your money, don't get any ideas about following me or coming near my house or near me before Tuesday evening. And you can stay away from my son too.' She stood up and stalked out of the café without looking back. Not even a glance towards Jeremy.

As she walked home her whole body shook, but she kept up a steady pace and didn't look back once. Yet she had to wipe away tears of anger and relief that she'd got through it. She hated Alf with a hate she had not realised was within her capabilities.

***

Ness sat in her kitchen resting her head on her folded arms on the table. It was the way she'd been told to sit in primary school, years ago, for a rest after lunch. 'No talking! Shut your eyes and think of nice things,' the teacher had said. Now it worked to a point, but she couldn't think of many nice things to think about.

The doorbell made her jump. Her heart thudded and she sat still until she heard a knock on the door, and then his voice, 'Mrs Proctor, it's only me.' Jeremy. She must tell him to call her Ness. She'd been calling him Jeremy in her head since the last time she'd seen him.

She welcomed him into the hall and suggested they sit in the front room.

'Are you all right?' he asked as they walked through.

'To be honest, it was awful and I'm a bit shaken up, but I'll get over it. I never realised quite how nasty he was, although I had a good idea. He didn't follow you here, did he?'

'No, I made sure of that. You were very brave. I couldn't hear everything you said but I did manage to pick up some of it. You looked strong when he confronted you. I wanted to intervene when I saw him grab your arm but you dealt with it brilliantly. I'm assuming you managed to talk him into coming to meet you at your office?'

'He's coming next Tuesday at six. He wanted tomorrow but I said no. Would you like some coffee or tea, by the way?'

'No thanks, I've drunk a bucketful of tea in that café. I don't need anything. Let's get down to business.'

He pulled out his notebook. It all seemed very surreal to Ness, as though she was watching a detective in a film – as though she was in a film, in fact.

'I've discovered that Alfred James Taylor was born on 10th September 1916, which makes him thirty-seven last week. Maybe that's why he's decided to visit. He'll be wanting to set himself up before he's forty.'

Ness wasn't sure if this was a joke or not, but she didn't react. Jeremy carried on, 'His ship *did* go down in the Med, but he survived. I'm not sure why his name was on the casualty list, but during the war there was a lot of confusion. I've not had enough time to find out everything about him yet, but I do know that after the war he became involved in some petty criminal activities. Theft, conman tricks, and he mixed with the general low life in London. Still lived with his mother in Southall, but she passed away in '47. I think he went completely off the rails then—'

'He told me his mother had died,' said Ness, 'but not when. He made it sound like a really sad story.'

'Yes, well, I think he'd like everyone to feel sorry for him. I imagine he's one of those people who believes the world owes him everything.'

'He's despicable.'

'Yes, well now, let's carry on,' Jeremy found his place in his notes. 'He married in '48 but they're not together now. He went to prison for two years in '51, and he's only just come out. I haven't had time to visit his wife yet, but I intend to go tomorrow. I might be able to find out more.'

'Can I come with you?' asked Ness.

'Certainly not. These things have to be handled carefully. I will take my lady detective with me though. She only works part time, but I've found it handy for a woman to be involved in the occasional job, and this one definitely falls into that category.'

'Where's Alf living at the moment, and is he working, do you know?'

'He's in Tottenham, working in the paper factory there, in the warehouse. I think the prison got him the job, but most men of his calibre don't hang around long in one place. Anyway, don't worry, I have a feeling we'll deal with him on Tuesday and you won't see him again.'

Ness tried not to feel anxious. Jeremy seemed to know what he was doing; she was impressed by how much information he'd gained about Alf in just a couple of days. 'What am I going to do on Tuesday? I could get the money, but—'

'Well, Mrs Proctor—'

'Please don't call me that. I'd much rather you called me Ness.'

He paused for a second, smiled and said, 'I thought your name was Eunice?'

'It is, but everyone calls me Ness.'

He gave an awkward laugh, 'Ness, then, and you can call me Jeremy. We *are* getting on well, aren't we?' His voice was kind and Ness felt comforted – but then, 'Sorry,' he said, 'that was a stupid thing to say.'

In a businesslike tone he went on to explain to her how they'd catch Alf in the act of blackmail next week. It all sounded very cloak and dagger, and Ness had to stop herself from laughing aloud. The scenario he painted she thought preposterous, but she trusted him. He told her he'd done this many times before, and often with blackmailers demanding much higher ransoms involving kidnapping and other heinous crimes, far greater than Alf was capable of – he was just a minnow. She had no need to worry about anything. By Wednesday next week it'd all be over and she wouldn't see Alf for dust.

'I would like you to come to my office on Monday so that you can meet Liz – she's my right-hand woman, the detective I just mentioned. We'll talk you through everything, and rehearse what you have to do, and say to Alf.

'Well, that's everything, then?' Ness was hoping he would stay for lunch or ask to go for a walk or something.

He must have read her thoughts, because he leant forward and spoke gently. 'Ness, I would like nothing better than to take you to lunch or a show or something over the weekend. You've made quite an impression on me but ... I'm a professional and I think, at least until after next Tuesday evening, we should keep things strictly on that level. I shouldn't have been so forward last Monday, but I couldn't help myself.' He smiled and looked Ness directly in the eye.

Ness was disappointed but also impressed. He was saying the right things, and she appreciated the sentiment. She could wait another week.

'I understand completely. Let's get this business out of the way first.'

Fifty-four

Monday 28th September 1953

Once again Ness found herself outside the office door of King's Investigation Bureau. This time she was more confident and looking forward to seeing Jeremy again. Last Thursday they'd had a long chat over their coffee, and Ness had enjoyed his company immensely.

On Friday night she'd telephoned Eileen to bring her up to date with what was happening, and Eileen had detected a note of excitement in Ness's voice when she spoke about Jeremy.

'Oh it's Jeremy already is it?' with a note of gentle sarcasm. 'Don't lose your head, now.'

Ness assured her she wouldn't, but as she readied herself on Monday morning she took a lot more care than she might have done previously. She wore a suit she'd made earlier that year in the spring, dark blue with a peplum jacket, the waist nipped in. The pencil skirt accentuated her figure. The whole outfit was good to wear, and she looked well in it. She wasn't a fan of hats, even though people normally wore one to go out, so although she'd worn them in Ridley, she didn't bother with one now.

At King's reception this time another woman was waiting. She smiled at Ness and walked towards her, greeting her with a handshake.

'Hello, Mrs Proctor, I'm Liz, and the guv'nor has asked me to help him with your problem. He's ready for us now, so we're going to go in and see what's what.'

Ness liked Liz immediately. She came across as a strong woman. She wore grey trousers and a loose-fitting dark green jacket with three-quarter-length sleeves. Ness didn't imagine she was too bothered about keeping up with the latest fashions. Her hair was cut short like Audrey Hepburn in *Roman Holiday* – Ness had seen the film with Ray. The style would be practical for Liz in her line of work. Yet she still looked feminine. Ness wondered if she ever had to wear wigs and disguises. She couldn't wait to know more about Jeremy's work.

'He's waiting for you,' said June, and Liz led the way into the office.

Jeremy gave them a big smile. Ness felt it was aimed at her; he was being discreet but still signalling that he liked her.

'First of all, Ness, I can report to you that I saw Taylor's wife yesterday. She's not a happy woman at all. It seems he was a pretty terrible husband. He wasn't too bad at first – he'd told her he was getting over the death of his mother and it had hit him hard, and that she – his wife, that is – was the best thing that had happened to him in ages. He wanted to settle down and have a family of his own. But even though they tried for a few years nothing happened.'

Jeremy sipped some water. 'At that point they were rubbing along all right, but his wife made him go for a test. She was desperate for a baby. Taylor told her he'd had mumps as a child, so what she wanted to make sure of was that it was him and not her who had the problem. I don't know the details about how they do these things, but the fact was, the test proved ... how can I put this? He doesn't have enough ammunition ... to have children.'

'What? Are you *sure?*' asked Ness.

'Absolutely,' said Liz. 'Which is really good news for you, isn't it?'

Ness didn't have to think about it for long. Now she could be certain that Ray was Robert's son. 'That's the best news I could ever have heard,' she said, and felt the tears pricking her eyes. She opened her handbag and fished out a handkerchief.

'Now then, Mrs Proctor. Do you need to take a moment?' asked Jeremy.

Ness said she was fine.

'I don't want you to be at all worried,' Jeremy continued, 'about the procedure for Tuesday. Liz and I have done this several times, with much bigger amounts of money involved and with nastier, more dangerous, people. What we need to do is get Taylor to admit what he's doing and to also admit to other crimes he might have committed. That way, we'll be able to confront him and hopefully scare him off for good. He won't know that we've discovered that he can't have children, so that's a trump card for us. If he tries to say that Ray's his son, then you can categorically say he is not. As for the sexual assault, he only has his word against yours. If you're not scared of him, we can take the wind right out of his sails. Ray is not his son, and he's got no evidence against you. You have never written to him or had any contact with him for over ten years until last week. He's flying after something he can't possibly achieve.'

The three sat in the office for another two hours going over questions that Ness had prepared for them. Jeremy and Liz told her exactly the way she should behave when she confronted Alf in her office. They would both be there, too, in the next room.

Liz left, and Jeremy asked Ness to wait in his office for a moment longer. She wondered if he was going to go back on his 'professional' promise, but he didn't make any attempt to come closer to her. 'I just wanted to mention that you look wonderful today. But I think you should wear something plain and simple for your meeting with Taylor.'

Ness didn't know what to make of this last remark. But in any case, she hadn't planned to dress up for Alf.

'I've been in this game a long time,' Jeremy continued, 'that's all, and I know how men think. I'll be outside the door when he's with you, so you won't have to worry about anything. If he tries anything physical I'll intervene. I don't trust him at all.' Jeremy punched the air.

'Thank you, Sir Galahad,' Ness laughed. 'I'll be ready and dressed in the most boring outfit I can muster. Roll on tomorrow!'

Fifty-five

Tuesday 29th September 1953

Ness told Ray she'd be out later than usual, and to get his own tea; a sandwich or something. She wasn't sure what time she'd get back, but hoped it'd be before eight.

She dressed in what she thought would be suitable clothing for the encounter with Alf. She picked a plain wool skirt and an old blouse with an open neck and two breast pockets. The pockets made her laugh as much as the dated style. *How ironic*, she thought. She teamed the whole thing with a cardigan of a dubious green colour. It didn't suit her at all, but as her mother had knitted it she'd kept it.

The night before, she had spoken to Eileen for the third evening in a row, keeping her up to date with the plans. She even rehearsed what she was to say to Alf.

But Eileen didn't help much; she thought it was all a bit over the top and dramatic. 'It's like a bloomin' film, Ness – honestly, you'll be able to write a book about it afterwards. Just you watch out that Jeremy isn't after one thing.'

Ness smarted at that. She knew he wasn't that kind of man. She said as much to Eileen, and told her how helpful he'd been, and the bit about him wanting to keep things on a professional level for the time being. Eileen said she wasn't convinced – she was only looking out for her friend. 'Be careful and good luck,' she said.

Now, on Tuesday evening, after all her staff had left the office, Ness sat waiting in her office. She had gone over and over everything with Jeremy and Liz.

There was a knock on her door and Ness jumped, her heart thumping like mad.

'It's only us,' came Jeremy's voice, followed by his head round the door then the rest of him.

He was wearing a khaki warehouse coat and a flat cap and looked ridiculous in them. He was carrying what looked like a large canvas tool bag. It completely threw Ness and she laughed aloud at the sight.

'You like my disguise, then?

'I thought you didn't do disguise,' said Ness.

'I do make exceptions, and this is one of them. I don't want to look too obvious outside the building.

Liz was wearing a pair of high-waisted three-quarter length trousers and a polo-neck sweater. She looked fashionable, but at the same time it was practical wear for someone who might have to be active.

'We haven't got time to waste. Liz and I have already done a recce of the outside, I just need to check out the workshop and the back door. He looked at the door: 'This goes to the main work area, yes?'

'Yes,' said Ness.

'Is there another door that leads into there?'

'If you go back out of the door you've come in through, then turn left in the corridor, there's a door facing you at the end.'

'Nothing else?'

'No. The main warehouse door's locked. And the back door's locked.'

'Right. So Taylor will have to come in through the front door, which you'll have left unlocked. Is the door at the end of the corridor locked?'

'Yes.'

He began to pace around: 'Give me the key, please. Liz'll wait behind that door, and once he's in here she'll slip back through it and wait outside the reception door so she can hear everything. I'll stay behind that door.' He indicated the one leading directly from the reception.

'It sounds as though you know what you're doing.'

'Yes. We do this sort of thing all the time.'

Ness wondered how many times he'd said that to her now.

'Right, Ness, you know what you have to do, yes?' asked Jeremy.

She nodded.

'Here's the tape recorder.' He pulled it out of his bag.

He and Liz had been all through this with Ness the day before, so she knew how to work it – but now it was real she felt a panic run through her ...

'It'll fit under your desk, and he won't be able to see it because of the modesty panel.'

'I wish we'd done a run through here, in my office, not just in yours,' Ness said.

'Just pretend it is my office. You practised it there and you did well. We'll tape the microphone and lead under the top of the desk so he won't see those, either. Now then, remember, it only records for about fifteen minutes, but I'm hoping it'll all be over in five.'

'What if it doesn't work? What if I panic?' asked Ness.

'I'll be right outside door that door,' he pointed to the door from the office to the workshop, 'and Liz outside the other one, and we'll be recording too, with our Dictaphones. One of us will get him. Now then, are you ready?' He squeezed her hand in encouragement.

'Yes, I think so.' Ness looked at her watch. 'It's five-thirty. He might be early.'

'I'll get into position. Liz, into the workshop and stay behind the door. Once he's in here, you can move forward so you're outside this door. I should be back by then anyway. I'll go out through the back door now – and then, when I see Taylor approaching, I'll come back in the same way.'

The next half hour dragged then at just gone six Ness heard the front door open. She prayed that Liz and Jeremy were in position, and pressed the recorder buttons. Her fingers were damp and shaking – but the reels began to turn. She was aware of the sound, but only slightly, and prayed that Alf wouldn't hear it. She decided to stand up to face him as he came in the door.

'Well, nice little setup you've got here. Of course I've seen it before, did a little walk around outside at lunchtime, saw a few people coming and going, but they've all gone now, right? Wanna show me around inside?'

'No I don't, actually.'

'Where does this door lead to, then?' He made to open the door to the workshop.

'It's just the workshop, but nobody's there now.'

He ignored her and walking across, opened the door and looked through. He took a step or two across the threshold and had a good look around. Ness was petrified and then equally worried, as there appeared to be no sign of Jeremy. She knew Liz couldn't be seen as she was around the corner – but where was Jeremy?

'Sensible girl. Just the two of us. How cosy.' He walked towards her.

'Keep your distance, Alf. Stay that side of the desk, please.' She opened the drawer of her desk and took out an envelope full of £10 notes. Jeremy had told her that it was important for her to have the money.

'Nice one. You've come up trumps indeed.' He put his hand out to take it.

Ness put it back in the drawer. 'Wait. How can I be sure you won't come after me again? How can I be sure that you won't ask me for more money?'

'Well, I am partial to a little blackmail, that's for sure, but ...'

'You mean I'm not the first person you've done this to?'

'It can be quite lucrative. You know what I mean? Plenty of blokes in London breaking the law in a variety of hotels and clubs.'

Ness was disgusted. 'I don't believe you. You're not a ...?' Ness couldn't say it.

'A queer? Well, I do dabble. Not fussy, me, and you'd be surprised what a man will pay to save his reputation and keep it from his wife.'

'And what does your wife think about all that?'

'She only found out because I was charged for it. I got a conditional discharge for that, though. But I did do a bit of time for petty theft. I'm quite the man, I am.'

'I wonder what your wife would think about our encounter?'

'What, you mean the fact that I had my wicked way with you back in '42?'

'Like I said before, it was *rape,* Alf.' Ness could feel her face going red. Instead of gaining confidence as the encounter went on, she was getting more anxious.

'If you say so. I suppose I did get a bit carried away. I'd just been let down by another woman, and you were letting me down too.' He gave a fake sigh, 'but looks like I've got a nice son for my trouble. I reckon he'll grow quite fond of me once he gets to know me.'

Ness wanted to speak again, to shout at him, he was despicable, but she found her mouth was dry and the words were stuck in her throat as though she'd been gagged.

'Now then, let's cut all the friendly chat here. Gimme the bloody money or I'll fucking well have you again!' He lunged towards Ness and as he did so both doors to the reception area flew open. Jeremy and Liz appeared.

'What the f...?' Jeremy grabbed Alf and pushed him against the wall below the front windows. He held him fast, with his arm across his neck.

'Shut up with the prattle now, will you? We've heard enough.'

'Easy, mate. I don't want no trouble. I don't know what this lady's told you but I just came to have a little chat. Who are you, anyway? You're not the cops, are you? D'you work in the warehouse?'

Jeremy was still wearing the khaki coat. He released his hold on Alf, then swivelled him around and whipped an arm up behind his back. Alf knew he couldn't go anywhere. And Liz was standing guard at the exit door, with her arms folded, and a nasty-looking leather cosh sticking out under them.

'Come on, Ness, what's all this about? We're friends, ain't we?' Alf's wheedle hung in the air.

Jeremy spoke. 'Done this before, have you? Threatened a few men unfortunate enough to get involved with you? I think you've been a bit of conman, too, haven't you? You've tried to extort money from Mrs Proctor in the most *vile* of ways. We've witnessed you trying to frighten her into paying you money so that you won't bother her again – but I know men like you, and you have every intention of coming back.'

'I just want to get to know my boy, that's all.'

'Ah, but he's not *your* boy, is he?'

'You don't know that. I could prove it – they can do blood tests, you know.'

'What I do know is that you *can't* have any children. You're sterile, Taylor, and I have a statement from your wife to prove that. So that's the end of that little game, and if you don't want to go back to prison you'll leave here and never come anywhere near Mrs Proctor, this place, or the boy ever again.'

The shock on Alf's face was palpable. He turned white and sagged at the knees. Jeremy released him, moved around behind the desk, opened the drawer and took out the tape recorder, then began to play the recording.

They didn't even get to the end before Alf spoke. 'It's okay. I get it. You can shut that thing off. I get what you're after. Will you let me out of here now?'

'Not before you've signed this agreement and a copy. It says that you'll not come anywhere near my client ever again. You'll never ask her for money, nor make any attempt to contact her son. Sign it, and I'll wipe the recording.'

Alf leant on the desk, gave a cursory glance at the words and signed both sheets. Jeremy signed it too, and Liz witnessed both signatures.

'One for you and one for me.' Jeremy handed Alf his copy, 'Take this with you, you can leave right now. I'll show you out.'

He walked Alf out of the office and through the front door.

Ness burst into tears.

Liz made her sit down. 'It's okay – it's over. You did so well, not many women would have stood up to that man like you did. I think you need a strong cup of tea now. Is there anywhere I can make one?'

Jeremy came back into the room as she spoke. 'Tea's a waste of time, Liz. I'll get this excellent disguise off, and we'll take Ness to that little pub around the corner for a debrief.'

Fifty-six

Tuesday 29th September 1953, Evening

The three of them spoke in depth about how successful it had been and they discussed a few other similar cases that King's had solved in the same way.

'Although,' said Jeremy, 'we make an agreement with the blackmailer – that if he desists from his activities the tape will be destroyed – it isn't, of course. As you can't trust a man of that kind, you don't worry too much about keeping your own word.'

Ness was a little shocked by this admission, but could understand why he would take this attitude. She had a lot to learn.

At eight o'clock Ness said she had to get back home. Jeremy offered to walk her there, and told Liz he'd see her in the office in the morning as he had another job for her.

'It's an insurance claim a man's making against his firm. He was injured in an accident at work, and now he's saying that he's disabled and can't walk. Liz will be able to find out if he's telling the truth. Often, we stake out a subject's house only to find them running around the streets like an athlete.'

Ness was intrigued, but Jeremy stood up and guided her out of the pub before she could ask any more questions.

***

When the two of them got back to Ness's house, Ray was asleep. Ness set about making tea for herself and Jeremy. He sat in the kitchen and watched her as she boiled the kettle, warmed the pot, got the cups and saucers, filled the milk jug, and arranged everything on a tray.

'Haven't you seen anyone make a cup of tea before?'

'Not in the way you do. It's quite a performance – I can't take my eyes off you.'

'I noticed that. Well, here you go – make yourself useful and carry the tray into the living room. Are you hungry? I could make a sandwich if you like. It's been such a day, I haven't even thought about food.'

'I did have lunch, but a sandwich would be most welcome. I don't want you to go to any trouble, though.'

'It'll take me five minutes, honestly. Cheese and homemade chutney, okay?'

'My favourite,' he said, and took the tray.

Sitting at the dining table, a good distance apart, they chatted about the weather, Ray's schoolwork, what foods they liked and what card games they knew, neither of them wanting to make the first move.

Then Jeremy stood up and began to pace the room, fidgeting with the waistband on his trousers and his face twitching a little. Ness wondered what he was going to say.

She was about to ask him if he was all right, when he blurted out: 'Do you think we could move over to the sofa? It might be a little more comfortable.'

'Yes we can, as long as you don't think that too unprofessional,' she smiled.

Even though Ness had joked about it, when she sat down beside Jeremy, she just couldn't relax; she was a bit stiff and felt a little awkward.

But then he held her hand and spoke: 'I absolutely know how hard this is for you, and I won't be rushing you in any way. You're the best thing that's come into my life for a very long time, and I don't want to ruin things before we're even over the first hurdle. I like you very much indeed, and I hope you feel the same.' He stopped for a moment as though working out his next move. His mouth twitched, then he continued, 'I'm completely out of touch with the sort of things one should say or do when courting, so you'll have to forgive me. I'm extremely nervous.'

'Me too,' said Ness.

He squeezed her hand gently, then bent forward and kissed her gently on the cheek. Ness put her free hand on his cheek and kissed him on the lips. There was an instant connection, and as they kissed again her body melted.

After a moment she pulled away. 'I like you very much, too. But as you said, let's take it slowly, shall we? It's getting late now, and I must call Eileen, I promised her I'd let her know how things went today and she'll be anxious, waiting to hear what happened.'

They went out to the hall 'Thank you for the tea and sandwich,' he said. From now on I'd like to see as much of you as possible. If that suits you.'

'It does suit me. It suits me very well,' said Ness. She pulled him towards her and kissed him with a mixture of relief, excitement and anticipation.

The End

About the author

Ninette Hartley has an MA in creative writing, and has been published in three short story collections. Her memoir, *Dear Tosh,* published in May 2021, was short-listed in the Selfies Book Awards and long-listed in the Dorchester Literary Festival Writing Prize 2022. From 2008 to 2016 she lived in Italy on an olive farm, returning to the UK to live in Dorset for eight years. Never a person to stay in one place for long, she has recently moved to France where she plans to continue writing more works of fiction and poetry. *Loose Ends* is her debut novel. You can read more about her on her website: http//www.ninettehartley.com and you can also follow her on social media.

Ninette Hartley
Photograph Will Hartley

Printed in Great Britain
by Amazon